"What Are You?" Lauren Asked, Careful Not to Look at Him.

"I thought you knew. You act like you've got me all figured out. You're thinking: here's a man who has some talent and the best way to treat a guy like this is to keep him in his garret with his paints, pat him on the head, rev up his ego now and then—and avoid him on any personal level."

"Now who's sounding defensive?" she responded defiantly, although his words had made her uneasy. His points were legitimate.

"Me. I resent having been discounted as a man because of what you've judged from the outside. Maybe all you're seeing is the reflection of your own fear."

Dear Reader:

Silhouette has always tried to give you exactly what you want. When you asked for increased realism, deeper characterization and greater length, we brought you Silhouette Special Editions. When you asked for increased sensuality, we brought you Silhouette Desire. Now you ask for books with the length and depth of Special Editions, the sensuality of Desire, but with something else besides, something that no one else offers. Now we bring you SILHOUETTE INTIMATE MOMENTS, true romance novels, longer than the usual, with all the depth that length requires. More sensuous than the usual, with characters whose maturity matches that sensuality. Books with the ingredient no one else has tapped: excitement.

There is an electricity between two people in love that makes everything they do magic, larger than life—and this is what we bring you in SILHOUETTE INTIMATE MOMENTS. Look for them wherever you buy books.

These books are for the woman who wants more than she has ever had before. These books are for you. As always, we look forward to your comments and suggestions. You can write to me at the address below:

Karen Solem
Editor-in-Chief
Silhouette Books
P.O. Box 769
New York, N.Y. 10019

A Season of Rainbows

Jennifer West

Silhouette Intimate Moments

Published by Silhouette Books New York

America's Publisher of Contemporary Romance

SILHOUETTE BOOKS, a Division of Simon & Schuster, Inc.
1230 Avenue of the Americas, New York, N.Y. 10020

Copyright © 1983 by Jennifer West

Distributed by Pocket Books

ISBN: 0-671-47133-3

First Silhouette Books printing July, 1983

10 9 8 7 6 5 4 3 2 1

To Matt and John

A Season of Rainbows

Chapter 1

LAUREN LESLIE TAYLOR CUT HER YELLOW PORSCHE convertible between a large Mercedes and a new Rolls-Royce. Santa Monica Boulevard was jammed. Since she had come to Los Angeles six months ago, she had determined that there was no time of day when the city's transportation corridors were not filled with a steady river of automobiles. It was a nuisance when you had to be somewhere quickly, as she did now.

A strand of hair broke free from its sleek chignon and whipped across her face. Her hair was thick and so dark as to appear black in contrast to the seed pearls decorating the simple, elegant hairstyle. Like the paintings she offered her clients, she, too, bore an international flavor. It had always been a private source of amusement to her that foreigners would ascribe her appearance as being typical of their respective countries. Her eyes were a brilliant cornflower-er blue: "Definitely Irish!" The raven-colored hair was attributed to the recessive genes of a Far Eastern ancestor, high cheekbones obviously Scandinavian in origin, and the oval delicacy of her face was "most typically French—and Parisian, one could be sure!" One day, she had managed (with a perfectly straight face) to tell an adamant Hungarian expatriate that she was not a Magyar, but rather a salamander.

She turned her wrist to glance at her small Piaget watch. The circle of diamonds, substituting for numbers on the dial, glinted under the sun. It was two o'clock. She swallowed hard, forcing away panic.

One of the richest men in America was now waiting for her.

But it couldn't have been helped; the dismal meeting with the bankers had dragged on and on and, in the end, no decision had been reached to extend her credit line.

Blast it, she muttered under her breath and downshifted to take her chance to slip into a faster-moving lane.

A black Ferrari kept pace at her right, the car's driver appearing familiar to her. She recognized him as this season's heartthrob, the star of a mindless television car-chase series. Hype had it that he'd come from the Midwest a year before and was discovered while delivering a singing telegram dressed as a chicken to a producer's home. That, at least, was the story.

But Lauren knew that the City of the Angels was built of hyperbolic fictions. It was less a geographical place than a state of mind; a city constructed entirely of dreams.

Some dreams were fantastically good. Yet, there were those other doomed fantasies, the ones that turned into personal nightmares and left men broken without even their souls intact.

She shivered, pressing away the disturbing thought that her own hopes would not be realized.

Eleven years would have been sacrificed. The struggle, the superhuman effort to amass first the knowledge and then, with the expertise, the money—all of it would be wasted.

She did not even want to think about the toll her career had exacted from her personal life. She was twenty-nine, and there was no husband, no children, no real home. She told herself it didn't matter, but sometimes, when she lay alone at night on those few occasions when she allowed herself to drift into the dangerous regions of her heart, she felt the ache of loneliness. She tasted doubt.

Everything she had done and been these past years had been for the moment that was now only two weeks away. She was standing literally and figuratively before the fabled Golden Gates of Success. If she failed, there would be no second chance. Beggars did not get another opportunity to enter the very special world she now approached.

The line of cars inched forward, agonizingly slow. Another red light.

A young boy stepped between cars offering roses for sale at four dollars a bunch. The light changed, and he jumped back to the curb. She saw him kick the scarred trunk of a palm tree. *No sale*. Anger and desperation radiated from his glance as the parade of luxury cars rolled past. Lauren said a silent prayer for him, wishing him better times and, with her eyes fixed straight ahead, she repeated the same words on her own behalf.

The city of her destiny was a magnet to crazies and a mecca to those of true genius. Sometimes the dividing line separating the two was thin. But she felt she belonged here.

So what did that make *her*? One of the crazies? Perhaps. She'd be the first to admit that it took a bit of insanity and more than a dollop of nerve to risk everything on this million-dollar crapshoot—an art gallery the media was already hailing as the ritziest, glitziest salon ever to open on the West Coast.

Or could she be bold and pride herself on *Time* magazine's recent assessment? *Lauren Leslie Taylor, twenty-nine-year-old, raven-haired beauty, with the business acumen of a Wall Street wonderkid and the impeccable taste of a Renaissance doge . . .* , etc., etc. What to believe? *Believe in yourself, Lauren,* she cautioned and took in a fortifying breath. The very air seemed to pulsate with energy. It was as if people here moved in time to some inner music. *The beat was always sensual, the rhythm building to a climax, then ebbing, but yes,* she thought . . . *it was always sensual.* The climate, the city, the people, stirred something in her. There was promise inherent in every moment.

Wherever she looked, her senses were invaded by beauty, dazzled by ostentatious luxury. She was being seduced at every glance by life in full ripeness. If you can't drive it or wear it or make love to it, then it ain't worth your time. That was the credo of the Sun people.

She stopped at a red light. Ahead of her was Century City and perhaps what would be the single most important meeting of her career.

The sky behind the towering buildings had the blue serenity of a Van Gogh horizon. Only a nasty streak of brown tinted the moving canvas, where smog marred what would otherwise have been a climatological paradise.

Her paradise now. God willing.

She stared up at the potent May sun. *Please,* she beseeched fervently, wishing she had the naiveté of an ancient Egyptian to believe in the god Ra behind the glowing yellow ball, *make me a miracle and move this bloody traffic.*

And at once there was a break in the traffic's flow.

The yellow Porsche zoomed forward, the sun gaily reflecting off the chrome and glass.

She was off to see the Pharoah.

If your office was in Number One, Avenue of the Stars, you were rich. You might also be famous. Generally, you would be a combination of both. Century City, they called it, the area dedicated to high-rise, monolithic office buildings set amid miles of emerald lawn.

She was cleared for her appointment by security, then guided to the private express elevator. It rose without a sound, without so much as a hint of movement. But it took only seconds to shoot to the top floor, which was the West Coast domain of Phillip Whelen Lloyd.

The doors parted, and Lauren stepped into an expansive reception room.

Her eyes darted mechanically to the paintings: a Gainsborough on one rosewood-paneled wall; on the far, opposite side of the room, an oil that portrayed haunted, impressionistic figures. German. Definitely by Erich Heckel. There was no doubt both paintings were originals. It was all she could do not to examine them up close.

But a woman had risen from behind a Regency desk, her smile directed at Lauren.

"Mr. Lloyd was afraid you had some trouble."

"Just my stupidity for scheduling an earlier meeting. I haven't quite gotten used to the traffic flow yet. Rather, the nonflow."

The woman laughed. "We don't measure distance in miles here. We go by minutes."

She was led into another chamber, an inner office where the only sound was that of their shoes caressing the luminous silver sea of carpet. A second woman,

introduced as Lloyd's administrative assistant, announced her arrival on an intercom.

Lauren felt her stomach muscles tighten in apprehension.

"You're expected," Lloyd's assistant said, smiling
as warmly as the first woman had.

It was an auspicious sign. Nice people hired nice
people. The old birds-of-a-feather adage calmed her,
but only for a second.

An electronic buzzer was activated, and the woman
swung one of the unmarked double doors wide.

Lauren took a deep swallow and stepped forward.

Light. Everywhere there was light. A wall of plate
glass expanded the room's boundaries into a celestial
landscape of scudding white clouds.

As she moved into the room, a man rose from
behind a desk of chrome and marble. His hair was
silvering, his eyes friendly and blue, masking the
shrewdness that had served him well in building his
financial empire. Lauren fought the impulse to genu-
flect before Lloyd; his stature commanded something
more than the smile she exchanged with him.

With an athletic bounce in her direction, a second,
younger man left his chair opposite Lloyd's desk.

"The late Miss Taylor, I believe." Senator Riff
McIntyre greeted her with a light, affectionate hug.
His hazel eyes contained approval of her navy blue
silk dress. Appearance to the senator was always of
primary importance. She caught the smell of marine
lacquer and knew that he must have come from his
ketch docked at the Marina del Rey.

With his arms still around her, he turned to Lloyd.
"Are formal introductions in order? No," he answered himself, emphatically. "Both your reputations
precede the flesh. Thanks to our ever-vigilant press,"
he added sourly.

Lauren noted the slur and its irony, coming as it did from a man who veritably worshipped journalists, or rather, the power they wielded.

It was Riff's expert manipulation of that immense influence that had put him into office. One day, she knew, that same despised press would be enlisted by the McIntyre clan to support Riff in his expected bid for the United States presidency.

"My apologies," Lauren offered to Lloyd. "The traffic."

"Good people, like everything else that is excellent, bear waiting for." Lloyd smiled, and Lauren could have sworn the room became even brighter.

"I can assure you, this visit today is entirely my honor." She was being sincere.

Lloyd waved the compliment aside. "I hope you'll still bear that sentiment when you leave here today. I'm afraid my motives for seeking you out are entirely selfish."

Lauren knew he had not "sought her out," but she restricted her response to an enigmatic smile as she accepted the seat Riff offered opposite Lloyd's desk. Lloyd took what was obviously a transatlantic call, speaking rapidly in French.

She did not doubt that she was equipped to handle any professional needs Lloyd might have. She was good, positive of her ability, totally confident of her worth. But she also knew that this meeting had been engineered through the machinations of Clarence McIntyre, Riff's father and senior patriarch of the powerful McIntyre dynasty.

The McIntyres were obviously worried about her.

She herself had spent more than one sleepless night gnawing on her knuckles while she balanced the risks of her endeavor against the rewards. It was easy to envision the McIntyres seated along their baronial dining table in their Shaker Heights estate outside of

Cleveland. She saw them, their collective brows furrowed, their computer-minds weighing her chances of success against the debacle of her failure.

The scene rose in sharp, animated focus as Lloyd spoke on the telephone.

There would be Madeline McIntyre, gun-metal gray hair perfectly coiffed, seated ramrod straight at one end of the table. Clarence would reign across from her at the far end. He was a big Irishman with a tumult of white hair and dark eyes as penetrating and alert as a hungry crow's. Riff's two older brothers, along with their obedient wives, would shore up the flanks on either side of the table.

From Madeline, Lauren could imagine hearing, "I would have been far more comfortable had Riff's young woman have chosen a less flamboyant assault on the art establishment."

"We went over this six months ago. Ad nauseum, as I can recall. We made our decision—the Taylor woman would be appropriate. So why chew over past history when we have the opportunity to create history?"

"The consideration was that she was to imbue Riff's public image with an aura of refinement, not—"

"Damn bloody West Coast yokels!" McIntyre would bellow, remembering the publicized barbs made by opposing candidates. Riff had been painted as a man of shining white teeth, a splendid California tan, an enviable tennis backhand and scant intellectual prowess.

To her husband's outburst, Madeline would counter calmly, "I realize, Clarence, that we decided Lauren Taylor would provide our son with the necessary accouterments of taste and a dash of intellectualism through association. I realize this quite well. But, at that time, we had no inkling as to the extent of her ambitions. Now we find she's opening a place on one of the most expensive streets in the world. If she fails, if things go sour, then our son is going to have to bear that taint. The press will have a carnival at our expense."

"Riff needs to be noticed," McIntyre Senior would grumble.

"Well, if she fails, I can assure you he'll be noticed. But not in the way we want. I do not want the odor of failure wafting after our son. We cannot chance it, Clarence. And what this young woman is doing is potentially dangerous."

"No, dammit! It's heroic. The woman has guts. And that's the image we're going to get our son. Voters will see him as larger than life. May I remind you that we are building a legend? I have never in my entire life known of a single legendary man to waste himself on mousy enterprises or to keep company with mousy women. Riff must be seen looming, Madeline, looming high over the masses of mediocrity!"

"Then we had better be certain that she succeeds in her vision."

"When do you last recall a time a McIntyre failed?"

"We are not speaking of a McIntyre. We are speaking of a woman who is not related, whom we do not own through favors or through the compilation of information about her past and of whom we subsequently cannot control."

"Then when, tell me, has there been a person we could not arrange to control?"

"All right, then do it," Madeline would snap.

And that would be that, Lauren knew, except for the arrangements of the details. This meeting, she wagered, was the unfolding of those plans to bring her into their camp. They would insinuate themselves into her professional life until she was no longer merely morally obligated for favors rendered, but was also financially entwined.

They had cast out their net to ensnare their fish, but the McIntyres would be surprised; she was going to be a very slippery fish. She had weathered some rough waters inhabited by a great many sharks. They bore smiling faces, those maneaters, and they wore suits and diamonds and spoke in velvety tones of deals and chances and friendships and countless opportunities she should not miss. She would have floundered on rocky shores by now had she listened to those friendly voices. But she hadn't. And now she was wise as well as being slippery.

Riff sat beside her, beaming his winning-candidate's smile her way as Lloyd replaced the telephone in its cradle.

"A stroke of good fortune that my parents thought Lauren could be of assistance," Riff was saying. "My father's always envied your eye for art, Phillip. Guess he felt if he couldn't own a collection like yours, he may as well help add to it."

Lloyd took no notice of Riff's play at ingratiation.

Instead, Lauren saw that he was studying her intently. "Riff told you why you were invited here today?"

"Only that you have some paintings you'd like to exhibit on consignment at my opening." She had thought perhaps they'd be contemporaries. Reputedly, Lloyd was building his old masters' collection. He might be cleaning house. Her thoughts upon hearing that he wanted to see her had immediately danced to names like de Kooning and Lichtenstein. Surely Lloyd would know she would consider nothing less for her gallery.

Lloyd nodded. "There are two works I'd like you to present."

His gaze dropped to a small framed photograph on his desk. From where she sat, she could not make out the image, but she saw that the millionaire's eyes had softened. His thoughts appeared to dissolve into the past, where he seemed to wander among sweet times before suddenly becoming mired in what was an unbearable sadness. He wrenched his attention from the picture back to her.

"My personal opinion is that both paintings are excellent. My wife—their discoverer—used the term 'extraordinary.' But I'd like you to judge for yourself." Lloyd rose and moved to a door opening to a walk-in vault. He returned with two unframed canvases and positioned them against the wall. Standing back, he waited for her reaction.

Lauren crossed the room with Riff following along beside her.

Halfway to Lloyd, she stopped. A small shock traveled through her spine. For a moment, she wondered if she could be mistaken, if what she was looking at could possibly be that good.

Lloyd motioned her forward.

Closer now, she saw there was no mistake. It was not a trick of lighting, nor was it a kind of distortion of distance that gave the two oils their integrity.

"Who did these?" she asked. "Where did you find them?"

"The artist is Christopher Reynolds."

"Reynolds? I don't know him," she whispered, wondering how she could not. This Reynolds was no beginner. She stepped back, drinking in the brushwork, the use of colors, the refined shading.

"And to answer your other question, Buffy ferreted them out from a Santa Monica gallery. 'A second-string affair,' was her unlikely description of the place." Lloyd smiled. "I hadn't been aware she knew about football. After thirty years of marriage, the woman still surprises me."

"I'll say one thing, she's got an eye for art. These are amazing." Lauren stepped back and forth, viewing each painting from a different perspective. The background of the first was a deep brown, brooding, warning of shapes hidden in its depths.

She could not see the shapes as much as she sensed them there. A blue emerged from the brown. It came at her like a mist, a swirling force that appeared to gather energy as it spun ever outward. And in the foreground, one was assaulted by violent electric colors—red, yellow, a strange green, colors that seemed to dance together as figures, pagan and free.

Sweet Lord, Lauren thought, understanding at last exactly what *primal* meant. The artist had cut to the bone. He had struck bedrock soul. *What kind of a man possessed feelings like this?* she wondered. *What man could hold this degree of emotional power within him?*

"The artist needed money for motorcycle parts," Lloyd said.

Lauren thought she had not heard him correctly. "What?"

"Motorcycle parts. He repairs them for a living."

Beside her, Riff feigned interest. Lauren knew his body was there with her, but sensed his thoughts were either on his next sailing trip to Catalina Island or engaged in a future campaign strategy.

"I know this is going to sound sinister, but I had him checked out. It's general policy with all my dealings with new people," Lloyd said. The explanation was not an apology.

Lauren was not surprised. "Well, it does smack a bit ominously of cloak and dagger." She smiled slightly. "But I understand." With Lloyd's multinational holdings, he was an easy prey to various terrorist groups. It was a common and frightening phenomenon to men in his league. But his necessary precautions contrasted jarringly with her own world in which art reflected man's highest spiritual nature.

"And me?" she asked. "Did you also have me checked out?"

"I did," he answered gravely. "And discovered you were a desperado of the first order. Better to have her on my side than against me, I thought."

His attention trailed back to the paintings. "Reynolds lives nearby. In Venice. His place is a block or two from the beach."

She was familiar with the various suburbs adjacent to Los Angeles. Venice was a beach area sociologists would label as an area in transition. Ocean-front shacks costing a million dollars and up and nineteen-forties stucco boxes further inland going for half that amount nestled beside ghettos where the violent content of graffiti predicted murders occurring as a matter of daily course.

"He's what I suppose you would call a starving artist," Lloyd went on. "As Buffy generously put it, his digs are romantically Bohemian."

"Translating to morbidly pathetic?"

"I'd say that might be a fair real-estate assessment."

"Personal life?" she asked abruptly and immediately felt foolish.

Lloyd registered surprise.

"Professional curiosity," she explained. "That is, with his work being so dynamic, I thought he might have an interesting . . . that is I felt—"

"Yes," Lloyd broke in. "Buffy did, too. She was, in fact, shamelessly blatant in voicing her admiration of his . . . shall we say, his sensed other talents? If I can recall, she said, 'Now there's got to be one sexy dude lurking behind that brushwork.' Yes," Lloyd reflected, "those were her precise words. You can clearly see that money has not spoiled my wife's enjoyment of life's more basic pleasures."

And she did see. She understood that Lloyd was amused and proud of his wife. The woman who presided over world-class social functions was very human. Personal honesty was priceless. Lloyd knew it.

For a second, a wave of sorrow engulfed her. She had longed for a union with a man who could accept her just as she would likewise accept and revel in him. She was envious of Lloyd. It was possible for a man to have a woman beside him on *his* way up; the same selfless devotion in reverse was not a luxury frequently offered a woman.

Riff was suddenly interested in the conversation. "Really?" he commented and stepped forward. "You can tell all that about a man's nature just from looking at his work?" Riff was always interested in unraveling clues to the human psyche. He scrutinized the paintings like an inveterate connoisseur of fine art. "How can you tell?" he pressed.

"You feel it. Inside," Lloyd offered. But he had directed the statement more to Lauren. "Isn't that right, Miss Taylor?"

"I'd say so, yes." She held his glance. "You can feel the artist through his work. Fundamentally, that's what this business is all about—feelings. Some people think it revolves around money. They're wrong. Others take a snobbish delight in owning art, even in hoarding it—a ridiculous attitude, trying to capture beauty. And to some it's a technical game that ultimately ends in sterility. But what it all boils down to is very simple, basic and beautiful. Art has to do with inner feelings expressed outward and shared.''

She hadn't realized it, but the last words came out softly like a prayer. When she had finished, she heard her voice echoing in her mind and was slightly embarrassed for disclosing her reverence. She had always held her feelings for art close to her like a secret lover she met passionately, with commitment, in quiet personal moments.

Riff shrugged. "Whatever turns you on, I guess. I see squiggles and swirls."

But Lloyd had understood her. And she suddenly understood him. He had baited her with the expectation that she would be getting masterpieces from him. Had he told her she'd be coming to see work by an unknown artist, she never would have made the trip. Time, at this point in her life, was a precious commodity. Lloyd knew human nature. He knew that after she had seen Christopher Reynolds's paintings, she would not be able to resist them. One reason was the work. It was brilliant. But there was another reason, and it made her blush inwardly to think that Lloyd understood this about her. It had to do with feelings. It had to do with being a woman. Rare art was one thing; a rare human being was quite something else. Lloyd had known, somehow, that she would recognize that Christopher Reynolds might perhaps encompass both ideals.

"Will you show Reynolds's art in your gallery?" Lloyd asked.

"Of course." There was no hesitation. "As you knew I would."

Riff looked surprised. "I thought—"

"That I wouldn't take less than a Warhol."

"I'm really quite amazed." Riff studied Lloyd. "I guess I naturally assumed they'd be those of a recognized artist." He turned to Lauren. "And I thought you'd think the same thing." He sounded almost hurt.

"I did," she said.

Lloyd was looking at her, the smile behind his eyes struggling to remain veiled.

"Well, perhaps the abstracts just turn her on," Lloyd said lightly. "To quote you, Senator."

Chapter 2

LLOYD WENT OVER THE DETAILS OF THEIR ARRANGEMENT to exhibit Reynolds's work in her gallery. After five minutes of listening to their discussion, Riff decided he had had enough.

"A press interview," Riff explained, tapping the face of his Rolex, "at four. Would, of course, love to stay. To me, art has always been so, it's been so—" He searched vainly for an adjective.

"Boring and dull?" Lauren assisted him sweetly.

"You got it." He winked, the professional, boyish charm that captivated his female constituents coming through. Pumping Lloyd's hand vigorously, he said, "If we don't get together before, I'll see you on the big night." He threw another wink Lauren's way.

"Your parents will be there?"

"Parents and their whole eastern entourage. A regular invasion."

Riff bestowed to Lauren a parting pat on her shoulder and left in search of more exciting conversations—namely, his own oratory to the press.

Lloyd drew his attention back to her. "You make a handsome couple."

Lauren grimaced. "We make an absolutely ridiculous couple."

"Then why?"

"Why, indeed?" She had wondered that enough times herself.

Sitting behind his desk, Lloyd suddenly appeared to her as the absolute image of the father confessor. It was very tempting, this opportunity to unburden herself.

"Convenience," she said, at last. "For Riff, but also for me. It's not just a cliché that a career and love don't make it. Not for a woman, that is." She hoped she didn't sound bitter.

"In other words, the senator's heart is committed to his political career and yours to Michelangelo."

"Umm . . . something like that."

"Still," Lloyd said, eyeing her with the potent stare of a grand inquisitor, "you're a beautiful young woman. It's hard to believe you haven't lost your heart to someone."

"My heart, Mr. Lloyd, has belonged to many men. Great men," she intoned mysteriously.

"Fascinating." Lloyd leaned forward, playing the game with her. "Would you care to offer any of their initials?"

"Better than that," she said, "I'll give you their full names." She relaxed in her chair, ticking off the men's names on her fingers. "There was Renoir. And Matisse. I had quite a thing with Degas for a time. Yes, you see, my life has been filled with men."

"And, it would appear, your bed unfilled." Lloyd broke off. "Excuse me. Please. That was totally out of line. I had no right at all to say that."

"Your curiosity's understandable. I'd like to be able to brag that my life is ablaze with passion, only it's not. I made a trade-off. And I'm hoping it's been the right one. Anyway, in a couple of weeks, I'll be able to say for certain."

"So you and Riff put on a show for the press. A rather good one, too. Of course you realize that everyone assumes you two are lovers."

"There's nothing going on between us. It's just an arrangement, a tacit agreement we have that's mutually beneficial. The media gets lively stories and the opportunity to develop another cult figure. Riff gets all the free political exposure he wants because we make good copy. Glamorous copy. I'm sure you realize that the underlying motive for his attraction to me—or rather his family's attraction to me—is that I add a touch of stability to his playboy image."

"And what do you get out of the relationship?"

Lonely nights and unfulfilled longings, she mused, but answered, "Introductions to men like Phillip Whelen Lloyd."

Lloyd accepted the compliment with narrowed eyes. "We would have crossed paths on our own eventually. I buy art, and you sell the best. No, the McIntyres merely expedited the inevitable."

"Tell me," she asked, feeling the need to move the topic from herself to something safer, "why does an important man like Phillip Lloyd decide to become a guardian angel to an unknown artist?"

Lloyd was pensive for a moment, then reached across his desk and turned the small, framed picture around to her. "My son," he said, his voice barely audible. "You may have read about it."

Lauren's mind spun back through time. "He was—" The words froze on her lips.

"Killed. It's all right, I've anesthetized myself to the word. My son was murdered." There was no rancor in his voice, only a weary, futile sense of having experienced life's capriciousness in its cruelest form.

Lauren remembered the incident well. Carey Lloyd had been an innocent victim, a senseless casualty of a military junta in a volatile South American country five years ago. It had been a big story in all the papers and on television. The president had even imposed temporary trade sanctions on the country in retaliation for the unwarranted barbarism.

"My son was a totally pure human being," Lloyd said. "The news carried stories about him, of course, but no one account really ever captured the essence of what Carey was all about. He was like his mother. He was true. Real. And instead of taking my route in life—passage on Lear jets to boardrooms and mergers, he chose to walk a simple path. A footpath." Lloyd looked down at his hands, opened helplessly to the fates that had taken his son. "Carey helped people. He taught the Indians how to irrigate and how to plant disease-resistant strains of wheat to stop rampant hunger. And one day, when he was walking along on his simple path, he was cut down by a bullet fired by an automatic weapon."

"I'm so very sorry," Lauren whispered, feeling his pain as her own.

"Something not too many people know," Lloyd went on, "was that the gun that killed my son was made by a company on which I sit on the board of directors."

He turned the picture back, looking into his son's smiling face. "So now you can see why I have a selfish interest in trying to carry on my son's good works."

"For him," Lauren said.

"No. Not for Carey. I do it for myself—as penance." Lloyd reached into his side file drawer and pulled out a manila folder. Opening it, he removed the papers it contained. "You were recommended highly by the McIntyres, whom I realized, of course, had a proprietary interest in you. So I did, in fact, investigate your background. And what I found out is the actual reason you're here today—not because of your association with the senator."

"Would it be cheeky of me to ask what you found out?" She wasn't certain if she was flattered, amused or resentful that her life was on open display.

"I found out where you studied, where you worked. I looked into your family background and how you managed to get to the top of the heap at such a young age. And then I sifted away all the facts until only the core of Lauren Taylor remained." He put the papers down. "You're a creature of dichotomy. By the most stringent of standards you're certainly a lady, but I also happen to believe that you could turn into a mean little streetfighter if it was necessary. I see a woman who is a realist and a romantic. Most of all, I find a woman who is totally, absolutely committed to doing the best possible work in her field." He patted the manila folder closed. "The whole story's in here, although mostly between the lines."

From his top drawer, he removed another paper. Referring to it, he added, "This is a memo to my bank in Zurich. They've been instructed to send a Rembrandt drawing—an original, of course—to your gallery. It will be available for sale at your opening."

"A Rembrandt?" Her voice came from somewhere far away, lost in a preposterous dream she had once had. In it she had offered grand masters to the public from her own gallery.

"As I understand it, this will be the only original drawing by Rembrandt for open sale on the American market."

"That's correct," she confirmed, too stunned to even offer her thanks.

Lloyd stood. "I'm afraid I've a plane waiting at the airport. Something bothersome in London. You have done me a favor, Miss Taylor. Lauren. And I am

merely doing you one in return. I want to make
certain your opening will draw a crowd. I have a
special interest in this artist. Of course, you'll see that
the proper advertising surrounds your acquisition.
And one more thing," he said before seeing her out.
"This is Reynolds's address in Venice. He doesn't
have a telephone. You'll have to go there in person.
I'd like you to take a look at any other work he's
finished and report back to me. Oh, and I definitely
want him at the opening."

Chapter 3

IT WAS A FULL DAY LATER BEFORE LAUREN FOUND THE time to leave the gallery and drive to Venice.

The address she held in her hand was repeated in rusty metal letters affixed to the side of a two-story white frame building.

"Excuse me," she said, standing at the opening of a cluttered one-car garage. She hugged her arms, shivering from the gray mist that carried with it the scent of the ocean a few blocks away.

The man she spoke to was bent over a disassembled motorcycle holding a wrench to what appeared to be a hopeless tangle of chrome pipes and rubber tubing. But the apparent mess was obviously important to the man who finally looked up with annoyance.

His initial reaction changed almost at once from aggravation to startled recognition.

She watched him withdraw, reassemble his emotions. Her appearance on his doorstep represented power—hers. It also augured hope for him. She could understand his wariness. There was little more painful than hope shattered, especially when a person may have hoped for a long time.

"You look lost," he said.

His voice was soft and deep, the tone shaded with the same promise Lauren had experienced in seeing his paintings—the hint of passions waiting to be spent.

So this is who you are, she thought, but said, "I'm looking for Christopher Reynolds."

He considered the name with exorbitant gravity. "Reynolds . . . Reynolds . . ."

He rose to his feet, and she saw that he was tall, six one, or maybe an inch more. His physique was lean and hard, with muscular thighs evident beneath denim jeans and arms that appeared to have hefted more than a paintbrush. There was no trace of the wan ascetic about him. But, of course, she had known there would not be.

"Christopher Reynolds, the artist?" she prompted.

Dark eyes smiled at her. "Ah, that Reynolds. I know him. Hell of a guy."

"No, no," she dismissed. "Couldn't be him. This one's a wretch. And a tease."

They both smiled. Contact was made.

"Hi," she said and held out her hand. "I'm Lauren Taylor."

"And I'm the wretch." He threw his wrench into the toolbox, extended his hand, then withdrew it apologetically to wipe the grease on a rag. "Out slumming this morning?"

"Treasure hunting, actually." She opened her purse, and as she fumbled around inside it, she felt his eyes appraising her. It was the man—not the artist—who took in her anatomy in the white St. John knit dress. Her shoulder-length dark hair had been worn loose that morning. It fell forward, shielding the outline of her face from his gaze, and blessedly hid the slight color that had risen to her cheeks.

She looked up and handed him her card, which was

taken from a thin gold case—a gift from a shiek grateful to her for securing a rare Daumier.

"I consider myself fortunate. I've been introduced to your work, Mr. Reynolds."

He looked briefly at the card, then back to her. "How could you know my work? My entire fan club consists of a tomcat whose taste runs to fat mice and the admiration of one male friend. Rick's generally too drunk to see the nose on his face, let alone judge potential genius." More seriously, he added, "I haven't shown anything of mine for four years, and that was only a one time shot at immortality. The occasion was not exactly a milestone in the annals of art history."

He brought a hand up, raking it through a thick mass of wavy, dark hair. His was not the image of sartorial splendor, and yet Lauren had to admit he bore himself with the same elegant, slightly ironic arrogance sought by advertisers in the looks of top male models.

He had on tight, well-worn jeans and a faded and frayed light blue dress shirt with the sleeves rolled up to the elbows. There was a streak of black oil down the front, which somehow looked more artistic than grimy to Lauren. His shoes were scuffed motorcycle boots splattered with dried oil paint. It was preposterous, but she thought he looked marvelous.

"Two of your paintings were brought to me. You sold them recently to a gallery in Santa Monica."

He winced, remembering. "She drove a hard bargain."

"But you were desperate," Lauren replied, matching his melodramatic delivery.

He cocked his head to where the ailing motorcycle stood. "I had my beast to feed."

"Why?" she asked, incredulous. "You're damn

bloody good at what you do. You don't have to
scratch around for a living."

"No?"

"No. Don't be so afraid. Everyone has to take the
gamble once. Otherwise, what's it all for?"

"It's you who should be afraid. I'm a glutton for
compliments. I was just about to ask you up to see my
etchings."

"Great, I'll take my chances. Besides, the word's
out that I've a pretty mean tennis backhand."

The building in which Christopher Reynolds made
his home was a white frame duplex. The sea air had
chiseled away at the paint, and the siding buckled as if
it cringed in shame.

Lauren went with him up side stairs that ended at a
small landing. The door to his apartment was unlocked, and he held it open for her to enter.

"It's not Park Avenue," he explained.

She looked around.

His small living room had a single upholstered
chair, a monster that must have been left over from
the early fifties. There was a standing lamp, minus the
shade, a round wooden table, the top piled with old
paint palettes, tubes of half-used oils, several moldy
cups of undrunk coffee, a couple of beer cans with
their sides crushed in, and in the center of it all sat the
biggest, meanest-looking orange cat that Lauren had
ever laid eyes upon.

"What do you think?" he called, leaving her to
enter the small galley kitchen.

"You're right," she said. "It's not Park Avenue."

"But it has a lot of charm, don't you think?"

"Umm . . . a definite ambience."

"Some people say it reminds them of the Bowery."

She was staring at the cat when he came back.

"Meet Cavalier Cat." Christopher picked up the
animal, holding him out for his introduction. The cat

hissed and spat, and Christopher put him on the floor. "His friends are few. I make it a point never to intervene in his social life, so it's up to you two to form your own relationship."

They watched Cavalier slink to the screen door, shove it open with his paw and exit.

"Rude critter." He shook his head. "I'd offer you something, coffee at least, but I'm out."

"A look at those etchings would be fine."

"Yeah, sure. The paintings."

Lauren felt for him. He looked miserable like a parachuter just before his first jump.

"They're in here," he said, starting away. "I have a studio of sorts a few blocks away. It's got light and space and cheap rent. Another artist and I pool our resources for the overhead. When I'm finished with my masterpieces, I haul them back here so I can concentrate on their flaws at my leisure."

"What flaws?' she said, standing just inside the bedroom. Most of the floor space was taken over by a king-size mattress, but every other available inch was occupied by his art. Unframed canvases hung on the walls, and others leaned against each other, stacked on the floor.

It took her about twenty minutes to examine each one carefully. During that time she had forgotten Christopher, except to notice in a vague sort of way that he would watch her for a moment, then leave and pace back and forth over the hardwood floor in the living room.

At last she was through. She turned to find him in the doorway.

"You wanna be a star, kid?"

He passed a hand through his hair. "You think there's hope?"

"Hope? They're magnificent," she said, this time with seriousness.

"I don't know what to say."

"You've already said everything. In those."

He turned from the doorway and moved back into the living room. She found him staring out the front window.

"I don't get it," she said, coming up behind him. "In order to paint like this, you've got to have critical judgment. And if you've got critical judgment, then you've got to see how good these are."

He shook his head with his back to her still. "It's been a long haul," he said with a reflective sigh. "I can't believe it."

"Believe it," she said. "Besides, if anyone knows about long hauls, I do. But when you've earned your reward, you've got a moral obligation to enjoy it. Lighten up, Reynolds. I just told you I was going to make you a shining star."

He turned, looking at her. They were very close. She was aware of his height and of her small stature beside him. He smelled good. Musky. Naturally masculine, without needing the scent of this season's male cologne to define his sexuality.

There was a split second when she knew they both felt the same urge to lean into each other.

It was Christopher who made the decision for them. He stepped away, creating a space of sane propriety. She was relieved and also disappointed.

"Do you have any idea what it's like?" he asked her with pained amusement on his face. "I had fear sitting on my shoulder for years, like some hoary vulture mocking me as I wasted time. No," he revised, "time was wasting me."

"I know that bird," Lauren said. "He's had many a good meal at my expense."

Christopher stared at her. "That's hard to believe. Your bio reads like the life and times of a storybook princess."

"Umm, this princess had a good press agent."

"So how'd you get that son-of-a-bitch bird to fly away?"

"I stopped with the free handouts. Doubt was his favorite meal."

"Message received." He smiled, but the mood was fleeting. His eyes became darkly pensive again as he searched her face. "You're like some splendid fairy godmother, you know? I knew who you were the moment I saw you standing there. You had to have come about my work, but I couldn't believe it."

For a moment, neither of them moved. Under the power of his eyes, she experienced the same wave of emotional fire the paintings had radiated.

"I've got to go back," she said. "Appointments. And uh . . ."

"Sure, yeah . . ."

But she didn't move, and neither did he, the two of them remaining rooted in their places. "Oh, uh, the paintings!" She laughed and touched her hand to her head. "I don't know what's the matter with me, I'm like in a fog."

Now they both laughed, and she felt as if she were dancing in his eyes. She looked down.

"So," she said, "I'm planning on showing your two paintings at the opening. I'd take more," she rushed on, glad to have something concrete to anchor her thoughts on, "but I'm afraid I don't have the space. Maybe, umm, you know, in the future. Sometime."

"Oh, sure. Sure. Two paintings in your gallery sound great. Great. And the future, too. That's also great."

"And you're invited to the opening. I'll see that you get a formal invitation to present at the door."

She then left immediately, hurrying down the steps and mentally chastizing herself for coming under the spell of a starving artist. Above her, the screen door creaked open and slammed. She turned to see Christopher on the landing.

"About the opening," he said, "I don't have anything to wear."

"That'll be fine. This is L.A., isn't it? Just come."

He saluted her, and she walked the rest of the way down the stairs with the feel of his eyes on her.

Chapter 4

IT WAS SEVEN O'CLOCK BY THE TIME LAUREN RETURNED home from the gallery. Meeting Christopher had been the definite high point of her day; the remainder of it being memorable only because it had gone straight downhill.

One of the contractors for the private upstairs salon had refused to lay the flooring until she gave him a check for half of the materials in advance. She could not oblige him. The bank had still not made a decision on the extension of her loan payments, plus they remained mute on the additional $150,000 she had requested to borrow.

The telephone was ringing as she turned the key in her door. It shrilled through the dark emptiness with a nagging urgency that made her grit her teeth and dash to get to it before it tipped her beyond the edge of sanity.

Her mother's voice crackled over the wires as Lauren held the receiver to her ear.

"Can you hear me?" Dina Taylor shouted.

"Yes! Please don't yell." Lauren felt for the nearest light switch.

"Oh," her mother said, sounding like a normal person. "It's the storm. Unbelievable. I can hardly hear myself think from the thunder. I only wish we could be out there in all that sun, rather than here in Philadelphia with this . . . this monsoon. Which is why I called, incidentally. We're not going to be there for the opening. It's definite. Your father was unable to reschedule court dates. I read today the McIntyres will be there. They're bringing their whole pedigreed gang along. What's happening with their son?"

Ah, the weather report was not the reason for her call. Lauren repositioned the phone to her other ear, her grip on the handle tightening. "I'm not sure what you mean." Of course she was absolutely certain what her mother meant. She only played dumb because it annoyed her mother as much as her mother's question irritated her.

"Lauren," Dina Taylor said, dropping her voice conspiratorially. "Your father's career would not be hurt if you and Riff were to—"

"My father's career seems to have been going along fine for the last thirty years without any help from the McIntyres."

"The man is obviously very serious about you, Lauren. There are pictures in all the papers. Magazines, too."

"That's because being the darling of the Associated Press is Riff's stock in trade, Mother. On a personal level, it has the same value as a big, fat goose egg."

"I don't believe that," Dina snapped. "You have never changed, Lauren. Never, never, never. You were stubborn when you were two, a snitty pain in the ass when you were fifteen—when for your own good I wanted you to take dancing and equestrian lessons— and you are still every bit as obstinate at twenty-seven."

"I'm not twenty-seven. I'm twenty-nine."

"Oh, my . . . you're getting so old. Just do me this one favor, Lauren. Don't go telling people, all right? My new tuck and lift is only six months old. Let me steal a couple of years."

"I'm not going to play out your fantasy of marrying me off to Riff McIntyre just so Daddy can wear black robes to work. He looks perfectly nice in his three-piece suits." It had never been enough for her mother that her husband was a successful criminal attorney. Once the money from that profession was securely in hand, she had lusted after the social status that came along with being the wife of an appellate court judge.

"Just answer me one thing, Lauren. Truthfully."

"What?" Now Lauren could hear the pealing of thunder in the background. She took it as an omen.

"If the senator asked you to marry him, would you?"

"No."

"No?" A beat of silence followed, heavily laden with maternal disappointment. "Why?"

"It's quite simple. I don't love Riff McIntyre."

"You have never loved anyone—anyone alive, that is. You are a very strange woman, Lauren. You are gaga over all those dead Frenchmen and those Italians from the fifteenth century molding in their graves, but you will turn down marriage to one of the world's premier bachelors."

"It's my life, Mother."

"Then what the hell do you want in a man, Lauren? And when, I'd like to know, are you going to want it?"

Lauren didn't answer. She was staring at the paintings leaning against the leg of the table. They were Christopher Reynolds's abstracts, brought home after her meeting with Lloyd.

At her mother's question, a curious thing happened. She became blank. And suddenly she felt very lonely and tired and more than a bit sad. She didn't know why, only that she thought she knew what it was like to be an empty canvas. She needed desperately to be filled with the colors of life.

"Are you still there, Lauren?"

"I'm here, yes."

"Darling, I'm sorry for picking. It's just that my job is to be the mother, and your job is to be the daughter, which means listening to me. Now, daughters are supposed to fall in love, get married and live happily ever after."

"I've heard that one, too. Only I'm sorry to inform you that that particular fairytale is out of print. I've got to run now. Kiss Daddy for me and tell him not to work so hard."

She let the phone drop into its cradle, but did not move. Her eyes traveled around the part of the apartment she could see from where she stood. She loved her apartment as much as any woman could cherish a vine-covered cottage with a white picket fence.

Moving out of the foyer, she entered the living room and flicked on all the lights to dispel the shadows. It was a beautiful room, the carpet pale peach and shimmery, blending into the soft pastels she had chosen for her furniture's upholstery. Each piece of furniture, every small accessory—some of them wildly expensive antiques collected over the years, had been selected with loving devotion. In a way, she supposed the apartment represented the children she had never borne, the husband she had sacrificed for the life she led. It was a beautiful environment fashioned out of forfeiture.

One of her greatest luxuries were the flowers she had delivered on standing order from a florist every week. They were living things and, to her, they were necessary to fill that nagging void she sometimes experienced alone at night.

A crystal Waterford vase was generously filled with irises and tiger lilies, and she saw that the container needed freshening. Lifting the bouquet from the coffee table, she stopped momentarily, struck as always by the magnificence of the small Monet framed in gilt behind her sofa. The soft colors bled together in a haze of pleasant summer memories, and one glance at the scene of trees and sky and young women frolicking in innocence always made her spirits rise.

More than once, she had longed to enter the canvas with them. And on an equal number of occasions she had sternly lectured herself on the frivolity of owning a painting that could be sold for a fortune. But it was not a fortune that she was hoarding; it was her soul that she was nourishing. The Monet warmed her against the chill of the outside world.

She rose early the next morning feeling better. There were a series of errands to run, which meant that she wouldn't arrive at the gallery until midmorning; lately, this had become the routine. There was no problem in this as she had had the good fortune to hire an excellent assistant. Jacqueline Boucher was a petite brunette, whose angelic face was complemented by placid hazel doelike eyes and whose demure public demeanor masked a passionate and mercurial disposition in private. She had come from France several years before, and her multilingual abilities had already been of excellent use to Lauren in dealing with foreign clients, artists and agents. Jacqueline was also fully capable of handling the work crews and miscellaneous business without Lauren's constant supervision.

At the sight of her gallery, Lauren's spirits soared.

Outside, the new facing of pale pink marble glowed softly in the warm sunshine, and the three-foot-high brass letters spelling out the gallery's name shone with bright promise.

But her euphoria was short-lived.

Upon entering, she found Jacqueline standing with a man in the main downstairs gallery. Her face signaled catastrophe as she looked toward Lauren.

The man also turned, and Lauren recognized him as the loan officer from the bank she had borrowed most heavily from to finance the opening of her gallery.

"I'm sorry I wasn't here to welcome you," Lauren said, the false cheer in her voice sounding strained, even to her own ears. "I had no idea you were coming to see your property." It was a weak joke.

"I have given Mr. Wright a tour while he waited," Jacqueline said stiffly. Lauren read the warning message in her assistant's eyes.

"We might talk privately?" he suggested, looking around.

"Of course." Lauren led the way to her back office. They passed workmen hanging an enormous crystal chandelier over the curved stairs leading to her private gallery.

When they were seated, she offered him coffee. He declined.

"There's a problem," Lauren said, taking the offensive. "We'll solve it."

He put a large envelope on her desk. "The figures are all there." Wright leaned back and waited.

Her eyes raced over the ledger sheets, scanning the numbers with full comprehension. She looked up. "I already knew I was at my limit. That's the reason I asked for the extension on paying back the interest."

"Your request was turned down."

She remained silent for a moment. At first she was

frightened, then she decided there was no need to panic. It wouldn't be the first time that things had looked hopeless, and she had subsequently turned the tide to her advantage. "You understand that my credit is excellent? Not only with your bank, but with my other lenders."

"You anticipated that the remodeling was going to run to half a million."

"It has cost more, true. But my initial projections were correct. Unfortunately, I didn't have access to a crystal ball. The economy's done a flip-flop. Everyone's in trouble, and everyone is gouging for more than their share, trying to stay afloat."

"Which is why we can't be of help to you." He paused and, with the relish of someone who could not afford the street, said, "With the economy nosediving —even on Rodeo, there are some nervous people at the bank."

"What do you know about art?" The question came out suddenly and took Wright by surprise.

"I know what I like," he said defensively. "We own a few oils, watercolors, like that. My wife's selection mostly. But my personal taste has nothing to do with your financial statement."

Lauren rose from her chair and walked around the desk to sit on its corner. Looking down at Wright from her perch, she said, "The people who come to purchase art from me don't buy what they like. They buy for investment. Art is not something they hang on their walls. Their kind of art is what they'll put in a vault beneath a sixty-room *schloss* overlooking the Rhine. To my clients, art is a way of removing hundreds and thousands of dollars across the borders of a country that does not allow the transfer out of hard currency. The kind of people who will visit this gallery, particularly my upstairs salon, don't bite their nails over the fluctuations in the economy that affect us. Their concern is to protect what they have and, at the same time, see it appreciate. And," she added, "those people will not come to a mediocre establishment because they do not want to—nor do they have to—do business in mediocre surroundings. Nor, Mr. Wright, do any of these people want to do business with a woman who will settle for anything less than the best."

Wright sniffed, looking at the rosewood desk and digging his heel into the thick carpet. "I hardly call what you've done here mediocre."

Lauren shrugged. "It's okay—just . . . okay. Unfortunately, okay doesn't cut it. I know what's acceptable, what's expected by my clients. And that's going to take another $150,000 of your money, matched by $150,000 of my money, to meet that criteria."

"I see."

She almost exhaled in relief. She had won.

"Still," Wright went on, "it's not up to me." He stood. "There can't be any extension on your payments. Good luck with your opening," he said. He saw himself out.

Lauren stared blankly at her closed office door. It was the first time in eleven years that she had felt truly beaten. And the killer of it was, she was so close. So close.

For the past six months, she had kept herself running on pure adrenaline. Now she was tapped out. She simply had no more physical or psychic resources from which to draw.

She sank back into her chair and closed her eyes. When she had been a girl, she had been too happy and too busy to cry over anything other than a scraped knee. It wasn't that life necessarily always went her way, but more that she chose to see life as going her way. Over the years, she had developed the capacity to find the best in every situation and to capitalize upon even the thinnest thread of hope.

But now she cried.

The tears came slowly, without assurance. It had been a long time since she had given in to her fears. The wet flow of escaping misery felt good as the tears slid from between closed lashes and trailed down her cheeks, tasting of salt as they hit her mouth. And finally she was sobbing, her shoulders heaving, bent inward, as she released years of bottled tension.

The door to her office opened. Jacqueline cleared her throat. "Pardon," she said as Lauren wiped her eyes. "I knocked. You did not hear?" They were both embarrassed.

"The men have finished," Jacqueline went on. "The chandelier is *magnifique.*"

For a fleeting moment, a swelling of pride filled the hollowness, but soon enough reality intruded. "And I owe them money."

"I did not like that man," Jacqueline announced with surprising vehemence. "It was bad with him, *non?*"

"I've had better times. But it's all right. He was a little confused about some of the established practices of our business. So I had to explain to him that we don't sell washing machines here, but Renoirs and—"

"It is not necessary to put on a brave face for me. Under certain extraordinary circumstances, it is allowable to be human. So be human. And don't forget, you have me."

"Thanks," Lauren said, wondering if Jacqueline had ever played *Jeanne D'Arc* in a school production.

"I appreciate that. Just do me a favor. Don't let a word of this little cash crunch get out among the natives, okay? I enjoy the reputation of being invincible." Lauren closed her eyes a moment, then finding her solution, spoke rapidly. "The chandelier was C.O.D. I can pay for it. But tomorrow I've got to pay for the delivery of the four paintings I purchased outright from that London dealer, and I can't back out on them, even if I wanted to. They've all been touted in news releases. "Oh, God." Lauren sighed, starting to wilt again. "And the day after that—"

"The day after that is not here yet. Give me the check for the chandelier now, because now is here. We can handle now. Then we worry about tomorrow when it comes."

Lauren made out the check. "Jacqueline, thank you."

But when Jacqueline was gone, she made a decision. She wouldn't wait; she would deal with tomorrow today. The main thing was she couldn't think about what she would have to do or she'd break.

She began by flipping through the roto-file containing her private telephone numbers of clients. No one saw this card file, not even Jacqueline, whom she trusted completely with all other aspects of her business. There were private numbers listed here that she could sell to the press and gossip-mongers for a small fortune. But she would never do that. Her clientele was built as much upon her trustworthiness as it was upon her stock and expertise in her field.

She took out the card she wanted and slipped it into her purse, then locked the roto-file back in her wall safe and headed into the gallery.

"Jacqueline, I was—"

Lauren stopped in her tracks, then recovered her composure. Christopher Reynolds stood just inside the doorway. He was obviously being grilled by Jacqueline, who had drawn herself up to resemble the formidable stature of a communist-bloc border guard.

Christopher looked over Jacqueline's head to where Lauren stood. He held a bouquet of flowers in one hand with a canvas tucked beneath his arm. Their eyes touched, and she felt that same odd shock travel through her as when she saw his work for the first time.

"Hello," he said tentatively, a smile starting in his eyes.

"Ah!" Jacqueline cried. "So you were telling the truth. I am sorry," she said, "but you cannot believe the stories people tell who want to show their work here." She finally noticed no one was listening to her. "I think I can become a manager again, not a police-man," she said and, with a shrug, diplomatically retreated to work in the back room.

They met halfway across the gallery. "Hello," Lauren said, a question implicit in the greeting.

Christopher handed her the flowers. "I read some-where that all fairy godmothers should be brought flowers."

"Thanks, they're lovely." They were awful. A pathetic array of daisies and dyed carnations, obvious-ly from one of the grocery store chains and, even more obviously, purchased on the brink of realizing their destiny in a garbage bin.

"I wish they could have been roses," he said. He looked at them with skepticism bordering on suspi-cion. "After I make a sale or two—I can bring you live ones, at least."

"It's the thought . . ."

"Oh," he said, "I almost forgot. I brought you a painting."

"Did you?" Her mind was on the call she had to make.

"This is one you didn't see. I had it in my studio. It was almost finished. As far as I'm concerned, it's the best work I've done. How's that for rampant ego? I thought maybe this one in place of one of the other two." He still hadn't shown her the painting, and suddenly, he stopped abruptly. "This is obviously a bad time to drop in." His eyes were dark, almost black. They were fixed on her with a directness that made her wonder if he couldn't see into her. It was a tantalizing notion.

"Okay," he said, "look, you're busy, so I'll just say what I've got to say. I brought the painting down because I wanted to see you. The opening's two weeks away, and I didn't feel like waiting. I was thinking, maybe dinner tonight."

She hesitated, and he broke in before she could respond.

"Of course. You probably have plans already. Then how about a cup of coffee? Fifteen minutes, that's all."

"Christopher, I don't have plans for dinner tonight. Only something's come up, and I've got to take care of it now."

"What's wrong?" It was a demand laced with gentle concern.

Her eyes flickered away from his. "Nothing."

"Oh, yeah? Well, I smell vulture." He searched her face. "I can always smell it because I've lived with it so long, so don't tell me I'm wrong."

She managed a half smile. "It's nothing I can't handle. Thanks for the flowers," she said, inching away toward the front door. "They're lovely, and I'll

take them home with me now, put them into water."
Her voice faltered, as she thought of her apartment,
of *home*.

He looked at her curiously. "Sure, all right. Glad
you like them."

Christopher stared silently after her, and outside,
as she passed in front of the gallery's front window,
she saw that he was still watching. She knew she had
been rude, but she couldn't help it. All she could
think of was that she had a call to make.

Chapter 5

SHE CLOSED THE DOOR TO HER APARTMENT. GOING directly to the telephone, she took the file card from her purse and dialed the private number of Keely St. Martine. As the phone rang on the other end, Lauren kept her eyes tightly closed, willing herself to be strong. Crying jags were pure indulgence; she didn't have the time for such luxuries.

Keely's Austrian maid answered on the fourth ring. Lauren gave her name, and Keely's voice responded seconds later.

"Lauren, my dear, dearest Lauren," Keely gushed. "Your name is everywhere. And, of course, your beautiful face as well. Raffael called only this morning. He's coming back from his Formula One race in Italy in time for your opening."

"Keely," Lauren began, getting to the point immediately before she lost her nerve, "how would you like to surprise Raf?"

"I'm always trying to surprise him," Keely drawled. "But just tell me what excitement a woman can give a man who takes turns at 200 miles an hour?"

"How about a Monet?"

"*The* Monet? *Your* Monet?"

"And anything, everything else I have in my apartment."

From then on, it all happened with lightning speed. Two hours after her call to Keely, Keely arrived with a personal check that Lauren knew was as good as solid gold bricks. It was for $270,000, which included payment for all of her antiques, plus a small Degas that would now furnish Keely's new, young husband's latest gift—a Palm Springs condominium. Lauren needed $300,000, but she'd cut corners if she had to. As it was, Keely's beneficence was a minor miracle— hell, it was a major miracle.

Before she left, Keely promised that not a soul would know of Lauren's financial plight, and she also agreed to have everything picked up and moved out of Lauren's apartment before the evening was over.

Two hours later, a van arrived, and in another two hours, Lauren shut and locked the door behind the team of movers. Leaning her head against the wood, she willed herself to look on the bright side of things. The empty apartment signified a successful future, not a loss. Finally, she screwed up her courage and surveyed what was left of her home. Not much.

Keely had left instructions with the men not to take her bed or the armoire. She had even told them to leave her dining table and chairs, but Lauren had refused her friend's largesse. She also knew that the only reason Keely hadn't left all the furniture was because it would have been perceived as a handout, and that kind of charity would have been intolerable to Lauren.

Standing in front of the wall where the Monet had so recently hung, she tried to visualize the girls frolicking amid the greenery. No image appeared. Instead she was left with a dull ache.

What she did begin to remember was a scene that had occurred in her own life. She had been eighteen then.

It was the day when Maxwell Kain had leaned over his wooden podium to deliver the speech that still haunted her after all these years. He was a small, effeminate man who spoke to his class with a resonant voice accented with broad, theatrical *a*'s. He hated his art history students as a collective entity. In turn, his students despised Kain as a professorial tyrant. But when he spoke, they listened with keen interest, for Kain was the Rona Barrett of the art world. Somehow he managed to collect data on everything and everyone connected to the art scene and, although a gossip, his taste was impeccable and his critical sense the absolute in refinement. The class that day was utterly silent as he scanned their faces—those loathsome reminders of his mediocrity.

"There are only two kinds of people in this business," Kain began. "There are those who dream, and there are those who become the dream. Now, most of you in here—you would-be artists, you would-be entrepreneurs of the arts—are dreamers. Maybe— just a slim maybe—one of you will make it."

He snapped his lecture notebook closed and looked out at his audience. Smiling, he said, "But I doubt it."

When he said that, Lauren felt a pain grow in her heart, the feeling of misery expanding until she was at its very core.

Kain's last words had been spoken directly to her.

Perhaps it had been because she was so young then that Maxwell Kain's pessimistic declamation had made such a lasting impression. Nevertheless, in the years that followed, there was a force within her, some slow, smoldering fire fueled by desire and stoked by determination that kept her moving relentlessly toward her goal.

She took her undergraduate degree in art history and received a graduate diploma in economics, all the while working part-time in galleries. The more she learned about the business of art, the more she came to realize and agree with Kain's vitriolic assessment of her chosen profession. It was a tough, frequently bitchy business in which only the best and most dedicated could hope to succeed.

She refused to give up.

During the summers, she took advantage of cheap student rates, spending vacations tramping through Europe and Asia until her parents feared she would overdose on museums and galleries.

At the Sistine Chapel in Rome, she stood among other awed tourists and gazed in wonderment at Michelangelo's fresco, *The Fall of Man and the Expulsion from the Garden of Eden.* An inexplicable sensation overtook her, which later she could liken only to the word "ecstasy." Her eyes had filled with moisture, her whole being seeming to react to the indescribable beauty and perfection contained in the timeless masterpiece. It was to her, as if the very essence of mankind's soul was reaching across the ages. She would know during moments like these that she would not, *could not,* waver from her resolve. She would not be cast out from the world of art, banished from her garden of Eden, by any amount of hardship.

And in the grandeur of the Vatican, Maxwell Kain's voice was diminished to a thin, inconsequential wisp, his prophecy rendered impotent.

She had persisted, studying in London where she spent a year of private tutelage at Sotheby Parke Bernet. Her mentor at Sotheby's explained that to know antiques was one thing, but to know the wealthy who were their purchasers was yet another realm to be explored. Promptly, methodically, he set out to teach Lauren how to address the aristocracy of high finance. She learned how to deal with the titled lords and with the instant oil billionaires from Middle Eastern principalities, men who bought on whim if they liked you, or took their millions elsewhere if they did not.

It was only after another year of abject slavery suffered under a prima donna gallery owner in New York (who paid her almost nothing, but taught her more than she had learned in her entire academic career) that she struck out on her own.

Her venture in Greenwich Village was more successful than even she could have dreamed. When she opened the Palm Beach gallery, she was twenty-six years old.

Two years later, *Newsweek* ran a feature article on what she had accomplished. She had learned early that there was money to be made from individual clients, but there were fortunes to be amassed from institutional buyers. She began by acquiring paintings for the corporate headquarters of Braxton Oil out of Houston. That year had also been extraordinarily profitable for the insurance industry. Two of the giants—Megaguard of Hartford and Unisafe out of Delaware—were in a frenzy to find tax shelters for what the IRS would surely interpret as obscene profits.

"What better plan than to invest in art?" Lauren asked and then explained, "Art is easily liquidable if you buy the best, which you can afford to purchase. It appreciates with the regularity of a metronome's beat. And it's always nice to gaze at an old master's canvas when going over a profit and loss statement in the boardroom on the thirty-fourth floor. "Wouldn't you agree, gentlemen?" And, of course, after putting a pencil to it, they did.

Now, as she stood facing the blank wall of her apartment where the Monet had so recently hung, the image of Maxwell Kain's pinched face took shape, looking as it had on that memorable day when she was a terrified eighteen-year-old.

"Forget it, Kain. Go peddle your fear somewhere else. I've made it," she whispered vehemently into the hollow emptiness of the room.

"Oh, not yet you haven't, Miss Taylor."

"But I will, Kain. You just watch me. In two weeks I'm going to open the number one gallery on the West Coast, and maybe someday it will be the number one gallery in America."

"But you have not done it yet, Miss Taylor," the wavering voice repeated in her mind, poisoning the silence with doubt.

"But I will, I will. . . ."

"And if you do, then you'll need to keep it. How will you do that?" Kain said, his laughing face dissolving before her as the doorbell jarred her attention.

It was a security apartment, and Christopher Reynolds's voice crackled through the intercom located outside of the downstairs lobby.

"I know what you're thinking," Christopher said before she could offer her objections.

He moved into the foyer, carrying a large brown paper bag with a grocery store's name emblazoned in red letters over its front. He had shed the jeans, and this time he wore slacks and a sports jacket with a navy blue turtleneck sweater beneath.

"What you're thinking is that you've got yourself involved with some sort of nut who's moving in on you like a shadow." He placed the bag in her arms. "This is for you. For us. Maybe I have gone a little crazy," he went on cheerfully. "It's the promise of success gone to my head. I'm not in the habit of coming on so strong."

She stared at him with dismay, then with curiosity looked into the bag.

"Dinner," he said. "Ours."

"Chris," Lauren said wearily, "I don't know what you have in mind or how you even found out where I live, but I've got to be honest. I'm really not in the mood for visitors tonight."

He was looking past her into the bare living room. "Who's your decorator? They must have been into their early imagination period. Total simplicity," he said and fixed her with a serious, questioning look.

"I've had kind of a bad day."

"I know," he said softly. "Which is basically why I'm here being so obnoxiously pushy. Here, give me that." He took back the groceries and found his way into the kitchen. She trailed after him as if it were perfectly natural that he'd taken over her apartment. Besides that, she was too tired to put up much more of an argument; it was easier to take any course of least resistance.

As he emptied the bag, he said, "I hope you like a nice, cheap cut of steak. And champagne. It was an excellent month," he said, holding up the bottle. "Could you shove this into the freezer? It'll chill faster." She reached for the bottle, but he held onto it, pulling her in to him. "Look," he said and, with his free hand smoothed away a strand of hair from her forehead, "I know this is very weird, me barging in on you. I've got no right, and I can see that whatever's gone down today has totally wiped you out. I knew it was bad when I was in the gallery. I did something nuts; I followed you. You said you were going home, remember? Anyway, when it finally hit me what an ass I was being, thinking I could do something to help you out of your bind, I went back to Venice. But that didn't help. I couldn't get your face out of my mind.

Your eyes had that look of . . . pain. Like your whole world had just caved in. So I came back, and there was a moving van outside your apartment. Nobody but you could own furniture that classy. I also figured you hadn't eaten, and there's nothing worse than misery on an empty stomach. So here we are, food and company." He had delivered the entire speech in a burst of cathartic energy.

Not knowing what to say, she pulled the bottle from him and placed it in the freezer compartment. She closed her eyes just for a moment and, leaning into the refrigerator as if it could offer more than just physical support, she decided to be honest. "This is going to sound odd," she said, "but I sort of wish you weren't being so kind right now. And not to be rude or anything, I also wish you'd leave me be."

"Go ahead, cry if you'd like." He made no move to come to her, yet his voice was deep and calm. If she hadn't opened her eyes, she would have sworn she was with an analyst.

"I already did." She looked at him frankly. "I've been working hard for a long time. I guess the tension just caught up with me."

"Okay. You don't have to talk about it, if you don't want to." He looked around. "Where's the frying pan?"

They ate on a tablecloth in the middle of the bare living room. Lauren dug out some candles, and Christopher made the steaks, which turned out to be so tough they could hardly chew them. The salad became her responsibility. There was something comforting in the two of them working silently together. In the final analysis, she wasn't at all sorry he'd come. The champagne made her giddy, and she caught herself in the middle of an uproarious laughing jag, sobering at once, as if splashed with cold water.

"What's wrong?" he asked, his own smile fading.

She stared down at her hands. Her legs were folded beneath her yoga-style, her back rigidly erect. "I shouldn't be this happy."

"Why not? You've made me happy," Christopher said, and when she looked up with surprise, he qualified his statement. "Showing my paintings in your gallery has given me something—something pretty fantastic to hold on to. In fact," he said, jumping up to take the dishes into the kitchen, "I hadn't realized before how much I wanted things. Nice things. Clothes and . . . hey," he called from the other room, "I even stopped by to look at a fancy sports car today."

He appeared back in the doorway, handsome and lean, his black hair mussed, staring down at her with eyes as soft and dark as cinders. "There was no sense in wanting things I couldn't have before, so I didn't want anything. And now I seem to want everything." He smiled, laughing at himself. "I want the whole world."

"You'll have it," Lauren said. "Someday you'll be famous." As she looked at him, it was as if she could somehow see into the future, and she saw another man in this Christopher's place—elegant, composed, even powerful. She wasn't sure if she wanted to know him that way. All she knew was that this man affected her as no other ever had. It was disorienting because she liked being in control. But when she was with Christopher, it was as if all the rules of the world she had spent her life growing to know so well had been changed on her, and she had to move blindly forward in a foreign universe.

"God," he said, "you look incredible. Hold it, don't move." He ducked out of sight, coming back a moment later with a piece torn off the grocery bag, a pen and a cookbook to write on. "Don't even blink," he commanded. In a few minutes, he presented her with the piece of torn paper.

He had sketched her rapidly, but the hand was sure and the eye exact. She noted the same indefinable quality of the drawing that appeared in his paintings. There was an undercurrent of passion, barely held in check.

"Thank you," she said simply, looking up at him.

"Someday, maybe I can do a real painting of you."

"Someday," she repeated, but she was thinking again of the next day and its problems.

Lauren had worked hard many times during her life. But it was during those last few days before the opening that she learned the full meaning of the expression "bone tired." Her eyes blurred and stung from lack of sleep, and she would have to drag herself to the salon's powder room to put drops into her eyes so that she could read over the fine print of the latest batch of contracts appearing on her desk. Now that her venture was being touted as a sure thing, with the tide of gossip flowing in her favor, there was a never-ending parade of eager sycophants available to share in the glory.

Six months ago, she had written polite, carefully worded letters to some of the heavyweight art agents in New York and Europe. The replies she had received ranged from cool dismissal—"The clients represented by my firm are unfortunately precommitted to showings elsewhere . . ."—to no replies at all. There was an inherent snobbery in her business that reeked of the old aristocratic arrogance of a Europe gone by—longevity, familiarity of name and a lineage of previous business triumphs were the credentials that mattered. Politically and economically, Europe may have choked on its outmoded snobbery, and although the barriers were being broken more and

more in her profession by upstarts with energy and
vision, the old guard still reigned supreme in the art
circles that counted most. Lauren's saving grace was
that, at the moment, she was the king's favored
mistress—the monarch of modern times being, of
course, the media.

Her name, her picture and stories about her gallery
had appeared all at once in a spectacular media blitz.
She and Jacqueline, in consultation with a public
relations firm, had planned much of the publicity
strategy months before. But Riff had charged onto the
playing field with his lance aimed full tilt at the media,
insisting that Lauren submit to a series of interviews
he had arranged with international magazines and
television stations—interviews in which he figured
prominently.

"I resent this interference, Riff."

"Sweetheart, it's for your own good."

"It's for *your* own good."

She went along with his plans, of course, because
Riff had been right to push for the extra coverage.
With a manufactured smile for each occasion, she
managed to squeeze in the extra time to accommodate
the interviewers who arrived in a steady procession to
greet the "Princess of Rodeo," as she had been
recently dubbed.

Riff was always there beside her. During more than
one interview, Lauren had winced, kicking him beneath the table to keep him from making an utter
horse's ass of himself, and her along with him, as he
expounded on her profession.

"I was thinking, Lauren," Riff said one day, after
they had completed a tour of the gallery with a
representative of *Art in America.* "I was thinking that
we ought to announce our engagement at the opening."

She almost dropped the clipboard she held. "What!"

"We'd get a fantastic amount of coverage. And my parents will be there."

She gaped at him incredulously. "Are you serious?"

"I haven't talked to my parents yet. But I'm sure they'll go for it."

"Well, I don't go for it."

"I didn't expect an elaborate show of enthusiasm, Lauren, but I thought—"

"I know exactly what you thought." She approached him, her pen pointed like an accusing finger. "You have this craving for some free publicity that will win you some nice new voters. Only I have no intention of prostituting my personal feelings for some free ink. I am not announcing my engagement to a man who I don't love and who doesn't love me."

"That has nothing to do with it," he said sulkily.

"Nothing to do with getting engaged? What do you have, ice in your veins?"

"I wasn't suggesting marriage. We'll only announce the engagement. We can play the rest by ear. If it works out to our advantage, and if we're in mutual accord at a later date, then we can carry the engagement forward to its natural conclusion."

"You sound like you're framing one of your bills on transportation!" she raved. "Why, you can't even say the word. The word is 'marriage,' Riff. Marriage? As in commitment. As in till death do us part? Does any of that have a ring to it, speaking of rings?"

"You don't have to be so sanctimonious," Riff said sullenly. "You've gone along with this relationship, too, and you're no more interested in any kind of real emotional commitment than I am. You've got a heart like—what's that stuff? Gesso."

Lauren glared back at him, too stung by his words to think of a fitting retort. It was the worst kind of insult, the type of remark she found completely odious because it was more true than false.

"I apologize," Riff said stiffly. "We've been straight about our relationship this far. I just thought you'd go along with my suggestion since we'd both profit from the publicity."

Lauren moved away so he couldn't read her broken expression. "I resent being made out to be some kind of cold, analytical machine."

"Well, you're no wide-eyed wonder from Kansas, either. If you're harboring illusions of Prince Charming on bended knee and vine-covered cottages in the country, you'd better cancel them. You passed up that fork in the road a long way back."

Instead of presenting the easy-going rah-rah-boy persona, Riff had taken on the aura of a tough, manipulative opponent. She had almost forgotten: Riff was a McIntyre. He was part of a family used to getting what it wanted—one way or another. She hoped to hell that he wasn't serious about wanting her.

"You're saying that I've lost my options on love because I've chosen to become successful."

"I'm suggesting that you'd better face certain realities. You're part of a different world, one that doesn't include some of your fanciful notions about romance." Riff took a deliberate, sweeping glance around the gallery. "You're going to need a very special breed of clientele to keep this place open."

"Well," she said quietly, catching the underlying message, "you're right about one thing. I'm not some country bumpkin who just fell off of the turnip cart. I know exactly what my business requires to survive."

"I hope so," he said and left.

The scene with Riff had left a bitter taste in her mouth. She understood perfectly well what Riff had meant. Every possible contact with money and prestige counted at this point. Riff had plenty of both. He had reminded her of that. No, he had warned her.

Jacqueline was in charge of three high school girls who had taken courses in calligraphy. Lauren found them in the back workroom laboring over the black velveteen invitations. Each invitation, embossed with gold-leaf lettering, announced the opening of the Lauren Taylor Gallery. She scanned the guest list, and finding Maxwell Kain's name, said, "Wait a minute. This one I address personally." To Jacqueline she added, "Make sure it gets mailed."

Her old nemesis, Maxwell Kain, was now the most powerful art critic in Los Angeles.

She hadn't seen Christopher Reynolds since the evening he had shown up at her apartment. Now she took the invitation addressed in his name and put it in her purse. "I'm saving on postage," she said to Jacqueline and drifted off mysteriously.

As she drove to Venice, she realized she was going faster than the speed limit. Her mind was racing as well. Riff's accusation that she had closed the door to her heart when she had opened the door to her gallery had upset her. She couldn't say that he was entirely wrong. There had been numerous men in her life whom she had dated, but the moment anyone became close to her emotionally, she pulled away. There had been some nice men, decent men, so she couldn't put the blame on the selection at hand. It had been more her unwillingness to enter into a relationship. She had been desired, but she, herself, had never burned for a man enough to give herself completely.

Christopher answered the door, looking surprised to see her, but not particularly pleased.

"Hi," she said, "I brought over your invitation." He had obviously just showered, and his hair gleamed shiny and wet. His shirt was unbuttoned, and he was without shoes.

He opened the screen door, but made no move to step aside for her to enter. Accepting the invitation, he tore it open and examined the black velveteen with its gold-leaf engraving. She caught the sparkle of admiration in his eyes. When he said nothing to her, she was disappointed.

"You could have mailed it," he said, slipping it back into its envelope.

From the time he had opened the door, he had barely glanced at her. First he had studied the invitation, and now he stared past her to the sky beyond.

"No trouble," she said. "I was in the neighborhood." He didn't laugh. "All right, I give up. What's wrong?"

"I was just on my way out," he answered.

"Oh, sure. Well, don't let me keep you." She started to turn away, feeling ridiculous. She had never thought of him as having a personal life that included a woman. She should have.

He caught her quickly by the arm. "Congratulations are in order," he said as she turned to him.

There was no hint of celebration in his face. "Really? For what?"

"Your engagement to the senator."

"My . . . where did you hear that?"

"My friend told me. Not the cat—the other one. The one who likes to spend his time in bars watching football on television. He caught your fiancé's act on an interview show this afternoon."

Lauren collapsed against the rail behind her. "It's not true," she said between tightly gritted teeth. "It's a damned lie."

"What is he to you?" Christopher asked abruptly.

"A pain in the ass."

"Seriously."

"I am serious." Lauren sighed, looking beyond the wooden railing to the skyline beyond. "He's part of a complicated business relationship."

"Does he know that's all it is?"

"Oh, yes. He knows it very well. That's what's so infuriating."

"Are all your relationships with men business oriented?"

"They have been, mostly." Somehow she felt as if she should be ashamed as she had just admitted to a severe lack in her character.

"That's what I kind of thought." He stepped back into his apartment. The screen door swung closed. Behind the gray metal netting, he was a faded image.

"I'll see you at the opening?" she asked.

"Sure. A deal's a deal, isn't it? You make me a star, and I make you a commission. That's the way it works, right? Of course, I'm not too familiar with these things. Maybe I ought to ask the senator how it goes."

"Christopher—"

He was waiting for her to continue, but she couldn't. After a beat, she said, "I'll see you then, at the opening."

Turning, she walked down the wooden side stairs, thinking that she had taken a wrong turn into an unfamiliar neighborhood. She didn't like being lost.

Lauren was in her bedroom. The doors to the armoire were opened wide, displaying the television screen. Standing with only her bra and half-slip on, she cradled the phone beneath her chin as she watched the end of an interview Riff had taped earlier that afternoon being replayed on the seven o'clock news. She was trying to concentrate on two things at once: the interview as it played and Riff's explanation of the same.

"That's ridiculous," Riff was saying. "I never said we were engaged."

"Not in so many words, you didn't. But you managed to do one of your coy little numbers giving the impression we were."

"Oh, Lauren, Lauren . . . you know how those things go. Reporters are so slick. They ask you a question, you try to give them an honest answer, and before you know it, they're twisting your words around so that they get the meaning they want."

"There has never been a person alive who has been able to twist so much as a syllable of yours around. We both know that, so cut the baloney."

"And you can cut the shrew routine," he shot back. "Probably half a million people saw that plug for your gallery this afternoon. At least that many. So you've got no complaints coming."

"Don't I? I'm not some chess piece you're moving around on your family's big political board. I want you to issue a retraction, and one that's clear."

"What's the diff? Lauren, it'll all blow over in a few days."

"You do what I want, Riff, or I swear I'll embarrass you every bit as much as you've embarrassed me."

"Don't threaten me, Lauren." His voice had slid down several octaves. It was chilling how fast he could change. Just as suddenly, he switched moods again. "Look, I can't retract anything I didn't say."

She started to object, but he overrode her.

"Incidentally, my father called just a while ago. Were you aware that Phillip Lloyd is going ahead with his plans to open his own museum? That could work out very well for you."

"No, no, I didn't know that." As Riff had planned, her grievance against him was momentarily forgotten.

"My parents have been speaking to some of their friends. You'd be amazed at some of the paintings that have been kept locked up in those old family estates for years and years. You'd be really amazed," he repeated. "So, anyway, I was thinking, wouldn't it be super if you got introductions to some of those people who might be willing to unload? I'd imagine Lloyd would be very grateful to anyone clever enough to root out some treasures for his museum." He paused just long enough for her to assimilate his message. "So, anyway, Lauren, getting back to the other thing—why not just let it slide? I'll watch my slippery tongue in the future. And, of course," Riff said placatingly, obviously sensing the match was not yet won, "your opinion is well taken."

"Understand one thing, you can't manipulate me. I'd appreciate it if you'd impress that upon your family, too." She replaced the phone, then thoughtfully considered Riff's news about Lloyd opening a museum.

There was no doubt that Lloyd would consider her services to acquire paintings on his behalf; but other dealers who had been in business much longer than she had would have an edge over her, merely from the standpoint of their longevity in the art field.

They had cultivated a social and business network that gave them access to art that others less well-connected would not be privy to. Many old-line families might sell paintings long held in their estates, but these offerings were done in secret transactions, as if the implication of selling off personal possessions was shameful and denoted weakness.

The McIntyres could help her a great deal. She was,

however, afraid of what their assistance could ultimately cost her.

The last conscious image she had before drifting off to sleep that night was of a fish circling a piece of bait. There was a faint shimmer of a lethal hook just beneath the lure.

Chapter 6

ON THE MORNING OF THE OPENING, LAUREN STOOD beside Jacqueline on a silver cloud of thick pile carpet surveying the special world she had created.

She had ordered the wall-to-wall silk and wool blend from Edward Fields, whose Los Angeles manager had brought her five samples of custom-dye runs before she was satisfied with the shade. The inclusion of silk to the weave created the misty, shimmering effect found only in the finest Persian carpets. Even with her wholesale discount, the extravaganza had cost her seventy-five dollars a square yard. But now that she looked around her, she knew it was worth it.

Jacqueline adjusted a Jasper Johns abstract that would fetch $145,000 at the opening—give or take a couple of stray thousand.

"What do you think?" Lauren said. "Did we do it up right, or didn't we?"

"It will astound them all."

And Lauren had to admit that she really did agree.

"Only one problem," Jacqueline scolded, "there are some things here that are entirely too fine. Who knows what kind of people will walk in from off the street? And they will place their ordinary behinds in those extraordinary chairs." She shook her head, referring to the six nineteenth-century armchairs placed throughout the downstairs salon. The chairs' gilt wood frames contrasted opulently with the burgundy-colored antique velvet upholstery. A French sofa covered in Scalamandre brocade received the same dour glance from Lauren's top assistant.

"Not to worry," Lauren consoled. "There's enough Scotchgard on everything to survive a direct nuclear hit."

The scent of flowers filled the room. Lauren's florist had delivered the special arrangements of white roses that morning, each bouquet a work of art in itself and placed in the Waterford crystal vases Lauren had provided beforehand. The large workroom at the back of the gallery had been set up as an operations center for the French caterer and his serving staff of twelve.

"There is nothing left to do," Jacqueline announced. She sounded disappointed.

"Oh, yes, there is. I hate to lay this on you, but neither of us could take so much as third place in a dog show, the way we look now."

"I can take a hint," Jacqueline said. "Very well, I leave you with Rembrandt." She waved and departed.

Ah, Rembrandt van Rijin. The drawing had arrived two days ago, delivered by three armed guards from a security truck. The work of art had been hung in the private gallery upstairs, open to her invited guests only for this one night. After that, no one would be allowed in without a special appointment and clearance by Lauren. The room was designed for private showings only. Its function was to entertain those special clients, that half percent of the world's population that never entered a gallery just to browse. They did not buy for color nor make their selections for status. They would come to her gallery solely because they were aware that she had a certain work available by Chagall that no one else had. They bought for investment.

Those were the people whose soft Gucci soles would touch down on the antique brass floor that her architect had railed against installing. It was preposterously extravagant, unthinkable and impractical, he had ranted. It was exactly what she had wanted to hear. She had then insisted on the floor. He was somewhat appeased when she allowed him to put a finish seal of several layers of clear, tarnish-retardant lacquer over the surface.

The room's center was devoted to a sunken pit. A multileveled sofa had been constructed in the shape of a small amphitheater. At the bottom was a stage where paintings could be displayed against different textured walls, which were dropped like floating panels from a trapdoor in the ceiling. A special light grid operated by a computer was installed to duplicate the sun's changing intensity from morning to dusk. The upholstery was silk, in soft varying colors. Small inlaid tables had been built into the platforms at strategic points. One needed only to press a button on each table and a panel would open to expose a conference phone with a built-in calculator for quick figuring.

During the reception that night, Lauren would have two armed security guards circulating this salon at all times. Since the arrival of the Rembrandt drawing, she had been nervous about its safety, regardless of the room's massive door, which had the same special locking mechanisms used for bank vaults. Before leaving for home, she felt compelled to check the room one last time.

At the rear of the salon, a circular stairway wound its way to the level of the special salon. She took the stairs, which ascended in graduating colors beginning with amethyst, going to smoke and becoming a pale blue. The staircase was designed to appear as if it were a platform floating in space. It would lead clients to what Lauren intended would be the most exclusive private showroom for art on the West Coast and, perhaps, in all of America.

She pressed the coded computer panel on the wall beside the locked door and waited several seconds for the machinery to operate. Stepping into the salon, she saw the Rembrandt in its place of honor. Across the room from the drawing, she had hung Christopher Reynolds's paintings. Jacqueline had said she was insane and had looked at her queerly. "He is very attractive," Jacqueline had said cryptically. Then, more to the point, she added, "Starving artists are always three things: they are hungry, they are sexy and they are bad news. Do not make the mistake of falling in love with one."

"You have a peculiar notion about my professional interest in this man," Lauren had returned with pique.

"Mon chère, in this room you have a Rembrandt, you have a Chagall, you have a Braque. There is only one man represented here who is not lying beneath the earth. This is Reynolds. He has no reputation, no connections. Only one thing does he have—a lovely smile." Upon further consideration, she added, "And, I will grant, an attractive male physique."

"I wouldn't know about that."

"Non? Well, I think soon you shall."

Lauren let the matter drop.

On the low table between the two Reynolds abstracts, she had put the roses he had sent her that morning. There were twelve of them—all red, with long stems. Before she left the Rembrandt to change into her evening's outfit, she removed one of Christopher's roses. It would look nice at home.

At seven-thirty, the guests began arriving.

They did not come in a trickle, but *en masse*, in waves of glittery jewels, designer gowns, feather boas, high-fashion funk costing more than the haute couture originals, black tuxedos, velveteen dinner jackets trimmed in eel skin and styles yet too new to have been publicly named.

Outside on Rodeo, valets hopped to open the doors of the Rolls-Royces, the Jaguar sedans, a sampling of exotic sports cars and most often those of the ubiquitous Beverly Hills chariot, the Mercedes-Benz.

Each guest presented his invitation at the door where Jacqueline was posted behind a Louis XIV secretary. She extended warm greetings in each guest's language and, after giving them her expert once-over, allowed them to pass into the gallery. She had assured Lauren earlier that there would be no party crashers at this function.

At first Lauren had greeted guests individually, but within an hour the crush of humanity had swelled to proportions precluding this social nicety. Instead she drifted among small cliques saying her hellos and accepting congratulations and compliments with graceful humility.

For the occasion, she had worn a taffeta gown in a subdued wine color. It was fitted and had a low scooped neckline that displayed the antique ruby and diamond necklace at her throat—a gift from a favorite great-aunt. Her hair was slicked into an elegant and sensible chignon, and diamond earrings flashed as she turned her head in response to greetings.

Riff was impressed by her appearance. He was not a man who cared much for fashion other than the uniforms of yachting, but he knew "class" when he saw it. She had also passed muster with the senior McIntyres who had arrived with their group of twenty, a sedate parade of the obviously civilized come to mingle with the untamed natives of Southern California.

Madeline took her aside. "You're looking well, indeed," she said. Clarence joined them immediately.

"Thank you. Have you seen the Rembrandt upstairs?"

"Yes," Clarence said, "and we were delighted to have arranged for it."

Lauren bit her tongue to keep from responding that they could stuff their help, which had nothing to do with the Rembrandt at all. "I'm so pleased that our world still has true patrons of fine art."

Riff grabbed her by the elbow to meet a reporter from *Artnews*.

"Who is he?" the man asked breathlessly.

"Who is who?"

"The one upstairs with the others?"

"Ah, you mean Christopher Reynolds."

"I know his name. I can read," the reporter said testily, "but I mean, who the hell is he, and where the hell has he been that I've never run across him before? He's not German, is he?" the man asked, suddenly seized with inspiration. There had been a recent influx of flashy, new wave, neo-expressionist artists from Germany.

"American as apple pie. He's been in his garage repairing motorcycles."

She spotted Christopher across the room. He had found a black leather dinner jacket to wear, and it looked stunning. No matter what he put on, he wore it with *élan*. His shirt was white and open halfway down his chest. Improbably, he wore jeans. Instead of looking ill-dressed for the occasion, he seemed to

have created a style all his own that made others look
boorishly unoriginal.

"If you want to know more about Reynolds, he's
over there, the man in the leather and jeans."

"Oh," said the reviewer, "oh. He does look intriguing, doesn't he?" He faded quickly away, and Lauren
watched, amused for a moment as he snaked through
the crowd toward Christopher. She saw Christopher
turn with surprise, shake the man's hand and look
momentarily lost as he moved off with him to the side.

Her socializing was interrupted to accept the sales
of several paintings, and when she had finished with
her customers she found Christopher in the upstairs
gallery.

He was not looking at his own paintings, around
which a crowd had assembled. Instead he stood off to
the side, eyeing the Rembrandt as if ready to pace off
for a duel.

"The dude had a fine eye," Christopher said as she
took her place beside him.

"So does this one," she said. "More champagne?"
She took two glasses from a passing waiter. "I'm
starting to feel little bubbles playing in my brain."

"Thanks." He took his glass. Looking into her eyes,
he said, "And thanks for that." He gestured to where
his paintings were displayed.

Lauren raised her glass. "I wanted you to be in
good company for your coming-out party. Oh, and
thanks are also in order for the flowers."

"They cheated me," he said. "I ordered twelve."

"Twelve arrived. I took one home with me."

He was quiet, as if analyzing her remark for hidden
implications. She felt herself growing warm under his
questioning gaze.

"I'd better be going . . . sales . . . that sort of
thing." She felt like a teenager again. The only thing
she didn't do was shuffle her feet.

"Lauren," he said, "you look beautiful."

"So do you." The remark came out unexpectedly. She laughed, covering her embarrassment, and moved quickly away. She felt his eyes on her and knew what she would read in them if she turned around. She wanted him, too.

Phillip and Buffy Lloyd had come and were perhaps the biggest surprise bonanza for the press. They shot pictures of Lauren with the Lloyds, Lauren with the McIntyres, Lauren with some of the Hollywood celebrities, Lauren with the European visitors and Lauren by herself.

"Hold it," she cried, in the midst of the exploding flashbulbs. "You don't want to leave here tonight without capturing history in your little black boxes, do you?" She dragged Christopher out of the crowd and, despite his protests, positioned him in the circle of media representatives.

"Hey! Who are you?" yelled one photojournalist.

"No one," Christopher said, blinking into the lights as cameras whirred and popped.

"He's somebody," Lauren assured them. "He's Christopher Reynolds, and this man's going to be the hottest artist in America within one year."

"Are you speaking personally or professionally?" one of the reporters quipped. Everyone laughed, including Christopher.

He hugged Lauren closer to him, suddenly warming to the circus that he had found himself the ringmaster of. "So, smile, already," he said to her, posing them this way and that, as if born to the art of publicity stills.

His arm was firmly positioned against the side of her breast. As they moved, he rubbed against her, and she felt a velvety tide of desire travel from the pit of her stomach to her chest and fill her with a melting longing for him. She was no longer aware of the crowd, but only of the warmth of his breath on her temple as he moved his face down to hers, accommodating the photographers who called out different shots.

"The champagne has gone to my libido," he said in her ear. "I want to take you out of here."

"Hey, hey, hey!" A chorus of photographers yelled, snapping shot after shot of them together. Christopher danced her through a series of inventive positions, each one requiring that they touch physically. Her whole body and mind burned from longing.

The corner of the room was a blue blaze of flashbulbs and spots brought in from vans owned by the local networks running film of the opening. She felt as if she were alone with him, trapped in a bubble.

"Say you'll go home with me," Christopher whispered, his tongue like the kiss of a butterfly on her ear as he swung her into another pose for the press.

"Stop it, be serious." She smiled into the camera.

"I want you. You want me. Admit it. I do."

"Fame has gone to your head. And I don't . . ." she added. "I don't want you at all."

He was smiling broadly as the journalist from NBC asked him a question about how it felt to be in the company of Rembrandt. He answered with humility and soberness. Lauren knew the champagne was just an excuse to make his outlandish comments to her.

"I'll make you feel wonderful," he said into her ear. "I'll form pictures in your head you've never seen in any gallery. I'll—"

"Make me crazy!" She laughed. Holding up her hand to the press, she said, "Enough, enough. I'm beginning to feel like a negative."

The laughter died on her lips as she saw Riff standing beside the McIntyres. Other onlookers were smiling at the clowning that had been going on for the cameras, but the McIntyres formed a funereal tableau.

Christopher was trying to lead her away, but she pulled back. "Please . . . no more. I can't afford games. This night is too important to me. Fantasy's terrific, but it has its place." She spoke sharply.

"Sorry," he said. "Funny how I had considered myself very real. Flesh and blood and all that. Or have you been too busy with business to notice?"

Although it was deserved, the rebuke stung. "I've been busy," she answered.

"Too bad. Then you've been missing out."

"Oh, Christopher . . . please, please don't." She pulled away from him before things could get worse, escaping into the emotional safety of her profession.

Jacqueline had written up the sales slips, and now Lauren took care of the appraisal papers and the certificates of authenticity of the art purchased that night. It was late, and she was exhausted. Inside her office, she could hear the muted strains of the string quartet playing on the second-story landing. It was with effort that she rejoined her own party.

Lauren had forgotten about Maxwell Kain. It came as a shock to see him standing in a corner watching her as she handed a client an envelope with the sales papers for an Andy Warhol.

"Mr. Kain," she said, coming to him, "I'm so pleased you could come tonight."

"It's been an interesting event," he said. "But then so many of these events are interesting and so few unique."

Kain still had his old talent for spoiling anything that could bring a moment's pleasure. "I consider my opening unique," she said defensively, feeling as if she were eighteen again.

"Somehow, I was sure you would. But you see, Miss Taylor, just because something is expensive and showy does not mean it has substance. Only substance can endure. You have opened your enterprise on a street that pays homage to fads, Miss Taylor. Fads come and fads go. Interesting that you should be attracted to this street, wouldn't you say?"

"Mr. Kain," she said sweetly, "every year I'll have a party, and I want you to know that every year I'll look forward to sending you an invitation."

Kain smiled, his thin lips taut strings of contempt. "I'll be haunting my mailbox, Miss Taylor—but I won't hold my breath."

It was four o'clock in the morning when Lauren closed the doors to the gallery and said good-bye to Jacqueline.

When she returned home, she had only just fallen into bed when the telephone rang.

"You made a fool out of me tonight. Don't ever let me see you with that man again," Riff said, his voice riddled with spite. "If it is going to cost me, Lauren, then I'm going to make damned sure it's going to cost you, too."

"You can't threaten me," she said.

"No threat, babe. Just the truth."

The line went dead. In the silence she could imagine Maxwell Kain's shrill laughter.

Chapter 7

THE OPENING WAS NOT JUST A SUCCESS; IT WAS A CLEAR triumph, both critically and financially.

In Lauren's office, the teletype machine ran with clattering regularity as it recorded offers from art agents in New York, Lisbon, Zurich and Rome. Each communiqué was scrutinized carefully before having her new secretary respond with her decisions on the artists' works she would exhibit.

There were follow-up interviews with the art media and luncheons with new institutional clients who had specific requirements in mind for long-term acquisition programs. Her secretary or Jacqueline fielded the junk calls and took messages on others, which Lauren would return during the last two business hours of each day.

Lauren scrupulously avoided taking or returning calls from Riff McIntyre, who had left for his Washington, D.C., office a day after her opening.

She did take one call immediately. Jacqueline did the forbidden, using her wisdom to interrupt Lauren in a meeting with a West German steel magnate being held in the sacred confines of the upstairs salon.

"Lloyd's calling from Milan," Jacqueline explained,

hurrying down the stairs with Lauren. "Rather, I believe he said he was flying over Milan."

"I was impressed," Lloyd began, his voice carrying a smile, even through the static.

"The checks for the Rembrandt and the two Reynolds's paintings are clearing the banks. I'll send the proceeds to your West Coast office, minus my commission, in a day or so."

"No. Send the artist all the money for his work," Lloyd ordered. "And I'd like to arrange for a one-man showing for Reynolds."

"I see."

"When would you be able to have it?"

"I can't."

"Sorry. I don't think I heard you correctly."

"Reynolds is a marvelous talent. And you have every right to want to promote him. I'll be happy to arrange something with another gallery for you."

"No," Lloyd said. She could hear the pique in his voice. "I want your gallery for him. I want the best. What's going on, Lauren?"

"Nothing, and I want to keep it that way." There was no sense in her being coy with Lloyd. He was not a stupid man. Playing games with him would only irritate him further.

"You haven't let personal feelings enter into your business considerations before this. I think it would be a mistake for you to begin now." His voice became firmer. "I'm a busy man, Lauren. That meeting in my office took more time out of my day than I had to give. You were carefully selected for a number of reasons. The time I spent with you was to establish what I had anticipated would be a continuing relationship. You knew that, too."

"Forgive me," she said. "I responded hastily. And foolishly."

She had been standing with the phone in her hand; now she sank into her chair, feeling defeated.

"Leave a message with the date of the showing with my office in Century City. Buffy and I will both want to be there, so we'll need advance notice to arrange our schedules."

The connection became more fuzzy, and they signed off.

Not wanting to see Christopher Reynolds had nothing to do with Riff's threat. It had to do with knowing that any kind of relationship between them would ultimately end in futility.

Her cravings for emotional companionship and physical satisfaction were as intense as any normal woman's. But love . . . she did not know if it would have a place in her life. For that matter, she did not know what love was.

Countless nights she had lain awake, throbbing with loneliness, asking herself that unanswerable question: What was love? Was love a myth? No. She had heard the songs, read the books of poetry exalting the emotion, seen the gleam of its existence too many times in the eyes of others—cursed or blessed?—not to believe in its reality. But eventually the sparkle of love always dimmed to a dull film in the eyes of countless friends she had known over the years. And eventually they would no longer move with the fluid grace of people who walked on air, but would drag themselves listlessly through gray days until the pain ebbed and once again they existed in an equilibratory state.

Eventually love would always leave.

Lauren had compiled evidence to the contrary that it was "better to have loved and lost, then never to have loved at all." It was better to exist without the pain and the pleasure, without the passion and the ice, without the thrill of the emotional roller-coaster ride that would send the poor, captive passenger spilling over the side or, perhaps even worse, have him come to a jarring, anticlimatic stop at the end of an exhilarating run.

Love, Lauren had finally decided, was an exercise in futility, a surrender to the brief madness that was the cause of wars, suicides, overpopulation and ruined businesses. That the same state of altered consciousness was also responsible for mankind's bliss, for its most magnificent art, literature and music, was viewed as inconsquential to Lauren, faced with her fear of becoming an emotional casualty.

She sent him a note in the mail, and two days later Christopher came into the gallery wearing a pair of slacks and a sports jacket.

The European-styled clothes appeared expensive and completely altered his outward personality. He could have been a rich Italian playboy, rather than the rough-cut Bohemian she had met a few weeks earlier.

"Looks like you went on a buying spree," Lauren commented.

"It was time, don't you think? Thirty-two years of looking like a reject from the markdown sale rack at a discount house is long enough for any man. What do you think?"

"Well, you look—"

"Fabulous? I'll settle for better."

"Different."

"Why do I get the feeling you aren't pleased with the new me?"

"I don't believe that clothes necessarily make the man," she said gently. She was aware that his change in style was not necessarily effected in superficial jest.

"Interesting. And yet the man that you—that you see—dresses impeccably. I'd call the senator's look kind of overgrown preppy, wouldn't you?" He paused, but the comment he was seeking from her was not related to fashion. She knew he was fishing for a personal response to her feelings for Riff. To cover himself, he continued with the rapid banter. "Not my style, however. I'm more the continental type. At least that's what the silver-tongued devil of a tailor told me. Do you think I'm an easy mark?"

They both laughed. She had prepared his checks, which she handed to him, along with her verbal explanation. "Phillip Whelen Lloyd is your mysterious benefactor. It's because of Lloyd I've asked you down here."

He seemed disappointed by her last remark. She turned away, going to her desk and, with a great show of purpose, pretended to gather papers together.

"I'm impressed that Lloyd's impressed," he said, his dark eyes fixed on her.

"Yes, well, Lloyd wants you to have a one-man showing."

"Good. I'm ready," he said.

She looked up, surprised by the note of confidence in his voice.

"I want you to make me rich—a star—like you said."

There was no humor in the remark. She knew he meant every word. "I thought you artists were committed solely to your work. Isn't your profession a religious calling—money being bourgeois . . . insignificant . . . even, I've heard tell, downright unclean?"

Christopher smiled. "Yesterday's gossip. There's a new tale on the streets. I've heard that money buys steak, vintage wine and fine new threads." Pointedly, he paused, looking at her, looking into her. "Yeah," he said, "money can buy a great deal, and I'm a man who has developed an incredible appetite for what life has to offer. I've been hungry for a long, long time. Just so you understand."

And she did; miserably, she understood. She just didn't know what she was going to do about her knowledge.

In the weeks to come, Lauren was to discover three things.

The first discovery was that Lloyd had the energy of several highly motivated men, the memory of an elephant, the capacity for detail of a recently graduated CPA and the organizational brilliance of a field general during an invasion.

He had decided to promote Christopher Reynolds into a major name, and nothing was going to stop him. Between the two of them, they decided that Christopher was ready for a one-man showing. Lauren was objective: Christopher's recent work was flawless; his earlier work was better than eighty-five to ninety percent of other painters, but not beyond critical reproach. He would need to create new paintings for his show.

The second new thing Lauren learned during this period was that not all artists touched with genius were emotionally crazed.

Rather than lash out with a show of temperamental histrionics as Lauren moved through his bedroom-gallery commenting on the suitability of each of his paintings for the exhibition Lloyd had suggested, Christopher merely followed her with placid acceptance. "Eight of these are up to the standard we want," she concluded and made notes to herself on a pad. "I'll need another twelve from you." She looked up, armed for a display of resistance.

"How much time do I have?"

"That's entirely up to you."

"Good. Then I'm going to work night and day. Six months, and I'll have them ready for you—if not before. How's that?"

"Pretty damn fast."

"I'm pretty damn anxious."

It was the first instance that Lauren had gotten an emotional response from him since arriving at his apartment that evening.

He turned and walked through the living room into the small kitchen. Lauren followed. From where she stood in the living room, she could read tension in his profile. The strong jaw had tightened, and the mouth was pulled into a grim line.

"You don't have to kill yourself," Lauren said. "A month or two or three more wouldn't matter. What counts is the final product."

"I'm thirty-two," he said, his voice toneless as he concentrated on the wine he was pouring into two water glasses. "Do you think I like serving a beautiful woman cheap Chianti out of glasses like these?"

Lauren accepted the wine from him. "I don't mind . . . really."

"Well, I do." His eyes drifted from her face, traveling almost of their own accord down the length of her body. They were filled more with longing than with male lust. He closed his eyes and drank deeply from his glass.

When she said she had to go, he didn't attempt to stop her. Somehow she was disappointed. But, of course, she realized it was all for the best.

The third new thing she learned came three days after her visit to Christopher's apartment. She had discovered that she did not know the nature of starving artists quite so well as she had previously thought; now she found that she did not know her own nature either.

Christopher called her from a pay-telephone booth. "You've got to come down here," he said emphatically.

"Christopher, I can't just take off in the middle of the day. I've got three dyed-in-the-wool art addicts here. They also happen to be on the board of one of New York's largest banks."

"Okay, okay. But come tonight. I mean it. I can't go on until you give me your opinion."

"You are one fantastic baloney artist. And a rotten actor to boot."

"But will you come?" he pressed her.

"Have some of that cheap red stuff available." She sighed. "Today's been something else."

She arrived at his apartment shortly after seven, forty-five minutes late. Christopher was pacing. She saw him through the screen door just before knocking.

"The spaghetti's ruined," he said morosely, letting her in.

"Sorry . . . I didn't realize." She stared in wonder at the table he had set. It was cleared of its usual debris, including the presence of Cavalier Cat, who sat in a corner staring at her with eyes of yellow contempt. There was a red-and-white checked tablecloth, mismatched plates, flatware atop paper napkins and candles, already lit. The flames danced gaily in the seabreeze flowing in from the screen door.

He wasted not a moment, but pulled a chair out for her. As she sat, his hand lingered on her shoulder just a beat longer than necessary before he moved back into the kitchen.

Tonight he wore light buff-colored slacks, and his shirt was a blue pullover, tucked into his belt and

pressed taut against his lean, muscular chest. She had
to look away from him, pretending interest in the cat,
afraid of what secrets he might read in her eyes. It had
been a long time since she had made love. Opening
the gallery had been a monumental distraction, but
now . . .

"I'm not used to this," he called, working in the
kitchen. He was as busy and noisy as a chef with a
hundred unexpected diners on his hands.

"You're joking, of course. I never would have
dreamed . . ."

He appeared at last with a tray and bowls containing the spaghetti, the salad and the Italian garlic
bread. Rather than the cheap, California varietal, he
flourished a fine bottle of French Cabernet. She also
noted the new crystal glasses.

"I thought I was going to find a suicidal artist this
evening, not a maniacal cook."

"These are fast times we live in," Christopher said,
offering her some lightly burned bread. "You hesitate
—you take your chances on what you find later."

"I'll remember that."

"You may want to," he said, and there was no trace
of humor in the remark. He poured wine for them
both.

The reflection of the candles in his eyes were
exclamation points celebrating her presence at his
table. "To our venture," he said, raising his glass.

"To your success," she said.

When she looked into his eyes, it always happened
that she felt vulnerable, afraid of being absorbed and
controlled.

"What problems are you having with the painting?"
she asked.

"I'm not."

"But you—"

"Lied. I lied because I wanted to get you over here, and this was the only way I figured I could do it. I'd heard somewhere that the way to a woman's heart is through her—"

"Christopher, please . . ."

"I guess I heard wrong." He was silent. After a moment, he said, "Look, what is it with you? I get these definite feelings from you, and then something seems to change."

"I shouldn't have come here. I wouldn't have, except that I honestly thought this was about your work. I'm sorry if I've led you to believe—"

"Have some more bread. More wine?"

"Yes, wine. Thanks."

"It's very good, don't you think? Much better than that plain-wrap stuff. Even Cavalier turns up his nose at that, and he'll drink almost anything." He stopped. Staring at her, he said, "Why don't we just quit playing the games? I'm an artist, Lauren, and from what you're telling me, I'm pretty good. That means that I've got eyes in my head to see what's going on in plain sight, but I've been trained to look beneath the surface, too. In other words, I don't just paint abstracts, I'm able to abstract—emotionally."

"Your abstracts are wonderful. Lloyd thinks—"

"Don't," he said. "Don't try to avoid this conversation. It was bound to happen sooner or later, anyway, so let's just get through with it. Let's decide what it's going to be, because we're going to be working together."

"Right. And working together is not—"

"Sleeping together?"

She pushed herself away from the table, suddenly feeling claustrophobic. She looked around for her purse.

"Your purse is in the kitchen, on the counter," Christopher said, his eyes boring holes into her. He looked amused. "I'm the crude, poor-slob artist, right? And you're the classy, uptown lady. That's the scenario we're dealing with here, isn't it?" He also stood. Moving around the table, he pulled her to him and lifted her chin.

Her breathing quickened automatically, and she felt a rush of hot desire.

But he drew away from her, the faintest outline of a mocking smile on his face, his color deepened from his own response to her. "You aren't afraid of me," he announced, almost with wonder. "You're terrified of yourself."

That was the end of the subject for then. Lauren felt as if he had worked out the whole evening to the last detail, and that she was being masterfully directed. It gave her a sense of being out of control, an experience that was uncomfortable and strangely pleasurable at the same time.

Rather than allow her to see the work he had done in his studio, he took her for a walking tour of the canals.

Venice had been conceived during the early twenties as an architectural replica of its Italian namesake. Planners had constructed deep canals, which time had since filled with dirt, so that now they were navigable only by rafts and rowboats. Narrow, arched bridges spanned the waterways. Sidewalks were mostly cracked and overrun by grasses along the banks.

As they walked along the edge of a canal, ducks converged upon them, demanding handouts from Christopher who had had the foresight to think of taking along the burned garlic bread.

There was a charming seediness to the area that appealed to Lauren. It was as if civilization had forgotten about the area, leaving nature to joyously reclaim its own. Some of the houses along the canal banks were hovels and some were modern palaces of glass and stucco.

"California modern Moorish," Christopher labeled them.

The moon had come up and, as they walked across one of the bridges, it played beneath them on the water like a drifting, luminescent ball. Christopher stopped in the center of the bridge.

"See that place over there." He pointed to a modern glass structure, all cubes and clean angles, with girders of redwood lending support where necessary.

"It's breathtaking," Lauren said. It looked like a crystal palace, the rooms lit up where wall-to-ceiling drapes had not been drawn closed against the night and unseen prying eyes like theirs.

"In the day, the sun hits the water and bounces against the glass. You get a wild, prismatic effect. Pretty spectacular. And, at night, when they've got the lights off, I've watched the moon float past in the sky and, the way the glass mirrors it, it's as if the moon enters and wanders through each room. Inside out, outside in."

Christopher was quiet then, and the only sounds were a gull and the water lapping against the banks. They leaned over the railing. Lauren saw their reflections dark against the water's color.

Turning his head, Christopher smiled at her. "It takes a lot of guts to live in a place like that."

"Yes," Lauren agreed, still staring at the dark shadows they made on the water's surface. "I would imagine it would."

"Being vulnerable takes a pretty tough person."

"What are you?" she asked, careful not to look at him.

"I thought you knew." He threw a piece of bread

into the dark water. "You act like you've got me all figured out. You're thinking: here's a man who has some talent and he lives in his place, which ain't so fancy, and he drives his bike, which is kind of macho, and the best way to treat a guy like this is to keep him in his garret with his paints, pat him on the head, rev up his ego now and then—and, baby, avoid him on any personal level."

"Now who's sounding defensive." She responded defiantly although his words had made her uneasy. His points were legitimate.

"Me. I resent having been discounted as a man because of what you've judged from the outside. Maybe all you're seeing is the reflection of your own fear."

He threw a large piece of bread in the water. It hit where their shadows were, and Lauren watched their images break and spiral outward.

Before new shapes could form again, she looked off. "It's getting chilly. Let's go back." She hugged her arms protectively against her chest as they started down the bridge's slope going toward the road.

Christopher came up beside her. Then, in the dark overhang of a tree's weeping branches, he stopped suddenly and drew her into him. Before she could protest, he kissed her. It was a certain kiss, forceful without being violent, possessive without being demanding, and the emotion behind it penetrated to her core. She felt as if she had been caught in the vortex of one of his abstracts and was being pulled ever deeper into the realm of his male power and urgency. Her body responded to his hardness growing against her, and she moaned at the brush of his hand along the underside of her breast. His palm moved lightly over the thin silk of her blouse, her nipples peaking in immediate response. She cried out softly, her mouth opening to take his tongue, entwining it with hers.

The honesty of the moment frightened her. Reflexively, she withdrew from the desire flooding through her, cutting off the emotions that could bond her to him beyond the physical sensations.

She pulled away from his embrace. "No," she whispered. "I can't." Sadly, she watched as he opened his eyes, dazed from the brief dream they had shared. She looked away, pretending the moon had captured her attention.

"Okay," he said, and that was all he said. Only that. He began to walk, then waited for her to catch up with him.

They continued along in an uncomfortable silence, the tension between them palpable, like an intrusive third party.

"We're going to be working together, so there's—"

"Oh, cut it," Christopher said wearily. "Just don't, Lauren."

"There's no sense in starting something that—"

This time he turned to her, grabbing both of her shoulders. "No sense in starting something that's already over? No, that's pretty dumb of me to even think that. Actually there wasn't anything there except in my own head—stupidity hurts sometimes."

"You aren't stupid. It's just that I have a career, and my life doesn't need to become complicated, or my energies diluted with emotional relationships that can't be anything other than transitory entertainments."

"Cute," Christopher said and laughed unpleasantly. He dropped his hands from her shoulders. Still looking at her, he said, "Transitory relationships. What do you think of me, anyway? That I was just some pickup out looking for a warm body? This is L.A. Warm bodies come with the ease of a newspaper delivered to your drive in the morning. You can get that kind of fun with about as much trouble as buying fries in a burger drive-through. I don't have to do a full-blown courting dance to get myself a little romantic excitement."

It was the first time she had seen him really angry, and she felt a different kind of power in him than the sexual impulses she had responded to a moment before. It was every bit as intense and real, however, and she flinched as much from the brutal honesty in his eyes as she did from the biting remarks.

"No," he went on, "the stupidity wasn't mine. That's all yours, the way your career is all yours, and your whole empty life is ultimately going to be all yours."

"My life is anything but empty," she replied. She turned and started in the direction of her car.

"Isn't it?" he called after her.

It took every bit of courage for her to turn around. With the same tone of voice and with the same dignity she would use in conversing with a foreign ambassador at a cocktail party, she said, "I'm truly sorry if you've misunderstood our relationship. I'll admit that I find you attractive, and I'll accept that I'm every bit to blame for this . . . this unpleasantness." The words were spilling out now, but he interrupted her.

"Very, very nice. I'm impressed. But you can save the rest of your speech. I got it already. We have a business thing going. And that's it."

He saw her to her car, making sure she was safely locked in. Rolling down her window, she called after him, "If you need to speak to me about your work, feel free to call. Anytime."

He had his back to her. He didn't bother to respond.

Chapter 8

JULY WAS A MARVELOUS MONTH FOR THE GALLERY.

The weather in Los Angeles may have been sultry, but Lauren's business was brisk. With Jacqueline on hand to tend the day's mundane duties, Lauren was free to offer her services to the community's cultural development.

It seemed to Lauren that the entire city of Los Angeles was ravenous to experience the arts. Like a western gold-rush town eventually settled into a complacent metropolis of respectability, a ragged-edged Los Angeles had boomed and now greedily sought the refinements available to citizens of New York and L.A.'s polished northern sister, San Francisco. Legitimate theater flourished alongside the film industry's offerings, and beside the garish billboards hawking Las Vegas show girls with and without their feathers, fine-art galleries had assertively edged into prominence.

Lauren knew that money alone could not buy lasting eminence in the world of art. Although it would carry you a long way for a short time, there were other subtle considerations, that in the final analysis, counted for much more.

Reputation for integrity was paramount to assure staying power. She worked tirelessly to integrate art into the public's daily consciousness. Without charge, she gave lectures at the University of California and at other colleges and for any organization that would grant her a platform. She spoke to docents at museums, unraveling the mysteries of the New Wave figurative paintings arriving from Germany. Her selflessness was noted in newspapers, magazines and during her frequent appearances on local television interview programs. In eight months, she had become a celebrity in her own right. The tourists who frequented Rodeo Drive for stolen glimpses of Jane Fonda shopping at Georgio's or Ali McGraw striding by in her tennis togs, would also stop to gape in the window of the Lauren Taylor Gallery for a peek at the media's newest darling. To anyone looking in from the outside, Lauren Taylor had it all: beauty, class, brains and independence.

To keep up the elaborate façade of her public persona, she maintained a manic pace, as if to stop would bring the devil upon her. Days were scheduled without a minute's lapse in activity; nights were spent with special customers, and if there was a break of two hours before her next appointment, she would take in a dance class or work out at her health club. But the energy she was working off did not elevate her spirits; rather it promoted the strain. She had become an adrenaline junky, existing off the excitement of each moment, terrified of the stillness that could trigger serious contemplation. She was running from herself, and like a woman on fire, her frantic exertions merely fanned the flames.

Christopher had not called her after their night together in Venice. At first she congratulated herself on her firm resolve to end something before it began, to keep her life uncomplicated. Then doubt arose to confuse her. She began to wonder if perhaps there couldn't be a compromise between them. They could see each other casually. Sure, sure . . . that would have about the same chance of success as a party for a bird organized by a cat. She was being ridiculous.

There was nothing casual about her desire for the man, not from the first moment she had set eyes on him. And she knew it was the same with him, regardless of what she had said. But desire did not necessarily constitute a basis for a relationship. She was damned if she did, and she was equally damned if she didn't. She wasn't able to sleep with him if she felt nothing emotionally, but she also couldn't allow herself to fully engage her feelings. It was too dangerous.

For eleven years she had watched other women. They, like her, had started out with their own big dreams. And then each one of her friends had met a man, dated, fallen in love, married and finally the dream was lost to the realities of household budgets and children and the responsibility of filling the needs of other human beings.

Once a friend had sent her a letter with a photograph of her family dressed up for Halloween. There were four smiling vampirish faces in that shot, and Lauren had stared at the picture for a long time, finally deciding that her friend had been consumed by these people and that there was nothing left of her original self. Lauren had shuddered, thinking of how easily a woman could fall victim to that same fate. Only it was curious that her friend was smiling along with the other little vampires. It was alarming to think that her friend could actually be satisfied, even happy, in her situation. Lauren finally rationalized that her friend had gone mad, had become crazed and no longer knew any better than to grin.

Some of Lauren's friends had chosen to live with their lovers, proclaiming liberation even as they hurried home from jobs to put chickens in their ovens. The relationships worked for a while and almost always floundered eventually. Then there was the hell of putting fragmented lives back together, the months of lethargy, when their work was lousy, the weight gain, the weight loss, the calls to Lauren at three o'clock in the morning to lament their pasts or to denounce their chances of ever having a future again.

At Christmastime, Lauren still received Christmas cards from young women she had studied with at Sotheby's or worked with in Soho. It seemed that on the bottom of each card there would appear a hastily scribbled personal message. "Carrie and Allison are great. In school now. Have been thinking of going back to work at a gallery." In succeeding years, the messages about the children became more detailed, and about themselves there was only "Am thinking of taking some brushup classes at the local J.C." That was all that was left of the original dream.

Still, on nights when Lauren was not lucky enough to drop off into an instant coma borne of a day's exhaustive routine, she would relive the moment when Christopher had touched his lips to hers. She felt the pressure of his hand on her breast, experienced through her fantasy his male desire hard against her, and she would burn to have him with her, in her, completely. On some nights she would sleep very little, tormented by these recurring impressions.

The morning after, she would feel like a fool and take care to fill her day's appointment book to account for every spare moment.

It was toward the end of July when Lauren was forced to admit that the month had not been in all ways satisfactory.

She had breezed into the salon after giving a talk at the Getty Museum in Malibu. It was after six o'clock.

Jacqueline was locking away the day's cash receipts in the safe when Lauren entered her office to grab her tote bag for exercise class.

"Hi, I'm back. Any important messages?"

"They are there—on your desk. They are always there on your desk," Jacqueline said, her weariness showing through. She twirled the combination lock and gave the door a firm shove closed.

Lauren riffled through the messages. "Nothing," she muttered.

"What do you mean, nothing?" Jacqueline pulled down on her wire-rimmed glasses and tipped them down over her nose to scrutinize Lauren. "There are calls from New York," she began with exasperation. "A call from Rome. And there is the message from that painter—the Italian Buddhist. He has come out of his meditative trance long enough to make this call—a call that you have been waiting for for six weeks, and you say 'nothing'!"

"Sorry, sorry. Poor choice of words. I didn't exactly mean nothing." She picked up her tote bag, ready to leave.

"I know exactly what you meant," Jacqueline said quickly, "and I think we should talk. Now. I will not have you run off on me again. All month I have tried to get you to sit still for five minutes. But you go here and you go there and you are like—what is it?—the cat on the hot tin roof. I am French. I know about these things."

Lauren slumped down into her desk chair. There was no way out of some situations other than total surrender. This was one of them. "You know about what things?"

"The heart." Jacqueline made a stabbing motion in the general direction of that organ. "So, let us be honest. It is that starving artist, *non?*"

Lauren examined her cuticles. "He's not starving anymore. He made enough money at the opening to eat very nicely. Steak, if he pleases."

"You have not heard from him all month. This drives you crazy. This is why you must fill every moment. You get messages from people who would make someone else jump up and down and scream with joy. But you? As you say—nothing."

Lauren hung her head, avoiding Jacqueline's penetrating stare. "It took me eleven years of giving up everything normal to get to this address, Jacqueline. You know that."

"So? You have moved in. You are a bona fide resident now. You can join the human race."

"I'm still only the new kid on the block. Businesses come and go on this street. Anyone who's got himself a big idea thinks he belongs here. As long as I owe money to the bank, I'm just another transient." She thought of Kain's words to her. "Maybe other people can accept me because of what they see on the outside, but I can't. I've got to be free and clear financially first."

"Your receipts are good. You are new, but already you attract the best customers. It is only a matter of time."

Lauren shook her head in disagreement. "I can't relax now. And I can't indulge myself personally." She rose, glad that the teletype machine had come to life. It gave her an emotional breather. She waited for the machine to print its message and to clatter out her confirmation code before ripping the yellow sheet off. Handing it to Jacqueline, she said, "I believe this was your project."

She resumed her explanation. "This career has been like a marriage to me. I committed myself to it totally. And I want it to work."

"Well, that is very fine. Except that you have a cold marriage partner."

"I can't take the chance of diluting my energies on a relationship that could cause me to lose everything I've worked for all these years." Lauren faced Jacqueline as if they were opponents in a life and death contest. "Christopher Reynolds is not the kind of man a woman gets partially involved with. He's not Riff McIntyre. He is a body and soul commitment. All you have to do is to look at his paintings to know that." She paused, thinking back to the first time she had seen Christopher's work in Lloyd's office. "I would lose myself in him," she said. "Totally. Physically, emotionally, intellectually—I would lose myself in him."

"What will happen to you?" Jacqueline said, shaking her head morosely. "You are already lost, and you don't know it."

"Nothing will happen to me," Lauren countered defiantly.

"Don't wait too late to become wise, my friend. This man Reynolds is not going to be in his little place in Venice much longer. He is, in more ways than one, too hot to turn down."

"Believe me, I know what Christopher is."

"Then you had better know that this man will be gone soon. Oh, you may keep him as your artist, but you will not keep him as your lover. There are women who will also discover his talents. They will not hesitate, as you have, and then, my poor Lauren, you will know what you have really lost."

Lauren grabbed up her bag. "Well, I can't think of that now. Don't you understand, the only thing I have the time and the energy to worry about losing at this point is this gallery? I've got a meeting with the bank in two days. This time it wasn't an invitation they sent me. It was a command that I appear with my accountant.''

There was also another meeting that Lauren could no longer avoid, and that was with Riff McIntyre. He had returned from Washington and a visit with his family in Cleveland, calling her immediately to get together.

For the past week she had put him off with various excuses that she was tied up with client conferences and seminars. This time she demurred on the basis that she had a day's schedule planned with the curator of the Los Angeles County Museum of Art, and that she couldn't possibly make it across town to lunch with him. He foiled that excuse by meeting her instead.

They walked together past the La Brea tar pits adjacent to the museum complex. Large cement mastodons stood frozen in eternal jeopardy, their trunks reared piteously toward other cement effigies of their species who watched safely from the banks. Gaseous bubbles rose to the surface, ballooned and exploded just as they had done a million years before when live beasts came to drink from the dark pond. As they passed by, a real melodrama was being enacted on the shoreline as a hapless bird struggled to rid itself of the gooey substance coating its wings.

Riff, however, seemed enmeshed in his own personal melodrama. He kept pace beside Lauren, his eyes hooded as he spoke about his meeting with his parents. "They've hired the top survey researchers to analyze voter preference in the area. Projections are going to be run every two weeks, and based upon certain variables they'll get a fix on my popularity standing.''

She noted immediately how different Riff seemed. There was a gauntness to his face that Lauren had not noticed before, and the perpetual California tan had faded during his absence. Even his voice was tense. The usual laid-back cadence, always an integral feature of his calculated charm, had been replaced with a strident edginess.

The restaurant was across from the museum and down a couple of blocks on Wilshire Boulevard. As they crossed the street, Riff almost stepped into the path of a vehicle making a lefthand turn. Lauren pulled him to safety just in time. He appeared not to have even noticed.

"Hey, you know you almost bought it just then," she said. "You may get a lot of voter sympathy, but dead men rarely distinguish themselves in office."

He wasn't even listening.

The Egg and I was a combination art gallery and restaurant, and its specialty was crêpes. It was always noisy and always crowded, and not the best place to have an intimate conversation. But, then, their relationship had never been based upon intimacy.

"The preliminary research shows that I've a high recognition quotient." He took a long, thoughtful sip of ice water. "But the public's concept of my image leaves something to be desired. It seems that Rod Stewart and I share the same place on the scale. I'm perceived as colorful and sexy, but no one takes me seriously. Needless to say, the response to this report in certain quarters in Cleveland was not wildly enthusiastic. So," he said, "there are going to be some changes. First of all, I am getting rid of the boat."

"Umm . . . that does sound serious." It was meant as a joke, but it didn't amuse Riff. He drank some of her water, having run out of his own by this time.

"I'm buying a home. Not in Beverly Hills or Brentwood or Bel Air. I'm getting a place in Santa Monica, something ordinary and middle class. Something unpretentious." He said the last word as if it were poison on his tongue. "If I'm going to make it another term, I'm going to need to become more publicly acceptable. I need a woman beside me and hints of a family to be."

"My God, you'd prostitute your personal feelings just to please your parents, just to get a few more votes so you can keep a job?"

He surveyed her with contempt. "It isn't just a job we're talking about here. Winning this next election isn't the end of the rainbow. I know that. And you're not stupid, Lauren. You've known all along that I'm being groomed to run in a presidential primary. And you can't be so naive as to think I'm doing all of this just for my parents. I owe favors, they owe favors, and the people whom they're beholden to also owe other people. We're all in this spider web together. Think of it this way: It's all just a large circle of people who are holding hands, and if one person drops out of that circle, there's chaos."

Riff's eyes, usually so lively, had turned to blank walls. The last trip to Cleveland must have really been something. She saw him for the first time, less as a character and more as a human being who had been systematically sapped of his own personality and stuffed with the demands of countless other people. Unfortunately, no longer did he seem just a parody of the plastic man; he had become the genuine ungenuine item.

"I know you don't love me, Lauren, so there's no use in pretending. I mean we both understand exactly what we are to each other. We know what it is that we want out of our lives." He paused, as if trying to remember rehearsed lines. "It has been suggested that you would make an ideal wife for a candidate for the United States presidency."

"No." She didn't even find it necessary to make it a

big "no." It was ridiculous to even consider his proposal.

"Well, I'm afraid that I can't accept that from you."

"And I'm afraid you're going to have to. Believe me, Riff, I am not going to marry you. In fact, as far as I'm concerned, there's no reason at all why we should see each other again."

"Lauren," Riff said, sounding even more tired than before, "the circle I told you about? Lauren, you're already one of the people who are holding hands. You can't drop out. You can't," he emphasized.

It was the certainty that she read in his eyes that alarmed her, that made her go so far as to question her own position. She had never signed any papers, never made any verbal commitments to anyone other than the bank. "I'm totally independent. I'm a free agent, Riff."

"Not entirely." His eyes wandered away from her. They drifted through the restaurant as if he would have preferred to disassociate himself from the person using his body, playing out his life.

"I owe money to a bank, which I'm paying back on schedule. No one else has any claim on me or my business."

At her words, Riff's attention returned. He leaned across the table. His gray eyes were cold. She thought of a frozen pond through which a person could see dim images of life flowing past beneath the surface. What she could make out was cloudy and murky and absolutely frightening.

"You accepted favors from my family. You profited from their power and their influence."

"They brought me clients, yes. But they did that for you."

"Still, you benefited."

"That hardly constitutes selling one's soul."

Riff's fist was clenched, but his voice did not rise from its dull drone. "People made an investment in you, and now they are going to collect on their investment."

"Sorry about the misunderstanding," Lauren said, rising from her chair, leaving her crêpes untouched. She held her purse tightly in her hand, her knuckles white. "I'm a human being, not a corporation. Tell whoever has to know that I'm not paying out dividends."

"Yes, you will," Riff said, looking up at her. "You really have no other alternative." He looked down at his food and took up his fork, as if to eat.

Had Lauren not been so frightened, she might have even felt sorry for him. He looked like a mechanical man who had been wound up, who could say his piece and go through the motions of living, but a man who would never be able to taste the food.

As she started away, he called to her. Turning, she met his eyes that no longer appeared frozen, but instead were melting with sorrow. "Please," he said, "understand that whatever happens, it isn't personal."

She nodded. "Like you said—it never was."

Larry Fine was her accountant. He was a young man, just three years out of business school, and working on his certification. He was as pleased to have her as a client as Lauren was to have him taking care of her books.

"You don't need to worry," he had assured her when the bank had called to have her come in for a meeting. "Everything's in order. Your books reflect a moderately strong growth curve, even though, of course, you aren't an established business yet. They'll just want to look over your profit and loss statement."

"Is that usual?" she asked. "When I've been paying on time?"

Larry furrowed his brow. "Well, no."

For the meeting, she had worn her official banking outfit. It was an Italian design, a two-piece, light-weight wool that worked in any season. Subtle salmon-colored stripes bled into a soft gray back-ground. Her blouse was tailored, a crisp white with an attached bow that softened the mannishness of the suit. She wore her black hair clasped at the neckline with a wide gold clip. Before she left the office, Jacqueline gave her the once-over.

"Who are you supposed to be?" Jacqueline asked. "Queen Victoria or the chairman of the board of IBM?"

"I'm late. If any millionaires drift in while I'm gone, make a sale," she ordered, walking from the gallery.

"I will offer our best champagne. And if that does not induce them, then I shall seduce them . . . I'll sacrifice my body."

"You're one hell of an employee." Lauren laughed.

The bank's conference room was as quiet and frigid as a tomb. The only sound was the air-conditioning blowing from the ceiling ducts as the loan manager studied a sheaf of papers before him. Next to him sat his assistant, a heavy girl afflicted with a nervous obsequiousness that had already caused her to spill one cup of coffee and to slosh a second one into forming a lake in her saucer. The third person sitting opposite of Larry Fine and Lauren was the attorney for her absentee landlord, a Saudi Arabian sheik.

The loan manager looked up. "Your financial state-ment appears in order," he began.

"I don't understand why you felt the need to call in

my books," Lauren said stiffly, feeling righteously vindicated. "There were no delinquent payments."

The banker's eyes moved away and flitted to the papers before him where he twiddled a corner of a paper with his thumb. "We've a right to inspect your books at any time. It's in the agreement."

Larry Fine almost rose from his seat. "But it isn't usual procedure. Not unless there's been a default."

The heavy girl gave off a nervous giggle, then stopped abruptly.

"Uh, Mr. Simonton, here, brought it to my attention that his client is in favor of executing a clause in his lease. The, uh, one that allows for an increased adjustment of rent based upon reassessed property values."

"And I'm assuming that the building my client leases has been reassessed?" Larry's voice was laced with anger.

"Yes, that's true."

The banker would not look at them. Simonton seemed bored with the whole situation.

"And who has made this assessment?"

"Our bank has," the manager replied in answer to Lauren's question.

"Usually an assessment like this isn't made unless there's refinancing involved." Larry pressed him.

"That's correct. My client has had an offer from a purchaser. He can either sell at the reappraised value or he can now raise his rent, according to the clause."

"What's the increase?" Lauren asked.

"He wants a third more."

The heavy girl sucked in her breath, barely suppressing another inappropriate giggle.

"A what!" This time Larry did rise. He slammed his fist down on the table's surface. "What are you, bankers or bandits?"

"Come now, this is common practice today," drawled the lawyer for the landlord. "Surely you're familiar with what's happening all over the city with apartment conversions. What we're doing is really no different."

"The only thing I'm familiar with is that there's something here that stinks. Something's wrong here. Why did you ask to see the books if all you wanted to do was to raise the rent?"

Larry looked about ready to climb over the table and strangle her three oppressors.

She interrupted, speaking softly. "It seems perfectly clear to me." All heads turned to her. "Yes, it isn't at all mysterious. You merely wanted to determine what amount it would take to break me. You could look at my current sales and then pick a figure that would blow me out of the place."

"I think you have a persecution complex, Miss Taylor."

"To be perfectly frank with you, Mr. Engle, I don't believe you have the ability to think for yourself." The banker colored profusely, keeping his eyes glued to the papers before him. Lauren stood and smiled at Larry. He had become pale and seemed to twitch internally with a barely controlled anger for the duplicity he sensed but was at a loss to understand. She knew her young accountant was perfectly capable of lambasting the trio on her behalf. His silence was in respect of her self-sufficiency.

"What is your decision then?" Engle, the banker, asked anxiously, watching as Lauren gathered together her papers and put them neatly back into her attaché case.

"You send me the bill, Mr. Engle. I'll send you the money for the rent. Just as always."

With Larry beside her, she turned and left.

In the parking lot, Larry put down his attaché case. Facing her, he asked, "What the hell was that all about?"

"Oh, that? That, Larry, was a marriage proposal."

"Funny. To me it looked more like a stickup."

"Yes, well . . ." Lauren sighed. "Some men send candy and flowers to convince a girl of their sincerity. And others . . . I guess they send bankers."

But when she returned home, her coolness had vanished, becoming instead a steaming, churning rage. As she looked around her bare apartment, she was almost glad she didn't have anything of value left to throw.

McIntyre had done this. She knew the way his family operated. They had their fingers in everything, obviously one was in this bank. The bank had, in turn, called the attorney, probably making some sort of deal with him to have him sit there like a dummy so everything would look kosher. Nice squeeze play, Riff. But she could match him in finesse.

Riff waited two days before calling her. When he did, Lauren took the call immediately, even breaking off a conversation with a client to speak with him.

"I was wondering if you might be my hostess at a fund raiser? First week of August. A Saturday night. It's at the Bonaventure Hotel in downtown L.A."

"Is it important to you, Riff?"

"Extremely."

She hesitated, then, with an audible sigh, relented. "I'll be there."

"I appreciate that." He paused. "Lauren, I'm going to see that things are going to work between us."

"I know you are, Riff."

She hung up. So . . . the Bonaventure . . . a lovely

hotel. There would be a great many reporters there. She would look her very best.

Jacqueline's face had gone a shade lighter than the oyster-colored paper she held in her hand. "This can't be true," she said, looking at Lauren who was seated behind her, tallying the day's receipts on her calculator.

"It's true."

"But we can't pay an increase in the lease like this! It is madness!"

Lauren stopped her figuring. Quietly, she said, "We'll pay it."

"How? We must do better than we are, and we are working up to capacity. You and I—and the rest of the staff, we give more than one hundred percent as it is. There is not an ounce more of energy left to squeeze out of me." As evidence, Jacqueline collapsed into a chair.

"Forget energy," Lauren said, standing. "Think charm. Think elegance, panache. Tomorrow, my friend, we're going shopping for me. We're putting your taste on the line, too. At last we are going to see if you're truly French, or . . . if you are an impostor."

"You don't need to spend money, you need to get money."

"Don't I just know it." Lauren bit her lip, thinking very hard. "Do me a favor. Tomorrow, go down to Christopher Reynolds's studio in Venice and tell him we're moving his show up to the second week in August. I don't care how many paintings he's got ready."

"But Lloyd . . ."

"Lloyd will understand. After all, once he said he thought I could be a mean little street fighter. Well, now he can see me in action."

* * *

Riff's eyes swept over her as she sat in the back of the rented white Cadillac limousine. She wore a gown of full-length pearlescent beading. When walking in the gown, the material flowed along with her in undulating waves. Curiously, it was as refined as it was provocative. The bodice was caught in a halter at the neck; the back was bare and plunging. It was the perfect outfit for what would eventually be the perfect revenge.

The vehicle's television was turned to a news program. Even as she spoke, she knew that Riff's ear was listening for the mention of his name.

"You look incredible. You've never looked more beautiful." Leaning forward, he poured sherry from a crystal decanter in the bar. "This evening is going to do a lot for us tonight," Riff said, handing her the drink.

"To a landmark occasion." She smiled back, and they toasted.

"My parents are delighted," Riff confided. "They're very pleased at your decision to come tonight. They see you as a supremely sensible woman—their highest compliment."

"Well, a girl can never receive too many compliments."

"You won't regret tonight, Lauren. You're a full member of the club now. You'll be taken care of."

He switched his interest to the television, turning up its volume now that the segment about him had begun. The topic was the fund-raising gala that night. At its conclusion, he was sufficiently elated to pick up her hand and lift it briefly to his lips. His mouth was cold. But, then, so were her fingers.

The room was jammed by the time they made their carefully timed, and late, entrance. A band struck up a raucous welcome, and Riff smiled boyishly, as if overwhelmed by the attention he had generated. Photographers followed them as they made their way through a central aisle, to a raised dais with a long table.

Riff stopped several times, shaking hands with guests and dragging Lauren forward to introduce her. With casual ease, he applied just the right amount of pressure on her waist or her elbow to keep her always facing the cameras.

Lauren played her role with aplomb. She smiled at the guests, she smiled at Riff and, especially, she smiled for the cameras. Her performance would be duly noted on the late news.

"Just keep smiling, love," Riff said as they took their places on the platform. "You don't have to open your mouth for a second. Just smile that beautiful, classy smile."

So she did. All through dinner and through Riff's perfectly delivered speech (she'd vote for him herself, based upon that spiel) she smiled, even through the media's questions after the speech.

"Are you going to give up bachelorhood, Senator?"

Riff leaned in closer to Lauren and waited a shy moment before softly confessing, "The . . . uh . . . the thought may have crossed my mind."

"Miss Taylor?" The press clamored, "Miss Taylor?"

Lauren did exactly as she had been told. She smiled.

At the conclusion of their evening, she received Riff's review. "You were perfect," he pronounced. "And tonight hundreds and thousands of my constituents—and future constituents—are going to agree with me. Damn," he said, "you make me look fantastic!"

She was still smiling when she went to sleep that night.

Chapter 9

Lauren was in the back workroom uncrating a shipment of paintings that had arrived late in the day from Vienna. She had changed into a pair of jeans and a thin T-shirt. Even Jacqueline looked surprised to see her in the outfit.

"You look like an ordinary human being," Jacqueline commented, returning from running several errands outside—including her visit to Christopher Reynolds.

"Looks can be deceiving."

"The framer can have both the Childe Hassams remounted in a week if he can get the stock locally. Otherwise, it may take a month. We may not be here in another month," Jacqueline said.

Lauren let up on her tugging and pinned her assistant with a dark look. "Why must you be so confoundedly gloomy?"

"Because I am realistic," Jacqueline said. "Facts are facts. You are so brave that you are sometimes, I think, a little stupid."

"I told you, it's all going to work out all right. We'll manage to hang on, and eventually things will build up for us so that we're even doing well. I got this far, didn't I?" Lauren knew she was whistling in the dark and so did Jacqueline. But what else was she to do? Fall to pieces? Close up the gallery without even giving it a fight?

"I feel like I am in a western," Jacqueline said. "We are being run off the range."

"We aren't being run off," Lauren objected, working a wrench against a stubborn nail to loosen the crate. "We're having a showdown. Like in *High Noon.*"

Jacqueline dragged a stool over to the worktable and sat. She was not dressed to assist in the uncrating. Dolefully, she said, "I don't remember who won that gunfight."

"Neither do I." Lauren paused to think, then shrugged. "But the good guys always win."

"I don't see any white hats around to distinguish us." Jacqueline was still not convinced. "All I see are the invoices."

Lauren brought out the first painting slowly. She finished unwrapping it on the large, flat worktable, taking time to carefully inspect it for shipping damage. There was none. "By moving up the Reynolds exhibition, we'll be getting extra income, plus plenty of publicity."

"There will not be a Reynolds exhibition."

Lauren's fingers strangled the feather duster she gripped in one hand. "What?"

"He is no longer interested."

Lauren looked around her as if the answer to the situation could be found floating by in the room's atmosphere. "This showing would make him a major name."

"Yes, that's what I said, too."

"And? What did he say?"

"He said that there were other things more important than to become a major name."

"What the hell is that supposed to mean?"

"It means, I think, that we are in very big trouble."

Lauren worked late into the night, going through the mechanical motions of cleaning and cataloguing the new pictures that had been unpacked. Her mind was not on her work. She thought only of Christopher, remembering his smile, the irony in his black eyes as she told him they were only to have a business relationship. And now, Jacqueline had informed her, they were to have no relationship at all.

That was not the way it was to have happened.

But, of course, she could see now that it could have happened no other way. The very reason she was attracted to Christopher was the reason she was now reeling from a terrifying sense of insecurity—even worse than her fear of losing her independence to a man. She was having to come to grips with the truth of her own nature.

She played at being independent; Christopher was truly independent. She had built the equivalent of a temple to honor the passions of mankind expended through the medium of art. Yet in her daily life, she shunned all intense personal feelings. Christopher embraced passion through his work, but this was not a sublimation. Heroically, in his refusal to be manipulated by the lure of fame and fortune, he allowed passion to define his life.

When he gave her the honor of showing his work in her gallery, he had also offered his soul to her. And in return, she had offered him green ink with dollar signs.

Green ink would never be enough for Christopher Reynolds. She only hoped to God that she would be. . . .

She did not go home to her apartment first. Instead, she drove directly to Venice as she was, and somehow the decision not to bathe or to apply perfume and powder and makeup and silk, to abandon entirely the superstructure that defined the public Lauren Taylor, seemed the greatest peace offering she could bring.

So she stood outside Christopher's door on the second-story landing, waiting for him to answer her knock. From within the apartment, a jazz flutist piped a sensuous refrain over the radio.

The door opened, and Christopher stood looking down at her, his expression through the screen door undiscernible. It was a warm night, even near the beach, and he held an open can of beer. His shirt was off, and he wore the paint-splattered jeans of their first meeting. They shared a moment of mute understanding before he opened the door for her to enter.

"I didn't know if you'd come," he said, closing the door, pensive hope etched on his handsome face, restraint edging each word. "When issuing ultimatums, you've got to have the guts to lose."

"But you've won," she said softly. It was she who dared to take the first step forward, and he met her halfway, driving his body against hers as she moved into him, her face pressed against his bare chest.

"God," he moaned, breathing deeply. "It was hell. I thought I'd never see you again." Lending credence to his words, he held her away, looking into her face as if starved for the sight of it. A shadow dulled the luster of his eyes, and he broke completely free of her embrace, going to the table. He slapped the can of beer down. For a moment he leaned both hands on the table's surface, considering something, then made his decision. He swept up a newspaper clipping.

It was a photo of her with Riff, one of the many photos taken of them that night at the Bonaventure. She was smiling, and Riff had his arm firmly around her waist. It shamed her to have him see that false smile.

"No, please . . ." She rushed to Christopher and tried to take the clipping from him, to crush the past between her fingers.

But holding tight to it, he said, "No. I want you to look at it. Be sure, Lauren. Think about what you're doing here tonight. Don't let this evening be another challenge in your life, because it will only end in disaster for the both of us."

"It isn't like that."

"I can offer you my talent as an artist, for whatever that's going to be worth in the future. But that's nothing compared to what McIntyre can give you. I can give you one thing—myself as a man. That's the only guarantee I can make good on."

"I knew that when I put my key in the ignition tonight."

It was Christopher who crumpled the clipping in his palm. He handed it to her, and she dropped it to the floor.

He kissed her then, softly. She had dreamed about this moment for so long that she could barely believe it was actually happening now. She looked up at him, her heart filled with wonder and love. *Yes,* she thought, *I love you, Christopher Reynolds, artist extraordinaire, man extraordinaire. And I will always love you, forever, forever. . . .* She clung to him as he lifted her like a bride and carried her to his bedroom.

"I used to lay in bed dreaming of having you here," he said, propped on his side next to her. The light from a single candle on the floor danced shadows against his lean, hard body.

"And I," she said, tracing her finger along the muscular contours of his chest, "was dreaming the very same dream."

"Only now it's real."

He was kissing her neck, he was making her close her eyes, making her moan softly, as he moved against her and their bare flesh touched for the first time.

"Why did we wait so long?" she whispered.

"One of us was very stubborn." He looked into her eyes, his fingers tracing the planes of her face. She could feel the tension in his body, the male desire held carefully in check—for her sake, she knew. He wanted her to know that this was special for him, too.

"Well that person has now reformed. She's ready." Lauren touched his shoulder shyly, inviting him with her eyes. "I'm ready."

He began to kiss her again, this time with more urgency. Suddenly, he stopped and turned from her.

"What's wrong?" she asked. "Did I do something wrong?" She stroked his back. "Chris?"

Slowly, he turned, looking at her with dark seriousness. "No, no . . . it's me," he said. "Lauren . . . this is all I have to give you. It's got to be good. The best for you."

She smiled, her eyes filling with tears at the same time. Could she tell him that when he looked at her, when he touched her face, when he let his fingers slip even lightly along her arm, she trembled with desire for him? Could she tell him that the sound of his voice vibrated in her heart, in her soul, in her body? No, words could never express feelings like that. She would have to find another way to tell him.

"I want to belong to you," she whispered. "Let me belong to you." She touched his chest lightly with her hand, trailing it lower until his fevered body trembled. The restraint was lost now, for both of them. Her initial self-consciousness was abandoned in her need to please, and his doubts dissolved in his natural male response to her body.

"My love . . ." she cried as they joined together.

From that moment, they moved as one, reveling in the spasms that racked both their bodies until the fire

waned and they lay locked together breathing softly
once again.

"Is it too early," he asked, rising up on his elbow to
study her face, "to say that I love you?"

"I thought you just did," she said, and the sight of
his handsome face made her want him again, even as
their bodies cooled.

"And you?" he asked, his expression changing
suddenly from adoration to anguish.

"Oh, Christopher . . ." She pressed her fingers
against his chest, guiding him to lie on his back.
Rolling atop him, she brought her mouth down on his
and felt his immediate response hard against her leg.
"How can you even wonder?" she asked.

"Say it," he urged. "Say the words aloud for me to
hear."

"I love you, love you, love you," she cried joyously, laughing through the great, real tears cascading
down her cheeks. "It's madness!" she said and
laughed and knew at that moment it was also the
deepest reality.

From that evening on, Lauren was to marvel at the
extraordinary change that had taken place in the
world. The very air smelled of perfumes that had
never been there before. She had long since abandoned popular rock music for the refinements of Bach
and Ravel, but now as she switched radio stations in
her car on route to an appointment or to meet Chris at
his studio, she paused to let the rock lyrics speak to
her soul. The once shallow messages of adolescent
feeling, of indulgent and mushy sentimentality, had
become poetry.

She felt as if she now operated on a special frequen-
cy, and to exist on this new wavelength was to live in a
state of perfect clarity and understanding. Life was
kind to her, and she was generous to each person she

met. There were no questions, only answers now. She had somehow stumbled upon the one universal truth upon which all other truths rested: that the world was comprised of love entirely—each particle, each moment, all feelings.

Christopher had made concessions to the twentieth century by finally allowing a telephone into his Spartan sanctuary. During the course of a single day, they would consult five or six or seven times on plans to grab a pizza that night at ten o'clock. In midsentence, one or the other would lose the train of their conversation, becoming lost in the wonder of the other's existence on the same planet at the same time.

She would arrive at ten to leave with him for the local pizza place. Yet, as frequently as not, their plans would change with the slightest touch of his hand on her waist, the brush of her mouth upon his lips. They would fall languorously into Christopher's bed, exploring, exciting each other, sharing and growing more in love.

On his return from Hawaii en route to New York, Lloyd stopped in Century City to meet with her.

She had brought along a portfolio with all the paintings that Christopher would be exhibiting in his show reduced to small prints. There was also an outline of all her preparations, including news releases, and a list of guests who had been sent personal invitations.

"You've invited all the top art critics. Good," Lloyd said, handing the folder back to her.

He leaned back in his chair, looking at her from across his desk. "Christopher Reynolds is going to become a major force in the art world."

"I know," Lauren said. Even his name stirred a fire in her. Her mind flashed to the previous night's lovemaking.

"I can continue to help him," Lloyd said. "But that's going to mean taking him from you."

Lauren crossed her legs, her outward composure intact. There was no sign of the inner apprehension Lloyd's words had caused her to experience. "What exactly does that mean?"

"That Christopher is going to be called upon to travel—Europe, the Orient, maybe a visit to South America. He may be commissioned to work on a major project in Rome. Or perhaps he might take a guest teaching post at one of the major universities. But he's not going to remain a nonentity in Venice. He's got to move while he's new and hot. Otherwise, he'll be finished before he's begun. He'll fade back into the woodwork. You know this as well as I do."

"Then why make such an issue of it?" she snapped.

"Because I've the impression you might let your personal feelings cloud your professional judgment. That would be a shame—for Christopher, mostly. And I would be lying if I told you that I wouldn't be extremely disappointed on my own account. I've made a considerable investment in both time and energy, and even in dollars, in laying the groundwork for Christopher to realize his full potential in the marketplace."

"Christopher is free to come and go, to pursue his life—" She broke off, her nails digging into the palms of her hands. Hanging her head, ashamed of her display of emotion before Lloyd, she said, "I don't know what's going to happen. To be honest, I can't even allow myself to think about it." She raised her eyes to Lloyd, who was looking at her with a kind of detached compassion.

"Reynolds is very special. He doesn't have the kind of talent that can be thrown away. If you hold him back, Lauren, he'll not thank you for it. He'll wither and die as a human being. His art is as much a part of him as breathing is to ordinary men."

"I'd never do that to him."

"I'm sorry, Lauren. I had no idea that this might happen between you two, although I suppose Buffy tried to warn me at the beginning. I thought that you were too dedicated. I remember our first conversation very well. You've changed a great deal since that time. Anyway," he said, "I will not abandon you. In return for taking Christopher, I will bring you other name artists. At least you can be assured that our relationship will continue."

"Things will work out with Christopher and me," she said. "There's always room for compromise . . . concessions . . ."

The look Lloyd returned to her said that she was kidding herself. Christopher and she would be as two different species: she would be landlocked, planted firmly on Rodeo with her overhead and her responsibility to artists and clients and employees; Christopher would take off, spread his wings and fly, a brilliant, mobile creature. Many doors would open to him, each door leading to an intriguing space beyond, each door leading him away from the life they now had together.

"What do you think?" Christopher struck a pose, the complete continental swank in his rented tux.

For a moment, Lauren said nothing, but only stared. It was as if she didn't recognize the man standing before her. He might have the same face, the same body and be standing in the same place she had seen him in a hundred times before, surrounded by the familiar clutter of his bachelor's apartment, but this man was not the Christopher she knew.

Lauren's reply to his question was to throw her

purse down on the table. She crossed into the kitchen and put the wine she had brought with her into the refrigerator.

"Hey!" Christopher called after her, good-naturedly. "You got something against basic black? I figured it was a smart move. If I'm a bust tomorrow night, I can always wear it to my funeral."

Lauren came out of the kitchen. "What's the big deal? You look like any other man who went out and rented himself an expensive, trendy tux. This town's full of men in black tuxedos. You'll be appropriately dressed. Okay?"

"Well, well, you sure know how to pay a guy a compliment."

Christopher faced her, looking like a soldier in a war he didn't understand.

"I'm sorry," Lauren said. "You look nice. Really," she said sadly, and then added, "absolutely gorgeous."

And he did, which was the whole problem. Her sexy, macho, diamond-in-the-rough lover had become a brilliant-cut solitaire, whose sparkle would eclipse any other male at the exhibition.

She would not be the only one to recognize Christopher's attributes. The press would notice, for they had a nose for the exceptional; patrons would notice the talent, sensing either through instinct or through actual knowledge that this was work to collect, work in which to invest; and other women would respond to the natural charm, the raw animal appeal of the man she loved.

Her feelings of jealousy and possessiveness were immature—shocking, even to her, in their intensity. But she couldn't help her emotions. Ever since her conversation with Lloyd when he had brought into the open what she had always known would happen once Christopher became a public commodity, she had been consumed with worry. She was so ashamed of her pettiness, she couldn't even look at Christopher.

He lifted her chin, forcing her to meet his hurt and bewildered look. "What's going on here?"

"Nothing. I had a bad day, that's all."

"Okay . . . a bad day. Let's talk about it."

"There's nothing to talk about!" she snapped, tearing herself away from his gentle touch. Breathing deeply several times, she tried to get control of herself. She went to the refrigerator and ripped open its door, pulling out the bottle of wine.

"You just put it in to chill," Christopher commented.

"It's cold enough."

She took a glass from the cupboard and poured it full with wine, but Christopher took it from her before she could drink.

"Stop this, dammit! What's going on with you? Tell me and tell it straight, Lauren."

"All right, all right . . ." She moved away. "I'm going to tell you. Okay?" She took in a deep, fortifying breath and began. "My gallery is barely making it. I'm making sales and they're terrific, but the costs of maintaining my image, as it were, is astronomical. And my rent's been raised. And I've probably been spending too much time with you and not enough with my business. So there you have it, the whole mess." He had the partial lie—the whole truth of what was worrying her would be too degrading.

"What if you lost the gallery?" Christopher asked carefully.

"What if I—? What if the world came to an end? It would be the same for me."

"And what about me? Don't I count for anything in your life?"

"You! What do you mean? You're standing there

dressed like some . . . some new movie idol, and you know damn well that the only reason you've gone to all this trouble is because you're going to be having a debut that'll change your entire life. You'll be moving out and on. And I'm going to be staying. I'll be waving bye-bye sooner than you can have your tux dry-cleaned. So don't ask me if you count for anything in my life."

He took a step toward her, and for an instant she was afraid the anger she sensed in him was deep enough to send her reeling across the small kitchen. But he didn't touch her; instead, he turned away and walked into the living room, where it appeared he fought to control his fury.

Her words echoed in her head, sounding like the shrill screeching of a fishwife. "I'm sorry," Lauren said miserably. She joined him in the living room and collected her purse from off the table. "I apologize for yelling, for the whole scene."

Christopher turned slowly. Looking at her, he shook his head. "I can't believe you." The expression he wore was akin to disgust. "Do you think that what's going on between us has been some game? Do you honestly think that my feelings are dependent upon the Rodeo Drive financial climate?"

She had never seen him angry before. His voice resonated with the dark shades of his paintings.

"Is that what you think?"

"You're just starting out," she said. "You have no idea of what your life is going to be like."

"No idea. Maybe I haven't hit your big-time scene yet, but, lady, I've been a human being for going on thirty-three years now, and I've established a few very real principles for myself."

"You're going to have to develop some new ones then if you want to make it. You can't have it all ways, Chris. Your life is going to change."

"I love you. Three very overused words, but not by me."

"I don't want to lose you," she said, her pride abandoned. "I'm so afraid."

He moved to her, gathering her into his arms and holding her against him. "How could you possibly lose me? How could you even begin to think that you and I could be parted?" He raised her face with his hand and peered deeply into her eyes glistening with tears.

She didn't answer his question. But she could have told him that the world was going to turn upside down, inside out for him. The worst part of the whole thing was that she had made it all happen.

Shutting her mind to the future, she let him lead her to the bedroom. That night, she made love with a passion and energy close to desperation. She savored his every kiss, responded to his lovemaking as if it would have to last in her memory for eternity.

Before going to the gallery the next morning, she stopped off at her apartment to shower and change into fresh clothes.

Her key was barely in the outside lock when she was gripped by the shoulders and swung around with force that sent her reeling hard against the door.

"Where the hell have you been all night?" Riff wanted to know, his eyes red-rimmed, a growth of stubble on his face. His suit was rumbled with his tie loosened halfway down and his shirt collar open.

"Let go of me," she ordered, shrugging off his hold on her.

Riff backed off. "I waited all night in that car."

Lauren looked past him to the street where his car was parked.

"Were you with him?" he shouted, waving a furled newspaper in her face. Seeing her confusion, he opened it quickly, staring for a moment at the picture with acute distaste before holding it up for her to see.

"That artist," he said, biting out both words. "You really should have better sense, Lauren."

It was a picture of her and Christopher, taken as a promotional for the exhibition to be held that night. This one had appeared in the *Washington Post*.

"Yes," Lauren replied calmly and pushed the newspaper out of her way. "Yes, I was with him." She turned, beginning to put her key in the lock again.

But Riff reached forward and took her wrist, swinging her around to face him. His voice was thin and cold as he spoke. "All right, you've had your fun, Lauren. We've been upfront with each other. You had this infatuation going, and it can take a while to break things off. But now—and I mean right now, from this moment on—it is over. Canceled. Fini. Got it?"

"Nothing is going to be over, unless I decide it will be over."

"Listen to me," Riff said, crowding her against the door. "Two weeks ago, you were with me at the Bonaventure, and every paper in this country ran shots of us together. Now you know the purpose of those shots. You know the reason it was important for you to be there with me, Lauren!" His voice had become unduly loud, and realizing it, he stopped and looked self-consciously around to make certain he hadn't been overheard.

"You wanted a hostess. I merely complied."

"No . . . not just a hostess. An image. A permanent image."

"Then you had better look elsewhere, because nothing in this world is permanent. Get yourself a woman carved in stone." She tried to leave again, but he pressed his hand into her shoulder, pinning her against the door.

"I sent you four clients during the past two weeks in payment for your services that night."

"You also arranged to have my rent raised," she shot back. "Why didn't you withdraw that little squeeze play if you were so grateful to me?"

"Smart girl," he said. "My parents thought it wouldn't hurt to keep the screws turned tightly on you, that's why. And it seems they were right. Now you look here, Lauren. You make me look very good, you see. And my family and I and a lot of other people who are counting on this boy going all the way in their country's government, are extremely pleased with the image you and I project together. Together. It would not do at this stage in the game to have me looking unstable by appearing with yet another woman on my arm. It would be disastrous for me. And," he added pointedly, "for you, as well. Don't be dumb, Lauren. Don't mess with other men."

"There is only one man. Just one," Lauren emphasized, finding it increasingly difficult to control her rising anger at Riff's crude, shakedown methods. "There won't ever be any other men, so you can relax on that count."

"Unfortunately, there are two men at the present time." He slapped the newspaper against his palm. "But you're going to make sure that only one man is left. And that man had better be me."

She began to object. He cut her off sharply. "Because, Lauren, I swear to you, if you aren't there to make me look good, then I'm going to be forced to see that you look very, very bad."

Lauren smiled contemptuously. "Oh, Riff . . . honestly. Do you think I'm dependent upon your handouts to survive? I spent eleven years working to get where I am. Rodeo Drive wasn't handed to me on a silver platter. I'm worth everything I've earned so

far, and I'm going to continue to make my own way.
I'll survive."

Riff backed down the steps, all the while looking at
her. "We are coming to your gallery exhibition
tonight—me, my parents and a few of our people.
You either do your stuff right, or I promise you, your
net worth is going to make the market crash of
twenty-nine look like an up day."

By eight that night there was barely enough room in
the gallery to maneuver. Lauren had opened the
upstairs salon where she was displaying all of Christopher's paintings. Guests lined the circular staircase,
laughing, chatting, sipping from champagne glasses,
nibbling on the canapés served by the uniformed
catering staff. Jacqueline had posted another gallery
staff member at the door, making it possible for her to
handle the sales on Christopher's paintings.

"Twelve," Jacqueline whispered in Lauren's ear as
she squeezed by, holding her filled champagne glass
high over her head where it was safe from being
bumped.

"Sold?" Lauren turned away from the group she
was speaking to, mouthing the word again for confirmation.

With a grin, Jacqueline nodded, gave Lauren the
thumbs-up sign and disappeared into the throng.

Lauren was about to start off in Christopher's
direction, when a crisp, commanding female voice
sounded behind her. She recognized it instantly as
belonging to Madeline McIntyre.

"Lauren, I want to speak with you."

Lauren turned. "Some other time might be better,"
she said, glancing at the crowd.

Madeline's features hardened. "Perhaps at your
age you don't yet understand the significance of time,

the significance of the ability to *buy* time." Pointedly, she glanced around the gallery.

"Perhaps not," Lauren replied. With exasperation, she added, "This may come as a revelation to you, Madeline, but there are some things that your money cannot buy. I'm one of them."

Madeline gave her a last searing look, but said no more.

Lauren searched the gallery for Christopher. She found him surrounded by members of the press. Off to the side, she saw Clarence McIntyre huddled with Maxwell Kain, who was nodding and wearing a tight, pleased smile.

She also caught sight of Lloyd and Buffy looking flushed and happy at the turnout for Christopher. *Chris may not know it,* she thought, *but he's been adopted by one of the world's wealthiest couples.*

For the occasion, Lauren had worn a strapless Chinese-red satin dress with a full, draping skirt. Her black hair was worn up, but not slicked into her more usual chignon. Instead, it was loosely coiffed in gentle waves, tendrils of curled hair wisping down her neck and at the sides. Her only jewelry was a diamond necklace borrowed from Keely St. Martine, who had already purchased one of Christopher's paintings for Raffael.

Christopher finally caught up with her. Standing behind her, he kissed her neck. The touch of his lips made her respond automatically, and she turned her face, returning his kiss with passion, forgetful of anything but his warmth. Around them, lights flashed like rockets being launched.

Lauren blinked and broke their embrace. Christopher laughed. He swept her closer to him, clowning for the cameras. But this time Lauren wasn't smiling. Beyond the reporters, Riff, Clarence and Madeline

stood like stone figures, watching her. Clarence broke
the tableau. He pushed his way through the crowd,
making way for Madeline who followed close behind.
Before going after his parents, Riff directed a long,
final look at Lauren.

Jacqueline, innocent of what had just transpired,
appeared behind the circle of photographers grinning
as she held up her hands and flashed ten fingers twice.
All of Christopher's paintings had been sold.

So, Lauren considered, *the night had been a landmark occasion. All the way around.*

Success worked as an aphrodisiac on Christopher.
Rather than abandoning her, his new-found financial
security, coupled with his public and social recognition, gave him an added confidence that only served
to increase his magnetic personality.

Two weeks after the exhibition, they lay together on
Christopher's bed. It was Sunday morning, and they
had spent the entire time making love.

Lauren traced her finger along the inside of his
thigh, laughing because for once she did not get an
instant response. "I knew it." She sighed.

"Knew what?"

"That you'd tire of me. But I hadn't thought so
soon. Perhaps if I had eaten more of your spaghetti
I'd look more like a Rubens' woman, and you'd find
me more appealing. Well," she went on, musing
philosophically, "I suppose I should just be fortunate
that you're not a king. I'd probably lose my head to
the gallows."

He slapped her soundly on the rump. "Get up here,
wench!"

Contentedly, she wriggled higher, kissing him deeply. He cupped her breasts, his fingers playing over her
nipples until they hardened.

Sometimes she was so happy it frightened her. If

she had dreamed him up, he could not have been more perfect. His lovemaking was natural and passionate, but never did he forget her, the person, while lost in her, the woman. And she pleased him equally. Of that she was certain.

A lightning thrill traveled like a shot up her spine when she touched him, felt him stiffen. "How do you know what I want?" he moaned. "Do you read my mind?"

"It's just that I want what you want," she whispered, slicking her tongue along his hard, smooth stomach. And, truthfully, she did. There was nothing unseemly, nothing too intimate of herself that could not be shared with him. "I want us to be like this forever," she said.

"Forever." He half-laughed, half-moaned, his pelvis arched beneath her touch. "I couldn't . . . last . . . forever." With that, he put an end to her teasing and tossed her upon her back, covering her mouth with kisses, his hands roaming silkily on her body.

She gave herself to him again totally, swept for long moments beyond thought by the passions he aroused in her. She felt so much a part of him that in moments of sheer physical exhaustion, when they broke apart, a physical ache tore at her heart. She did not know if he merely sensed this in her or whether he felt that way himself, but as his passion broke in her, he clutched her to him, staying with her long after the spasm of their pleasure gently ebbed.

She stroked his back, slick with perspiration. "I can't bear it when it's over," she whispered. "Did you know that?"

He kissed her neck. "I know."

"Is that why you stay with me afterwards?"

"Partly. But as much for myself. It's a cold, wrenching feeling sometimes when it ends, when we pull apart. More than physical."

They lay that way a while longer, locked together. She was in a warm, dozing state when he spoke next.

"You're right," he said, languorously kissing the lids of her closed eyes. "I am tired. What we need," he said, turning over and putting his hands beneath his head, "is a vacation."

Lauren's eyes shot open. "From each other?" Her heart was no longer beating, her entire consciousness primed for disaster.

Christopher frowned. "Of course not. I meant with each other."

The relief she experienced was only momentary. Again panic seized her as she thought of her obligations. "But I can't. I've the gallery to take care of."

"Let Jacqueline handle things for a while."

When her eyes clouded, he said more insistently, "Lauren, this is important to me."

"I'll talk to Jacqueline," she promised. But inwardly she was wondering if this wasn't just the beginning of the end prophesied by Lloyd and Madeline.

Chapter 10

ORDINARILY, LAUREN KNEW TO THE PENNY HOW MUCH money the gallery had taken in and how much had gone out in expenses. Since her involvement with Christopher, however, she had become lax in her vigilance. This was partially because of her constant high, which fortunately seemed to run concurrently with the streak of good fortune her business was experiencing, and partly because Jacqueline had proven herself to be an excellent administrator. Lauren went over the books twice a month with Jacqueline, and other than that, she dedicated herself to meetings with special clients and to the seminars she was now holding on a twice-weekly basis at the gallery, as well as her outside activities that brought new business into the shop.

Over the past few weeks, following Christopher's showing, she had missed her bimonthly business meeting with Jacqueline, putting her off several times when she wanted to discuss the sales' figures. "Are they up?" Lauren would ask on her way to a meeting. "Yes, but—" "Do we have a reserve for next month's rent?" "Yes, but—" "Fantastic!" Lauren would call over her shoulder as she yanked open the door. "We'll talk tomorrow."

The promised meeting had not materialized. Until now.

Lauren sat at her desk. Jacqueline peered over her shoulder, commenting as they reviewed the sales figures on the ledger sheet.

"I don't understand it," Lauren muttered, tracing the numbers with her finger. "You said we were doing all right."

"And we were. Christopher's show gave us the extra income to easily meet the lease increase, and there's still enough for next month as well. The publicity you two have generated in the press has been responsible for a surge in our walk-in traffic, and you still have your institutional buyers as a cushion. You've the figures on those, of course—but, as you say, there's something wrong."

Lauren analyzed the columns of figures, trying to put her finger on the problem. "Nothing seems to be moving with our regular artists."

"I have an idea why," Jacqueline said darkly. She left the office for a moment, returning with two newspapers and the latest issue of *Los Angeles* magazine. Handing them to Lauren, she said, "Call me paranoid if you want . . ."

Lauren skimmed the articles in the social section of the *Times* and the *Examiner*. There were references to three competing galleries that had thrown rather small cocktail/entertainment parties during the previous month exhibiting their artists. None of the artists were better than her own. Yet she noted that several of her most faithful and well-heeled clients had attended these parties and that they had purchased art from her competitors. In *Los Angeles* magazine, she found a picture of Riff attending a theatrical benefit for the Los Angeles Music Center. He was flanked on either side by clients of hers who had not been in the gallery since the night of Christopher's one-man show.

"Damn." Lauren pushed aside the offending periodicals.

"Perhaps we are being too sensitive," Jacqueline said weakly. "They were also friends of Riff's. It could be that these social engagements were coincidences."

"Sure, just like the bombing of Pearl Harbor was a coincidence."

"What will we do?"

"First, I'm going to make some luncheon dates. And then we're going to throw our own party."

"You'll need someone very special," Jacqueline advised. "Your Christopher will be a tough act to follow."

"I know. What about the meditator—our Italian? He's colorful as well as being excellent."

The lights came on in Jacqueline's eyes.

Out of the four calls Lauren made to clients who had previously jumped at the opportunity to lunch with her, only one accepted.

Nigel Croup was an Englishman on the downside of his fifties who carried his fate as a financially distressed member of the old British aristocracy like a cross on his back. His value to Lauren was not so much his ability to purchase art, but rather his up-to-date encyclopedic knowledge of social currents. He was an outcast from the world he longed to rejoin. And yet, as he circled the perimeters of his cherished land, he was in a position to have an excellent perspective of its inner workings.

Lauren could think of no one better to have lunch with that day at the Windsor Hotel. The occasion, which permitted Nigel the opportunity to observe the entrance of some of the city's worthiest citizens, installed in him a blustery, jubilant mood.

"But my darling girl," Nigel Croup said ebulliently, "you're the toast of the land!" To prove it, he lifted his wineglass to her.

Lauren managed a wan smile. "Then why is it that when the toast of the land invited three people to join me for lunch during the past week, all three were busy?"

"Who were they?" Nigel asked, suddenly alert, his energies engaged in his favorite pastime.

"Charlotte Hemming, Lawrence Rait and Kenneth Pentello."

"Yes, well . . . Charlotte Hemming inherited a nice, tidy sum of money from her fourth husband, which is invested in a mutual fund—"

"Overseen by McIntyre interests."

"Umm." Nigel nodded. "And let us see, Lawrence Rait? Ah, yes, poor, poor Larry. He lost a bundle, everything, as I understand it, on that land scheme of his in the desert. The McIntyres are putting together a neat little loan for him to make a fresh start. If it were swampland in Louisiana, he couldn't fail with that crew behind him. And Kenneth Pentello, whose career as a singer has waned, is thrilled that the McIntyres are using their influence to launch his daughter's singing career in the East. She hasn't a crumb of talent, poor little twit."

"Thanks, Nigel."

"My pleasure. Serves the rotters right to have their dirty laundry aired. Not one of them had the courtesy to invite me out, you see."

Lauren was thinking hard. "Would you care for some dessert, Nigel?"

"That would be nice. And perhaps an invitation to your next bash?"

"Well?" Jacqueline pounced, following Lauren into her office when she had returned from her afternoon's meeting with Nigel Croup.

"We're being surrounded by the Indians, and our reinforcements are being picked off on the way through the pass." Lauren threw her purse down on her desk.

"Not all of them. The Italian artist will get through."

"You've got him!"

"The one and only Mario Mancusso will arrive three days before the show. His paintings come a week in advance. The conditions are a might peculiar, however. He must stay in the local Zen monastery, for one thing. He's terrified that his karma might be set back three lives if he mixes with too many bad vibes from the local sinners. Fortunately, our American money gives off the right vibrational impulses. Also, we cannot choose the date of the show. It must be on a full moon, he insists. That means that we have two and a half weeks to get things ready."

Lauren sat down at her desk and began writing rapidly on a pad. "I want everyone who is anyone invited to this—even people who aren't anyone yet, but who might be in the future. Goodwill is needed from all quarters."

"What we really could use is money," Jacqueline muttered.

"Look, you scrape together every loose dime we've got around this place. We're spending it on this party. If this doesn't work, then we aren't going to have to worry about money in the future anyway. We won't be here."

*   *   *

"Chris, try to understand . . . I can't take off now."

They had been arguing back and forth about his vacation plans for three days.

"I thought the gallery is doing all right."

"It is, it is."

"Then why can't you take off?"

She couldn't bring herself to tell him about her problems. First of all, it was too humiliating to have him see her as the distressed damsel, and secondly, if she told him the truth about her finances, she'd have to tell him about Riff McIntyre. She was afraid of what Christopher might do, especially when he found out that her problems stemmed mostly from her involvement with him. His life had just taken off. She loved him too much to see his happiness jeopardized.

Her refusal to take the vacation with him led to their first real fight.

"You're obsessive, Lauren!"

"I'm not! I'm dedicated!"

"And so am I, but I know where to draw the line. I'm a person first—a man. And I've got a right to live."

"Then live—who's stopping you?"

He slammed out of his own apartment that night after dinner. She waited for an hour, but he didn't return.

The following day there was no call from him. The day after that, she broke down and rang his apartment, but got no response. She called him all day and when she received no response she became jealous, thinking he might have stayed with someone else; angry, thinking that he was purposely not answering her call; and finally fear entered her emotions, as she considered that something terrible had happened to him.

She canceled an important meeting at the Getty Museum to drive to Venice.

What she found made her blood run cold.

His apartment was empty. Everything was gone, not a trace of Christopher remained. Half out of her mind, she tore off to his studio, found no one there either, and worse . . . saw that all of his paintings had been removed.

She couldn't work after that. Instead, she phoned Jacqueline from her apartment, telling her she could be reached at home, if needed.

"You sound terrible," Jacqueline said.

"Any calls from Christopher?" she said urgently.

"No . . . no calls."

Lauren hung up. She spent a sleepless night waiting for the sound of Christopher's key in her lock, for the ring of the telephone beside her bed. There was nothing but silence.

Like a dead person, she went through the mail the next morning. There was a handwritten envelope with a return address listed as Venice, which made her think of Christopher. Her heart ached as she opened it, expecting it to be an invitation or solicitation from a do-good society.

It was neither. Hand-drawn on a piece of art-paper stock was the picture of a familiar building. She recognized it as the modern house she and Christopher always stopped to admire from the canal bridge.

Printed on the inside of the folded paper was only the day's date and "Seven sharp."

Christopher was watching her every expression. He had dressed for her visit. His dinner jacket was a soft velvet in a muted burgundy color. The shirt he wore was of the palest pink. Its cut was tailored, masculine.

"I can't believe it," Lauren said. She turned slowly,

admiring the living room's modern furnishings. A solid wall of glass fronted the canal. The sun was just dropping, and the sky was tinged with pinks and oranges. Across the waterway, lights had been switched on in homes. "This is so incredible . . ."

When she smiled at him, Christopher reacted instantly with the uncontained, innocent delight of a small boy. "Isn't it? It really is. It's amazing," he said, also looking around as if for the first time.

"But how?"

"A lease. The owners are in South America. So for a few months—six, anyway, for certain—this will be ours."

"Ours . . ."

"Of course. Ours."

They still had not discussed their disagreement of the previous night. She had been so happy to have received his card that the incident had been brushed aside. But now, at the new suggestion from Christopher, the conflict was reinstated.

"I have an apartment."

"An empty one. But that's not the issue, is it?"

"No," she answered defensively. "I guess not."

She moved away. Standing in front of the glass wall, she stared out at the water in the canal. Above, the sky had turned to a flaming red.

Christopher came up behind her. He touched her lightly on her shoulder. "Dinner . . ." he said.

Disappointment resonated in the word. She had spoiled his pleasant surprise.

She watched sadly as he crossed the long room. He had been so happy when she had arrived, and she had ruined it all for him.

She followed him into the kitchen where he was carving the roast duck. Taking one of the silver platters off the hotplate, she started toward the dining room.

"Oh no, you don't," he said, gently retrieving the dish from her. "I'm the host. You're the guest." He disappeared into the dining room carrying the platter to the table himself.

Lauren stood in the doorway of the kitchen, watching him. "I don't want to be a guest," she said.

Christopher had lit a match and was holding it to one of the candles. He raised his eyes, doubting what he had heard. She turned and went back into the kitchen, got another bowl and took it to the table.

Christopher pulled her to him, kissing her tenderly, then more fiercely. Before he could go any further, Lauren extricated herself from his embrace. Laughing, she said, "Don't you think we'd better get to the main course first?"

"Quite honestly? No."

Christopher's lovemaking was different. In fact, Lauren concluded, Christopher himself was different.

She lay on her back in the king-size bed, Christopher's breathing a dim whisper of relaxed satisfaction beside her. A thin sliver of moon cut the dark night beyond the wall of plate glass. The bedroom was on the second floor. Knowing that no one could see in with the lights off, they had made love with the drapes open, enjoying their departure from propriety.

She reflected that the change in Christopher was not only in the new clothes he had purchased, but in the assurance with which he wore them. There was an *élan*, a feline elegance to Christopher that was inborn, and the outer trappings, which he could now afford, supported it well. And now there was also the house.

He had made love to her with gentle, patient consideration of her needs and had fulfilled himself with the same driving, masculine force as always. But there was a difference to their lovemaking that had not been there previously. She had never consciously realized it before, but always in the past, she had felt that she was somehow making a gift of herself. He was a man, and she wanted him for that part of his nature; he was also an artist, and she admired him, recognized his genius. But in the past, he had also been a poor man, a struggling talent, and she had been the grand lady. Being honest with herself, she would have to admit that a vague sense of *noblesse oblige* had characterized her attitude toward their relationship from the very beginning.

She looked at the sleeping man beside her. His dark hair was touseled, his eyes closed. A sweep of long, black lashes curved high on the pronounced cheekbones. *He was so beautiful, so incredibly perfect,* Lauren thought, and her hand reached out instinctively to touch him, but she reconsidered, not wanting to wake him.

A tear born of deep happiness trailed from her eye. She would protect him. She would fight for this man's dreams, rally to see his hopes realized.

He stirred and, slowly opening his eyes, began to smile as he saw she watched him. "Come," he said, pulling her into him.

At the touch of his hand on her body, she felt herself respond instantly. It was always the same. It was always wondrous, this desire to lie with him, to be possessed by him, to have him enter her, body and soul.

And yet, she thought, washed by a sense of alarm, she would not have him be her master.

He was kissing her, surely, expertly. Her fingers, wrapped in his hair, suddenly stopped their gentle twining as confused thoughts took precedence over the physical sensations.

"What's wrong?" Christopher tried to read her expression.

"Nothing . . . nothing." She kissed him, moving her body hard against his, feigning a passion she did not quite feel.

He held her away. "Yes, there is." Worried, he sat up. Looking down at her, he said, "Look, you don't have to force yourself. I'd never make demands on you if—"

"But I want you to make demands on me . . . I do . . . I do . . ." she cried and brought herself up into his arms. Holding him tightly, as if for dear life—for that was what he was to her, she kissed his shoulder, the indentation of his collarbone, the smooth, hard planes of his muscular chest.

"You've convinced me." He laughed and lay down on the bed again.

The lightness vanished as they came together, their mouths hungry, demanding, their tongues meeting like hot bursts of fire. And each time that she had almost climbed to the crest, he would lead her on yet still another path, forever bringing her higher.

Within her a dim, small voice tried to rebel against the needs of her body, urged her to hold herself apart and away before she was lost to him forever. "Christopher . . ." she began, but as she felt the driving heat of his loins, her protest dissipated.

"I love you," he said, ". . . love you."

"Christopher," she tried again, needing to assert power over herself, over him, "I want you to know something."

"Yes . . ."

Only, as his hands moved over her breasts, down along her hips, caressed her stomach, she became lost to the sweet agony of Christopher's knowledge of her body and could no longer recall the nature of her protest. It had something . . . something . . . to do with being independent. And in control. But now she couldn't be sure. Contracting her muscles, she arched into him, merging and receding, spiraling and, at last, abandoning herself to his rule.

She slept contentedly, curled into his body, the drums of inner warfare stilled in her psyche.

The telephone woke them. The room was unfamiliar as she opened her eyes. Then she saw Christopher, recognized the shrilling of the telephone, watched him rise groggily, his body still nude, and she remembered the previous night's lovemaking.

"Yes . . . hello," Christopher said, leaning over the side of the bed and reaching for his shorts with his other hand. "Yes . . . yes . . . the connection is good."

Lauren heard a tiny voice buzzing over the receiver.

"Thursday, next. Yes, certainly. In the mail . . . fine. No, my pleasure."

When the conversation was over, he turned to Lauren, the phone still in his hand. "That was Vincent Pirelli. He wantes me to come to Rome."

Lauren hesitated. "Marvelous, Christopher. I told you, didn't I? That you'd be a star?"

She slipped out from under the covers and walked into the bathroom where she shut the door. Leaning over the sink, she splashed cold water on her face. Vincent Pirelli was a heavyweight art connoisseur, part collector, part social benefactor. His forte was in discovering brilliant young artists and bringing them out. The news of Christopher's work had traveled fast. But then she knew it would. Lloyd knew it. Madeline McIntyre knew it. What they all knew would happen was beginning. In fact, the sound of the telephone had marked the beginning of their end together just as surely as a clock had struck that time.

Christopher was dressed by the time she returned to the bedroom.

"I want you to go with me," he said.

She laughed. "Ridiculous."

"Not to me."

"We already went through that, didn't we? I can't spare the time for a vacation now."

"What you're really telling me is that you're never going to have the time, isn't that so?"

"I can't give up my life to follow you around the world."

"One trip."

"No."

Surprisingly, Christopher accepted her decision not to join him on his trip.

She moved her clothes into his leased house—their home, as Christopher insisted she call it, but she retained her apartment as a symbol of her independence.

During the next few days, they played house together. It was a game, and both of them knew it, although they went through the ritual of pretending permanency. She smiled and cuddled. They made love in front of the downstair's fireplace. Christopher prepared elaborate dinners for her, and in spite of her problems at the gallery, she made concessions in her schedule and took off early to be with him.

But the letter from Pirelli came toward the end of the first week in the house, and from that moment on, she could almost tangibly feel him slipping from her life.

Pirelli's letter listed Christopher's complete itinerary. There would be parties, private interviews with collectors, tours of the major museums, a side trip to Florence to meet another artist Pirelli was sponsoring and introductions to gallery owners and Italian art agents.

They would lie in bed at night, and Christopher would tell her the plans he had—all of them including her. She would respond affirmatively. "Yes, we can buy our own place." "Yes, we can talk seriously about marriage when you're more established." Yes, yes, yes. . . .

But the word "no" rang in her heart. On a subtle emotional level, she had already begun to withdraw from the relationship. There was no hope for them. Love might conquer a great many problems, but it could not survive a situation in which two people would be on the opposite sides of the world for much of their lives. A trip to Rome today; then a sojourn in Paris for six months. An appointment to join a university faculty in Lisbon for a year. Lauren had seen other artists' careers take off. Christopher was slipping from her.

She drove him to the airport, and they parted outside the airline's gate. "I'll call you," he promised, kissing her.

It was a week later before she heard from him.

"Lauren, Lauren . . . this is fantastic, incredible . . . it's unbelievable," he went on, cataloguing his experiences. "Can you come?"

"Christopher, no. The gallery—"

"I'm staying another two weeks," he broke in, and she had the impression he wasn't all that disappointed in her refusal to join him.

"Fine," she replied. "Enjoy yourself. Give me a call when you've made your plans to return."

His name appeared in several art magazines, a few newspaper columns, and a picture of him was found in the Rome paper she received a week late. He was shown with Pirelli and a gorgeous, young Italian artist—another protégée of Pirelli's.

"It means nothing," Jacqueline said to her upon seeing the female with Christopher.

There were other problems to concentrate on at the moment anyway. The Italian artist, Mario Mancusso, had arrived. He was very weird, very difficult, and spent the day prior to his showing chanting to clear the gallery of negative impulses. The odd thing was that the gallery did seem lighter after he was through.

But by ten that evening, the day's buoyancy had been replaced by a funereal mood. General invitations had been sent to their entire mailing list, and special invitations had been addressed to Lauren's most prominent clients and to the art critics in the area. Lauren had personally handled the advanced public relations drive for Mancusso and had felt confident that the showing had received ample media coverage.

But there were few of her special clients in attendance that evening, and only two minor critics from secondary news publications had arrived to review the exhibition.

"I do not understand it!" Jacqueline said, pulling Lauren aside and continuing to rattle off her opinion in rapid French.

"And I don't understand what you just said." Lauren glanced around them, searching in vain for faces that had not appeared.

The artist was in a rage. "There is no one here!" he fumed at Lauren in her office.

"Of course there are people here," she soothed, trying to make the best out of a horrible situation. "There are many people here."

"They are nobodies! Nothings!" He stalked back and forth.

"I thought you were into peace and going with the flow, all of that," Lauren said in weak defense as he launched another attack on her handling of his show.

"I am, but this is not one of those times. Now I want money. Money!"

* * *

Nigel Croup floated into the gallery at ten-thirty that evening, dressed impeccably. Lauren came toward him just as he had begun to sniff the atmosphere for its social content.

"Sorry, Nigel. There's no one here."

"Really?" he said. "I'm here. What do you call me? Chopped liver?" His eager eyes scanned the room. "My, it is a disaster, isn't it?"

"The *Titanic*."

"They're all at that other place."

For a moment, Lauren wasn't certain what Nigel meant. Then, when she understood, she could barely believe it. "At the Latham Gallery?"

Nigel nodded. "The chap they're showing isn't bad. He's not good either. That's the shame. You really should make things up with the senator. He doesn't seem to take well to public embarrassment."

"So I've noticed."

"How are the hors d'oeuvres?"

"Plentiful."

"Ah." Nigel sighed happily. "Failure has some compensating features."

So the evening had been a debacle.

Lauren closed the shop with Jacqueline, who was too glum to even summon epithets in her native tongue.

At home, Lauren changed into a white terry robe and sat on the patio overlooking the canal. It was almost two o'clock in the morning. There were no lights on across the way. The water, too, was dark; the moon hidden behind a sheathing of clouds. Periodically, Lauren would catch a grouping of dark shadows, ducks traveling silently by on the narrow watercourse. The water lapped against the shoreline; it, too, seeming to slumber. All the world slept, but she could not.

It was understandable that Riff could have assembled his supporters at the Latham Gallery in a bid to deliberately sabotage her exhibition, but how could he have influenced the art critics to stay away? They were an independent bunch, always eager to discover new genius. They traveled in packs, arriving *en masse* to an exhibition, not out of camaraderie, but because of insecurity. They watched their comrades, always afraid that the next guy would be one up on them. As in any group, there was a leader of the pack, and in Los Angeles, that person was Maxwell Kain. Maxwell had not shown up at her opening either.

A light went on in a house across the way—a single beacon in the darkness. Almost simultaneously, Lauren had a vital thought. *Maxwell Kain.*

The art critic would also be up now preparing his review of the Latham Gallery's artist.

Slowly, thoughtfully, Lauren rose and walked back into the house. As she ascended the stairs to her bedroom, she put together the fuzzy pieces that were beginning to form a whole.

Somehow, Riff had gotten to Maxwell Kain. She didn't know how, but that would explain why he and the others did not show up for her opening. Where Kain went, the others would follow. No doubt, Kain was hyping this new artist way out of proportion, but with his track record, everyone else would follow. It would be a classic case of the "Emperor's New Clothes" in action.

She could fight Riff's social power, but if she didn't have the critics to help her publicize her gallery to the general public, she would not only lose a portion of her business, but she would also lose some of the top artists who would want to show elsewhere. In the long run, she could build her international clientele and reputation, but she didn't have enough time for that. At the moment, she was dependent upon West Coast trade, the monied people who were intertwined with the McIntyres.

Damn, she thought. *Riff's gotten to Kain, too.*
Well, then . . . so would she.

Chapter 11

IT WAS CRAZY, HER DRIVING ACROSS TOWN AT TWO IN THE morning into the Los Veliz section of Los Angeles where Maxwell Kain lived. But it not only had to be done, it had to be done immediately.

Kain's home was an enormous, sprawling place, its architecture Monterey Spanish. The property was overgrown with shrubbery. A rangy olive tree was near the dark entrance, and a series of stately palms stood sentinel on either side of the drive she took up a small hill.

Leaving her car, she walked gingerly up the red-tile walk, finding it difficult to see in the dark. There was one light on, however, just as she had known there would be. That light would be in Kain's study. She could envision him now, hunched over his typewriter, pounding out his copy.

She leaned hard on the doorbell, not letting up until she heard the security shutter in the old oak door open. A second later, an outside light illuminated the area in which she stood.

Kain inched open the door. She made out his eye peering at her through the crack. "What in God's name do you want?" He sounded almost fearful to Lauren.

"I want to talk to you, Maxwell."

"You're insane. It's too late. I'm busy, anyway."

"Yes, I realize you are." Lauren took an unexpected move forward, shoving her weight against the door. Maxwell was pushed farther back into his foyer. He glared at her as she entered.

"All right," he snapped peevishly. "What the hell is it? Just spit it out and get it over with."

"First," she said, "I want to see your review—the one you're doing for the Latham Gallery."

Maxwell tightened the belt on the long blue robe he wore. "You can read about it tomorrow in the evening edition."

"No. I want to read about it now."

"Well, too bad," he whined childishly.

Lauren would have liked to have slapped him. Instead, she pushed past him, gauging the direction of the light she had seen in the window, and continued down a hall with Kain scampering after her.

"You're a pushy broad, aren't you? You want me to call the cops?" Kain hollered after her as she turned into his study.

"Call them. But in the meantime, I'm going to read this." She whipped the paper out of the typewriter before he could snatch it from her and, at the same time, gathered up the first four pages of his draft. Taking them to a chair, she sat down and read his review. When she was finished, she looked up at him.

His face was white, splotched with strawberry-colored spots of anger.

"You little snake," she said softly.

"He has talent," Kain said.

"He's a mediocre, run-of-the-mill artist. I know it. You know it. But what I don't know is how much

Senator McIntyre paid you to come up with this garbage."

Kain looked away. "Absurd," he said. He moved to his desk, fidgeting with pens, papers.

"All right." Lauren rose from the chair. She threw his review down on his desk. He quickly snatched it up.

"What can I give you?" she asked him.

"I don't know what you mean." But Kain looked slyly at her from the corner of his drooping lids. He was already making his plans.

"All right . . . all right . . ." Lauren began to pace, her mind working through possibilities, each of them becoming improbabilities as she recognized the insignificance of her position in relation to Riff's. "I'll introduce you to Phillip Whelen Lloyd," she said, trying.

Kain rolled his eyes. "My dear girl, you aren't the only friend of Lloyd's. In fact," he went on, "I've been led to believe that I may be invited to a very intimate gathering where Lloyd will be—a party where we'll be talking about a new museum he's thinking of building." Kain was almost purring.

"Look, we both know I can't offer you any money. And, like you said, the senator can introduce you to the glitterati just as well as I can, but . . ." A thought came into her mind. A fantastic thought.

Kain looked up eagerly, a jaded child expecting a totally new kind of present than he has ever received before.

"But I can give you Fredrich Wilm."

The critic's jaw hung slack.

"Yes . . . Wilm," Lauren repeated. Her heart was beating like a marathon runner's as she walked back to the desk and picked up the review. She held it out to Kain. "If you tear this up now, if you come with me to my gallery and take a look at my artist's work, which, incidentally, we both know is far superior. And if you write your review on my show for tomorrow's late edition, then I will see that you get an exclusive review of Wilm's show at my gallery."

"Wilm . . . in your gallery?"

"Of course. I've been working on the project for a year now. Not only that, but Wilm's doing an exclusive lithographic run for me. I'll be the only gallery in the world to have Wilm committed to the multiple-print market."

"My God, my God . . ." Kain looked as if he might drop. He staggered around his desk, falling into his chair and holding his head between both hands. "He's never, never let anyone run his work off before. "My God," he breathed again. "You'll be rich."

"And famous."

"Yes, yes . . . certainly you will. My God."

She watched Kain's expressions change to match his fleeting thoughts. She could see him weighing all his options, those presented by Riff and those offered by her. He looked to her like a thief caught in a room with gold coins on one side and rubies and emeralds on the other. He didn't know which to take out with him.

"Perhaps I might be able to get a special deal on say . . . an artist's proof?"

"Deals are always possible, if you have the right contacts."

"And this will be my exclusive, totally mine before anyone else can report on it?"

"Agreed."

He reached out. She handed him the review. He paused a second, as if reconsidering Riff's bribes for a final time, then tore the paper into several pieces and dumped them into his trash can.

"Let's go," Lauren said. "You've got an exhibition to review before the sun comes up."

"Mon Dieu, a miracle! How did you manage it?" Jacqueline stood in the doorway of Lauren's office. In her hand was the newspaper with Kain's review of Mario Mancusso's work.

"Simple bribery," Lauren said, continuing to go through her mail.

Jacqueline came into the room and closed the door behind her. "Bribery with what, may I ask? Certainly not bribery with money, because you have none. Your only other recourse is to offer your body, but Aphrodite herself could not stimulate that prune Kain."

Still working, Lauren said, "I traded Fredrich Wilm for the review."

"What?"

"I offered Kain an exclusive review of Fredrich Wilm's work when it appears in my gallery."

Jacqueline's hazel eyes were round saucers of disbelief. "You have signed a contract with Fredrich Wilm?"

"Well, no." Lauren rose and, coming around her desk, sat on its corner. "A slight problem, that." She bit the eraser of her pencil.

"How could you do this?" Jacqueline groaned. "You know, I know, everyone knows . . . Wilm speaks to no one."

"Yes. Another definite drawback to my plans. He's supposed to be quite a hermit. Some say he's a regular madman."

"Then how . . . ?"

"I haven't the faintest idea."

Lauren spent the next morning researching Fredrich Wilm. At the library, she made copies of all relevant personal information appearing in all of the digests and newspapers she could locate on microfilm. She then made calls to friends and even a few enemies in New York and Europe, particularly in Germany, Wilm's native country.

However, Wilm remained largely an enigma. By the end of the afternoon, she had assembled only two pages of hard information on the man, much of it already known. He was a mad genius, hailed as the successor to Picasso. He worked holed up in his decaying *schloss* in the mountainous countryside about fifty miles outside of Munich. There was even a photo of the place showing a filled moat. He had no art agent, but would periodically call a dealer of his choice and make arrangements for his work to be shown. The dealer would be required to purchase the paintings from Wilm outright, and there would be an additional bonus for Wilm after the sale, based upon the total take. He had never agreed to have his work run off for the lucrative commercial-print market. In art circles, to have a lithograph of Wilm's work in a limited-edition run would be akin to having purchased the initial offering of AT&T stock.

Wilm's personal life was weird. He had been married as a young man to a beautiful girl, several years his junior, a girl still in her late teens. She had left him for someone else, and he had never recovered from the betrayal. Soured by love, Wilm consistently kept himself supplied with the companionship of nubile young women. He alternately treated them miserably or showered them with gifts. His lavish compensation insured that there was never a lack of female company.

Wilm's present mistress was a twenty-three-year-old former rock singer—a girl with long, unkempt blond hair and enormous, radiant blue eyes (the origin of the sparkle, some unkindly people suggested, was artificially induced by drugs). Wilm had used the young woman as a model in a series of companion paintings shown on exhibition in Paris a year ago.

The general consensus was that the girl was both as crazy as her keeper and as shrewd when it came to the management of money.

However, none of the information Lauren received, either through gossip or through print, provided a clue as to how she could approach the reclusive Wilm with her deal.

Kain had begun to call her regularly, pressing her for details on Wilm's showing. "He's working like a fiend, Maxwell, trying to get out this new series."

Jacqueline had taken to muttering the names of saints. "You aren't even Catholic!" Lauren accused testily.

"We need all the help we can get."

Christopher waved as he caught sight of Lauren among the throngs of greeters as he came out of customs at Los Angeles International Airport.

She noticed he had grown a short beard. His original two-week junket had turned into a European odyssey lasting close to a month.

As he moved rapidly past other arriving passengers, she pushed through the crowd to reach him. For a moment, they stood looking at each other, as uncomfortable as strangers. Then he swept her into his arms, squeezing her so tightly she lost her breath. "God," he said, "I couldn't wait to get back to you."

She could feel him trembling with desire. "Really, why was that?" she joked.

"Let's go home, and I'll show you," he growled.

He was filled with news, and she drove silently, listening to his tales of Italy. Everything was wonderful, marvelous, uplifting, terrific, spectacular. Opportunities were raining down upon his head. And with each new item he related, she felt more miserable.

"So it's finally happening," Christopher said, opening his suitcase at home. "Everything you said would happen . . ."

"Is that new?" she said, referring to a sweater he had just removed from his suitcase.

"Yes . . . from Milan. Do you like it?"

"It's okay." It was actually gorgeous. She wasn't feeling at all generous, however.

She continued to help him unpack, putting away the other new clothes he had purchased in Rome, Paris and Milan. She scarcely commented on anything, except to force out affirmative responses when it seemed absolutely necessary and appropriate.

Christopher seemed not to notice her silence. He was lost in his own state of euphoria. By the time he had finished unpacking, she was feeling decidedly uncharitable. Not only was everything in his life skyrocketing while her own fortunes were plummeting, but he didn't seem to notice her except as an audience.

"I'm going to hop into the shower," he said, putting the suitcase in the corner. "I'll expect you undressed and insatiable by the time I get out." He kissed her quickly, then disappeared into the bathroom. He was singing happily to himself.

"Swell . . ." she muttered under her breath.

She loved him, oh, yes. Yet, as she looked down at his new clothes, at his suitcase in the corner of the room, at the small mementos he had brought home with him to recall his high times in Europe—times without her, she could almost hate him.

Wanting him physically as much as he seemed to need her, she also wanted to withhold herself from him, to punish him, to exert her will over his. Of course she was happy for his success. Of course. It was all mean and petty, she knew, these feelings she harbored, and she actively disliked herself for each uncharitable emotion. But, in the shadow of all his triumphs, she felt excluded, her self-importance was diminished.

When he came out of the shower, instead of finding her in bed eagerly waiting for him, she was in the living room going over the figures Jacqueline had given her for the month's sales and expenditures.

They did not look at all good. Riff's war against her had begun to take a serious toll. She could get by, but only barely. Absorbed in her plight, she did not notice Christopher standing a few feet away, watching her.

"So," he said cautiously, "you must have heard already." His voice was heavy with regret. She realized instantly that he must have attributed her obvious rejection to another cause.

Slowly, in question, she raised her head. She saw that he had on a new robe—yet another change in the old Christopher who had formerly been content to parade around in his underwear. Even his cologne was different. Everything about him was unsettling, and she suddenly saw him as the conquering hero returned to find her kingdom in ruins.

"Heard what?" she asked and turned the balance sheet facedown, where he could not see her state of disgrace.

Chris sat down beside her. "I've been asked to paint the fresco in the Milan opera house." His hands dropped between his parted knees. He looked ashamed—or was it disappointment?—rather than pleased at the offer.

Lauren drew in a silent breath. "No, I hadn't heard that."

"I didn't accept." He hesitated, then turned to her. "But I did tell them I would consider their offer."

Lauren looked at him as if he were crazy. "That's a once-in-a-lifetime opportunity."

"But so are you," he said. "Lauren, I love you. I can feel what's happened to us, just me being away these few weeks."

"Going on four," she said.

"I'd be gone a much longer time if I take the assignment."

So, she thought, her satisfaction at having projected the future correctly bordered on the masochistic . . . *it was the moment of truth.* She closed her eyes, assembling her response. Lloyd appeared against the dark backdrop of her mind. She saw him as he had been that day in his office, having just imparted his prediction that her relationship with Christopher would take this final turn. To be forewarned, however, was not to be forearmed. She felt like hell, like a wounded, pitiable creature. In conscience, she could not hold him back from realizing the success to which he was entitled. By the same token, she couldn't bear to have him around to witness what, according to the projected figures, would be her imminent decline and ultimate failure.

"I think you should take it," she said, sounding to herself like one of those nits portrayed in old movies produced during the second world war—one of those rollicking good-sport nits who tap-danced on the tops of tables whenever the going got rough.

"You honestly don't mind?" He was staring at her with a mixture of relief and condemnation for not objecting.

"Chris . . . you know I'll miss you. You know that," she said, careful to keep her eyes averted.

"No, actually, I don't." His eyes pleaded with her for confirmation.

"Oh, Chris . . . honestly. Don't be so melodramatic. We've both got careers to run. I'm busy, you're busy. We're part of the new and improved generation, remember? What's the matter? Are you stuck back in some archaic age? Haven't you read the latest? We're the generation that keeps it all together. Career. Personal life. The whole bit." Her speech came out sounding somewhere between ironic sophistication and the ravings of a demented pom-pom girl.

Christopher shook his head slowly, assimilating her words. "Then I guess that's it. I'll accept."

"Good. Great," she said, gutsy, good kid that she was. "So, uh, why don't we celebrate?" she suggested. "You get the champagne and bring it upstairs." Licentiously, she whispered, "And I will shower." *And,* she thought, as she went up the stairs, *I'll also have myself a nice little cry. But I'll emerge smiling, so you won't have to know, my love, that this love we shared together, was just a transitory, beautiful, illusive dream that is fading . . . even now.*

When she entered the bedroom after her shower, the champagne was on the nightstand. Christopher handed her a filled glass. "To our future," he said.

She lowered her eyes, saying nothing to him as she drank. He put aside his glass and removed the towel from around her. Lightly, he ran his fingers over her skin causing her nipples to rise. As he cupped both her breasts in his hands, a drop of champagne spilled from her glass. He bent to catch the champagne with his tongue and continued to lick, moving to her nipple, sucking one, then the other, until she trembled, pushing her body into his.

More of the liquid fell, trailing down her bare skin. "Please," she moaned, a catch of laughter edging the tone of her desire, "I've got to put down my glass."

Christopher took it from her, tipping it so the liquid created a small stream between the cleft of her breasts, and with his tongue, hot and velvety against her skin, he followed its course over her stomach. Her breath caught sharply, and she closed her eyes, her fingers running through his thick, dark hair. She was trembling and felt suddenly foolish, completely vulnerable and totally wanton. It had been such a long time for her.

But she was not the only one straining to maintain a semblance of control. Christopher's eyes were glazed, and his breathing as short as hers as he took her by the hand and led her to the bed.

"You'll forgive me, I hope," his eyes never leaving her body as he spoke. "But I may not be quite the proper gentleman this time."

He was on his knees, his hands clasping her hips as he brought her to him. Moaning slightly, she writhed under the tantalizing sensations his fingers and mouth released in her.

Her fingers pulled at his robe's sash. It fell open, and she saw him hard, wanting her.

"You'll forgive me," she said, "if I'm not quite the lady this time?"

"I'm in the mood to make allowances, if you are."

As he touched her, she knew that he was replaying in life many nights of male fantasy. There was an urgency, a strong, masculine demand to his handling of her body that she had never known before.

"Show me that you want me," he said, his voice low, almost a growl from his unreleased need.

Suddenly, she was touching him boldly, responding to his moans of approval, losing awareness of herself, so involved was she in indulging his passion, and hers as well. A fierce heat spread through her loins as his hands clamped around her waist.

"You're so beautiful," he whispered, holding her just above him so that her hair hung loose, dark and luxuriant against his gleaming chest. "Do you know how much I've wanted you—wanted this?"

"Yes . . . oh, yes." She kissed him deeply then, their tongues joined, searching, and together they moved into each other.

She tortured him, slowly moving above him, watching his eyes drink in the form of her breasts, her stomach, the roundness of her hips. Now and again, his eyes would close, and he would move beneath her, caught in an oblivion of bliss.

Finally, he held her to him, taking control, and the fantasies of all their nights were fulfilled in their driving need for each other.

Afterward, he lay partially atop her, his breathing subsiding into the steady rise and fall of sleep. Lauren stared beyond the wall of glass, seeing past the roofs on the opposite canal bank, watching the sky, its cloud shapes churned by the wind, its changing hues bleeding into an infinitely expanding canvas, until, at last, she slept.

When she awoke, she found herself alone, the room dark. A blanket had been laid over her, keeping off the chill that had arisen since the afternoon sun had died.

Pulling herself up, still groggy, she looked around. Beyond the window, a fine mist had risen up from the water. Lights from opposite houses glowed through the fuzzy, moisture-laden atmosphere. September had crept upon Southern California. The season, as well as her life, was changing.

She pulled on some clothes and descended the stairs. Several lights had been turned on in the living room.

"Chris? Hey, where are you?"

She waited for his reply, expecting that he'd pop out from the kitchen door or come striding in from the garage. But there was only continued silence, an absolute silence that reinforced the loneliness creeping through her soul. She would have to get used to not having him answer her.

Moving to the sofa, she lowered her eyes in contemplation, and slumped down, telling herself to snap out of it, to pull herself together so that when Chris did return, he wouldn't catch her being gloomy. It would do no good, after all. What was, simply was.

Suddenly, her heart constricted. The gallery's profit and loss statement had been removed from the coffee table. She searched for it beneath the coffee table, then thought maybe she had left it somewhere else. But she knew she hadn't.

She cursed herself as she ran to find her keys in the kitchen. They were there, of course, but the key to her gallery was missing from among the others.

Using her spare key, she unlocked the gallery and entered. A slice of pale light issued from her office as she made her way down the hall. She pushed open the door and stood looking across the room at Christopher. He was seated at her desk with her master ledger opened on it. "Did you have a good sleep?" he asked, not looking up at her, but perusing a page.

"I resent this," she said tersely, standing where she was.

"Do you?" His manner was mild as he raised his eyes to hers. "Well, I resent this, too." He stood, and now the passivity gave way to a contained rage. As he spoke, he ground his fist into the ledger book. "I resent that you couldn't have been straight with me."

"There was nothing you could do," Lauren answered.

"I've got ears. They listen."

"I need money. Not sympathy."

Christopher ignored her sarcasm and leafed

through the ledger sheets. "June, July, August—all these numbers tell me a strange tale of woe. Rent raised here," he said, tracing his finger along a column of figures. "Advertising and promotional expenses up, sales for your master artists holding . . . yes . . . and those for your special exhibitions were decent. But there's been a drop in your overall sales. And, well, it looks to me, that unless you get your act together and damned fast, it's going to be tap-city around here." He squinted, analyzing her. "Maybe I don't want to know this, but I'm asking anyway. How did all of this happen?"

"I wasn't quite as smart and as tough as I thought I was."

She crossed the room and, taking the ledger from him, closed it, wishing she could resolve all of her troubles that easily. Chris held on to her wrist.

"It has something to do with McIntyre, doesn't it?"

She looked away.

"I thought so."

"The senator has a great deal of pride."

"I can understand that. So do I." He released his hold on her. Anger sparked from the depths of his eyes. "I'd heard some gossip. I didn't want to believe it—chose, in fact, to ignore it. It made me feel like a damned heel." He slammed his fist against his palm. Looking at her, he said, "I'm sorry, Lauren. There's no way I'm going to give you up to that bastard. I'm too selfish—too male, maybe. Whatever." He shrugged. He moved to her, holding her against him. "Come to Italy with me. You've proven you can make it on this street. Leave it alone now. You're tough and you're smart, and I know that if you wanted to play ugly like those guys, you could do it and probably beat them. But you won't go all out because you're too good for that."

"No, I'm not," she said. "And I can beat them," she said softly.

Christopher held her away from him. He shook his head. "No, Lauren, it can't be done. There's your future, all neatly itemized in black and red ink."

"I've got Wilm," she said.

Christopher was caught by surprise. It took him a second to respond. "Fredrich Wilm? You've signed him for your gallery?" He seemed not to believe her.

"Well, I will. As soon as I can get to him."

Christopher sighed. "Don't you ever quit? You've got about as much chance of getting Wilm as you have of getting Rembrandt to rise from the dead. The guy is a total recluse. He's—" Christopher stopped in midsentence. Slowly, he moved away, his attitude thoughtful. Looking at her again, he said, "I think I can help you. I don't really want to, but I'll do it."

"You? Help me get Wilm?" She laughed, then saw that he wasn't joking. Next she experienced a rush of elation, followed by an unpleasant jolt to her ego as she perceived her self-sufficiency again being eroded.

"Yes. He has this . . . this companion. I met her in Rome. An ambitious barracuda, if I ever met one. She's something else," he said, his words trailing off as he seemed to reflect on the meeting. "She liked my work. In fact, she made a few proposals—"

"Of an entrepreneurial nature, of course?"

Christopher smiled. "Ah, I love it when you're human. Some were personal," he admitted. "But her main interest in me—or any man, I'll bet—is professional."

"You turned her down, naturally."

"On both counts. I could contact Wilm through her. She's supposed to be staying in West Berlin for the next couple of months while she makes some avant-garde film. Apparently, she's got the idea that her days with Wilm are numbered. She's frantic to feather her nest. If you were to make it worth her while, I'm sure she'd do what she could to promote you to Wilm."

"I don't have a lot of time," Lauren said.

"Don't fret, my love. This is a very fast lady."

Chapter 12

LAUREN HUNG BY CHRISTOPHER'S SIDE WHILE HE TRIED repeatedly during the night to put through a call to Wilm's rock'n'roll girl friend.

"Promise her anything," Lauren urged, then amended her instructions, "within reason, of course."

"I'll let you handle the dollar negotiations," Christopher assured her.

"I wasn't talking money."

"Oh. Oh! You don't mean that you would barter my body for a Wilm squiggle?"

"A girl's got to work with what she has." Lauren sighed.

"Now that I think of it, she's not all that bad looking . . ."

"Then don't think. Just dial."

Two days later, she peered out the window of the Pan American jet. It flew low—as specified by the international agreement between East Germany and West Berlin—through the narrow, restricted air corridor leading into West Berlin's Tegel Airport. Only planes licensed under the allies during World War II were allowed access to the walled city, which before the war was considered on par with Paris for style, culture and entertainment. In the shadow of the plane, she made out military tanks belonging to the East Germans, their guns pointed up in the firing position.

A few minutes later, she disembarked with Christopher. They followed directional signs printed in several foreign languages, including English. Christopher nudged her slightly. Looking straight ahead and smiling queerly, he said, "There's your lady. The one who looks like a Martian."

"An expensive one, though," Lauren commented, taking in the slender girl with her unkempt, blond mane falling over her shoulders and partially obscuring her face. Holly Adler leaned against a metal railing and puffed languorously on a cigarette. She seemed oblivious to the human traffic flowing past her. Her outfit was comprised of silver, skintight lamé pants, hot-pink boots and a silver jacket, much like those worn by aviators. Lauren hadn't spent time on Rodeo without learning that that much weirdness carried a hefty price tag.

As she and Christopher approached, the girl turned her head. Noticing Christopher, she smiled slowly. Now that Lauren could see the girl more clearly with her hair tossed aside, she saw that Holly was also quite beautiful. But, of course, Wilm would have good taste. He wasn't that crazy. Lauren shot Christopher what she hoped was a mean look, and he smiled back innocently. "Moon maidens are not my type," he assured her.

"So, we meet again," Holly said. She had a London accent, a trace of cockney.

"This is Lauren Taylor," Christopher introduced her.

"Sure," Holly said with a lopsided grin. "My Rodeo connection." She gave Lauren a cool once-over.

Lauren noted the cleverness in the girl's luminous blue eyes. For that shrewdness, Lauren was thankful. It would be that much easier to convince Holly of Lauren's proposition to run lithos of Wilm's work.

Lauren was not surprised that the girl was booked into one of the most expensive of Berlin's hotels—the Bristol Hotel Kempinski, off the Kurfürstendamm, which ranked as the equivalent of Broadway and Fifth Avenue combined, from what Lauren could tell of the street's appearance.

"After you've stashed your gear, I suggest we get together and chat this out in my suite. After all," Holly said, "there's no need to drag things out, is there? The deal's good or it isn't, right?"

"It'll be good," Lauren assured her.

Holly smiled without warmth. "Then you won't have wasted your time and money."

An hour later, Lauren and Christopher took chairs in the singer's suite. They both declined an offering of marijuana, accepting a sherry each, in its place.

Holly had changed into a long T-shirt, which ended equidistant between thigh and knee. To accompany the purple jersey, she wore orange-and-purple striped tights with low-heeled orange boots. "So," Holly said, lighting up a regular cigarette, "you'd like to show my Freddie's paintings, would you?"

"Not exactly his paintings."

Holly seemed surprised, as if anything could surprise a girl like her.

"Not exactly? What then, exactly?"

Lauren was pinned by the amazing opalescent eyes.

"Wilm has never committed his work to the lithographic process—"

"Lithos? Prints!" Holly rolled her eyes. Accentuating her low regard of Lauren's suggestion, she aimed a knife-thin stream of smoke her way. "Prints are garbage."

Lauren retained her composure, although she would have liked to have gotten up and walked out. "Fortunes have been made from that garbage," she replied.

"Love, those days are gone. The bottom's dropped out on that scam. I'll grant you the public is stupid, but not that stupid."

What the singer was saying was true. Anyone involved with commercial art was aware of what had happened during the past couple of years. From 1978 through 1981, the art market went crazy with galleries selling prints for inflated prices. For a while, the market held, and people traded upward. Fortunes were made before the bottom hit, which it did, and it hit hard.

But before that time, even the average consumer who had a taste for Dali could satisfy his craving for art by purchasing a signed lithograph for as little as $120, with the guarantee that he could resell it for twice that amount in six months, perhaps sooner. For the more serious collector, there were prints of blue-chip artists' work that ranged into the five-digit category and which brought triple their investment price within a year.

Lauren had at one time considered entering the market herself, but decided against making a fast buck at what would ultimately be at the public's expense. She had read the handwriting on the wall. It was a boom and bust situation. Eventually, the market became saturated, as she had anticipated. Artists and their managers had become greedy. They would run off a series of prints, number them up to 300, sell them to investors who counted on the work's exclusivity to drive up the initial investment price, only to discover that a second and third and fourth, even a fifth, edition of the same work was produced for mass marketing. What they had purchased was paper, not investment-quality art, as they had been led to believe.

But it was not only the disreputable practices of a few artists and their managers, in collusion with galleries, that killed the proverbial golden goose. The economic current in America—in the entire world—had shifted. People were more likely to pull in their belts than to pull out their wallets for a print of Neiman's skiers.

Even original paintings by name artists were not moving; if they did sell, they might go for as much as $35,000 less than the original $125,000 paid. The master artists remained stable, of course, for these were owned by a totally different category of collector —those who could afford to wait for the financial tide to shift when they wanted to dispose of their Monet or Wyeth or Chagall. And the purchaser who had a liking for a Gauguin original, which was picked up for $6 million, did not need to worry about his cash flow.

"Hear me out," Lauren said. "Fredrich Wilm is not a master artist—"

"He will be," Holly said and nervously ground out her cigarette, only to immediately light up a new one.

"That's what I believe, too."

"Yes, and?"

"And I'm counting on enough other people knowing that, so that when his lithos come on to the open market, they'll be perceived as an investment opportunity they won't want to miss."

Holly moved to the window, where she stood silently looking out at the Kurfürstendamm. A haze of white cigarette smoke hovered over her.

"All right," the singer said. "This is the way it will work."

Lauren felt butterflies batting up against the wall of her stomach. She was going to make it. She was definitely going to survive. Holly was marching back and forth in front of them, thinking the future out loud. "I am going to trust you to know your business," she said.

Lauren and Christopher exchanged glances. There was no conceivable element of trust in this girl's nature, and they both knew it. She'd probably had Lauren checked out before they had arrived in Berlin. "And," Holly went on, "you are going to have to trust me. Freddie is a very weird man. He must be handled just so. Just so," Holly emphasized. "But I can do it. I'm the only one who can do it. Now, anyway." She had added the last as an afterthought, more to herself than to Christopher and Lauren.

Going on, she said, "Your end of the deal will be to show Freddie's work. I want top prices. My job will be to see that the lithos are produced. Everything will be done correctly . . . the best quality."

"You know the process?"

"No. Not entirely. But I know people who do. I'll supervise them."

Lauren was uneasy with the arrangement. "I'd feel better if I could have a more active part in the printmaking."

"Sorry about that, love. I'm afraid those are my conditions."

"Why?" Christopher had not entered into the discussion before this time. He sounded hostile.

A wave of panic rose in Lauren. The girl was clever and greedy, that was true; she was also temperamental. Lauren was afraid of antagonizing her. Better, she felt, to agree with Holly's demands now and later work around them when the circumstances were better. She didn't want Christopher to blow the deal before it had been made.

"Didn't you know? Freddie's paranoid," Holly replied to Christopher. "Yes, he is. And he certainly wouldn't trust a soul other than me with his plates. Only me, ducks. Only me. So take it or leave it."

"I'll take it," Lauren said. She rose, extending her hand to Holly, who looked at it as if it were an alien object never seen before. She smiled up at Lauren. "I thought only gentlemen shook hands."

"Ladies, too."

"Ah, then, perhaps I shouldn't, love." Holly turned away, lighting up yet another cigarette.

Christopher excused himself from attending any of the additional meetings Lauren had with Holly the following day. When they left on the morning of the third day, he was notably quiet. Now that she thought of it, Christopher had been bordering on sullen the entire visit, only she had been too involved with her plans to pay him much attention.

"You're angry with me," she said.

"Not angry exactly. But I think you've gotten yourself into something that could turn out to be a mistake."

"Oh, you mean because Holly is having her way." Lauren shrugged. "I don't like it either. But what alternative do I have? And, besides, what could be worse than losing the gallery altogether? At least this way I've got a sporting chance."

"I doubt very much that there is anything very sporting about Holly."

"Oh, come on," Lauren said, snuggling into him. "You're just prejudiced against Martians."

Chapter 13

THEY HAD A FULL TWO WEEKS TOGETHER BEFORE CHRISTOPHER would pack to leave for Italy. It was agreed that she would stay on at the house until the lease expired.

"But I've an apartment of my own," Lauren protested.

"An apartment without furniture," Christopher pointed out. "I've got the lease for another three months. You may as well take advantage of the view."

"But—"

"And the ducks! Who'll feed them? If not for their sake—if you can be that cruel—and if not for me," he went on dramatically, "then think of your roommate."

"My who?"

"Cavalier," Christopher said, motioning to the sleeping animal on the living room couch.

"Oh, yes. That wretch." She wrinkled her nose, laughing. "How could I have forgotten him?"

"Search me," Christopher replied. He retrieved Cavalier, holding him out to her. "He certainly never forgets you."

Cavalier turned his head away, distaining to even grace her with a glance from his yellow eyes. "Sure. He hisses every time I come into the house when you're . . . when you're gone." She broke off and began to furiously plump the cushions where Cavalier had been resting.

"I guess that's something you're going to have to get used to," Chris said quietly, and they both knew he wasn't talking about the cat's bad manners.

As a compromise for not taking the trip Christopher wanted, Lauren agreed to take off half days from the gallery.

The weather in Southern California was generally unpredictable, and during the fourth week of September, Los Angeles found itself treated to a bona fide heat wave, with temperatures rising to 100°F. Venice had taken on a carnival atmosphere. Beach people returned in full force, renewing their faded tans, reveling in the reprieve from the autumn's diminished sunlight by roller-skating along the boardwalk in bikinis or garish Hawaiian trunks, their bodies dipping and zigzagging in time to the rock music issuing from their earphones. Seasonal burger stands reopened, doing a hefty business. Surfers abandoned their wet suits.

It was a time in which cares were forgotten, as if somehow nature had turned back time and everyone got a second chance to enjoy fully what they were too blind to see before it was gone forever.

That was the only sadness that Lauren experienced during those idyllic two weeks she had with Christopher. Occasionally, the bliss was interrupted by the ache of awareness that this would not last—that just as the heat had arrived, blasting the atmosphere with energy, it would just as suddenly depart, leaving a cold, deadened void.

Sometimes, while walking with him along the sand, she would slip into a space—just for a moment—in which the sun, the music, the colorful, drifting litter of humanity would fade and she would feel the chill of loneliness sweep through her. With Christopher gone, she would be like the beach in winter, deserted, desolate.

But in the present, there were so many good moments between them. With the prospect of the Wilm litho coup in her future, she could finally relax and enjoy life. Even Maxwell Kain's frequent calls to her no longer caused much more than minor annoyance, whereas before she had been catapulted into first-degree stress levels at the first hint of his terrifying whine, carrying its implicit threat that he could and would sabotage her career.

Christopher surprised her one afternoon, when she had just returned from the gallery, with a used dinghy purchased from a neighbor. The three of them—the nasty Cavalier included—would voyage down canals, sometimes drifting lazily beside the ducks who accompanied them like a noisy, protective convoy and, at other times, rowing purposefully to explore some distant bank that looked intriguing.

Christopher was the captain of their small craft; Cavalier bore the attitude of a disgruntled cruise patron, accustomed to far better accommodations; and she was the self-appointed social director, in charge of good spirits and the planning of their sumptuous feasts packed for each trip in a picnic basket.

There was the typical pirate fare of wine and cheese, fruit and cold-cuts along with heavy-crusted rolls baked fresh each morning at a local bakery. But the wickedest booty of it all was the assortment of confections that she and Christopher shopped for together, which became occasions for great debates

over the attributes of whipped cream versus choco-
late, versus fruit-filled, versus multilayered con-
coctions of indistinguishable contents. Diplomacy
triumphed in all instances, with both customers leaving with all items—the sinfulness of it all sending
them into gales of laughter as they walked back to
their boat. And then one day, the laughter stopped.
The mirage of happiness dissolved into reality. It
was the first week of October, and Christopher was
leaving.

There had been moments during that two-week
period when she had almost abandoned her resolve to
remain selflessly noble on Christopher's behalf. She
knew that if she asked, he would stay. She knew that
he would abandon his career—and sometimes, she
thought, his very life—to be with her. But she also
knew that their love would not endure under those
conditions. His talent was part of him, and he was his
talent. Could an eagle have its wings clipped and still
survive? No. Perhaps it was possible to cage a small
brown bird, a middling creature content to sit atop
clotheslines or to perch on backyard tree limbs, but
Christopher's wingspan was already far too wide to be
contained. It was his nature to aim for the top of the
mountain. He would need to cruise at the loftiest
altitudes, where few ever experienced the current of
the wind, the touch of the sun so close, the excitement
of being free to rise as far as he could push himself and
dared to go.

His entire destiny would be altered with two words
from her: "Please stay."

But, by maintaining her noble silence, she was
destroying a part of herself that could never be
recaptured again. Instinctively, as she had known that
day when she had first thrilled to the majesty of
Michelangelo's genius that there would never be an
artist of his equal, she knew there could never be a

love for her again that could match her love for Christopher.

On the way to the airport, she silently rehearsed the farewell address she would deliver. In her mind, she had pictured the scene as taking place outside the departure gate or in the waiting room—perhaps by a window, the light playing softly across their faces. But when they arrived at the airport, only passengers were allowed past security into the international terminal. So, instead of her poignant speech, she was forced to recite hurried lines several decibels above the dulcet tones of intimacy and beneath the cold glare of neon lights.

For both their sakes, she managed not to cry, adopting the bravest of fronts. She smiled, kissed him, hugged him, kissed him again, made two rather insipid jokes, promised for the hundredth time that day that she would call, that she would write—yes, of course, of course!—and returned a jaunty wave in the final parting.

They both knew their exit cues; both turned on their heels, good soldiers, chins up, marching off to their respective destinies. Lauren took several courageous steps before she stopped. Spinning around, she caught sight of Christopher disappearing down the long corridor that led to the international gates. Panic clutched at her. It was happening . . . it was happening now . . . but she didn't have to let it happen.

She pressed her way through a large tour group of Japanese. She stumbled on carry-on luggage, hooked her purse on packages, apologizing all the way as she elbowed her way through the polite, dense assemblage.

"Chris! Christopher!"

But he didn't hear her. He rounded a corner, disappearing from sight. Her chance had passed. On the way home, she told herself that, after all, she had done the right thing.

Wilm's first trial proof arrived by special courier two weeks after Christopher's departure. So far, Lauren had no misgivings about agreeing to work with Holly on her terms, rather than pressing for a direct meeting with Wilm. Periodically, Christopher would call, continuing with his negative admonitions, denouncing Holly as being "bad news." But so far, Holly's behavior had been exemplary. Lauren received progress reports on the form the series was to take, and now she had a quality product delivered at the appointed time, all per their agreement.

According to the terms she and Holly had worked out, Wilm was to supply her gallery with a total of ten original graphics with a limited run of thirty-five copies of each work.

The price they had fixed for each print was to be $25,000—the retail cost easily justifiable given Wilm's reputation as the successor to Picasso, along with Lauren's guarantee of the work's exclusivity. With a potential market of three-hundred million (only seven and a half percent of the world's total population), a print run of just thirty-five copies would translate into the most advantageous kind of investment for a serious collector.

In the art business, the one immutable law to consider was that of supply and demand. It was a work's rarity, as much as its quality, which determined its dollar amount. Historically, graphics presented by name artists were able to realize average price appreciation of 400 percent within a ten-year span—a point that Lauren intended to capitalize on, both literally and figuratively. Wilm would be perceived as a stellar attraction to collectors. Lauren had already begun to work out her promotional campaign. She planned to predict, but not promise, the amount of investment return a buyer could anticipate, astutely using past price histories as her guide. Research had shown that a collection of 435 aquatints of birds by Audubon sold for $3,880 in 1958 and in 1967 fetched an astounding $216,000 on the marketplace. The sharp buyer paying $700 in 1953 for Goya's *Los Caprichos* turned over his investment for $21,600 in 1970. Similarly, Picasso's *Bust of a Woman,* purchased in 1962 for $1624, was resold seven years later for $24,593.

Lauren's usual commission for an artist was fifty percent. In this case, Holly said Wilm would take his usual ninety percent, and when Lauren balked, Holly came back with a more favorable deal of fifteen percent for Lauren's profit. Before her overhead expenses, Lauren's cut would be $130,250 on each separate run of 35 prints and for the complete series of ten lithos, $1,302,500. But, aside from the money, she would be realizing a boost in reputation that would carry her forward into another decade. As much as Wilm, she would become a legend just for having been the one to introduce his work to the multiple-print medium.

Neither she nor Christopher had been naive enough to assume that Holly had not actually settled with Wilm for something less than the eighty-five percent commission split. Lauren's guess was that Holly had cut herself in for five percent; Christopher, laughing cynically, insisted the girl would be in for ten or nothing. Lauren, however, was not concerned with that aspect of their relationship; she was happy with her own profit margin, and if Holly looted Wilm on the side, she had no control over that.

"You're missing the point here," Christopher said

during one such discussion. "The implication, my beautiful, good Lauren, is that you are dealing with a totally unscrupulous personality."

"Gossip! Besides," Lauren scoffed, "how can she hurt me? Our deal is very straightforward. She delivers the work, I sell it; the money is paid to me, the commission comes off the top and goes to Holly to disperse to Wilm. So, really, what could she possibly do to screw things up for me?"

"I hope you don't find out the hard way," Christopher said, and Lauren had changed the subject to something more pleasant before he could elaborate on the horrendous possibilities.

The trial proof that Lauren looked at was flawless, as Holly had predicted it would be. Holly had flown back to Munich on her days off from filming in Berlin to observe Wilm's method of printing—an art in itself.

There were four basic techniques for printing graphics. For his series, Wilm had selected planography, more commonly referred to as the lithographic process. Lauren had studied the form in school, and when Holly related the steps of the process to her, she knew the girl was every bit as clever and observant as Lauren had originally surmised. Holly had watched Wilm draw the design onto a stone plate with a grease crayon. He dipped the surface in water, then rolled greasy ink over the entire surface. Because of the natural repelling qualities of water and oil, only the designed areas would absorb the ink. Paper was laid across the surface and both were run through a handpress—although it was possible to employ a mechanical press as well. The method was long and laborious, as each color would have to be done in turn and with exact precision.

One of the few disagreements Lauren had had with Holly was over obtaining Wilm's signature on each print. Lauren wanted the prints signed in his own hand after the run had been completed. Holly reported that Wilm found this unsatisfactory. He would instead sign his name in the plate. Holly attributed the decision to Wilm's general quirkiness, and in the end Lauren had to content herself with the artist's decision.

According to Holly, Wilm insisted that the craze of pencil signatures on lithos was a recent phenomenon. Until the 1930s, it was the custom to have the artist's name signed in the plate only. Wilm was adamant that he was as good as Dürer, Rembrandt, Whistler and Renoir—all of whom adhered to the plate-signing practice for their masterworks.

There was, in truth, no particular stigma attached to this; it would not lessen the value of the artist's work. But as a safeguard, to protect the exclusivity of limited runs, the plate would be canceled by the artist by marking it in some way to show that the run was complete. In some cases, even these plates were sold or donated to museums. Occasionally, a canceled plate would be reprinted, but the prints would not be under exclusive run and therefore would be unattractive as an investment to serious collectors who purchased numbered editions.

Wilm would be entitled to five artist's proofs, which would be marked "A/P" on the bottom, rather than bear a number. In the case of an artist of Wilm's stature, the proofs could be sold for even more than the numbered copies. Lauren's trial print, marked *"etat,"* would also be sold, but for $35,000.

Her responsibility was to her customers, to insure them that Wilm's edition would be limited as numbered and would remain exclusive. Documented descriptions of each work would subsequently be entered into catalogues to be used as future references for collectors, who would check to see that form and size agreed with the descriptions, when the prints came up for resale.

Lauren had scheduled Wilm's showing for two weeks before Christmas, a time when holiday nerves were not yet frazzled and good cheer still prevailed.

During the first days of Christopher's trip to Italy, Lauren spoke to him often. Either he called or she would call him. In between their calls, he sent her short letters with clever etchings included, representative of moments they had shared together in Venice. She kept each of his hastily drawn sketches, delighting in them for personal reasons and savoring them for their intrinsic artistic merit as well.

The days of Christopher's absence progressed into long weeks. His name became mentioned more frequently, often with a startlingly avid degree of interest, by artists' agents and clients in New York and Europe. Museum curators were anxious to see his work. The scent of a hot new talent had been picked up. No one had forgotten Andy Warhol's blazing, if unsettling, entrance into the pop art scene, and no one wanted to be caught with their taste for the future down again. It could be an expensive oversight.

She was pleased for Christopher when the first batch of photos of him, with their accompanying news captions, began to appear in Italy's *Europeo* magazine, in *Jours de France*, and even in the Portguese *Marchete*, as well as in the various foreign newspapers. They would both laugh when sometimes he would be unaware of his own fame, and she would be the one to mention that the paparazzi had caught him with a rogue piece of spaghetti dripping from his lip, with a splatter of paint on the tip of his nose as he attempted a glamorous smile.

Kain, as usual, had his finger in everything, and it

was Kain, who in the course of checking with her on the details for the Wilm exhibition, mentioned ever-so-casually that he was pleased that Christopher Reynolds was on such good, such close terms with Fredrich Wilm's girl friend.

"Awfully surprising, though. She comes with a rather raunchy reputation. I wonder what on earth he could be seeing in her? A man of his elevated taste and style . . ."

"What are you suggesting, Maxwell?"

"It's not what I'm suggesting, my dear girl, but more of what appeared in the *London Times* last Sunday." He rattled off the section and page. Did she only imagine that he was smacking his lips?

"Pity. My copy hasn't been delivered yet."

"Then I'll be happy to send you over my copy."

"Don't trouble yourself—"

"No trouble. I insist. After all, what are friends for?"

It was true, of course, just as she had known it would be. Kain was a snake, but he wasn't a lying snake. And the picture the *Times* ran of Christopher and Holly in Berlin was as damning a testimony of Christopher's infidelity as she had ever seen printed. Holly was snuggled up against Christopher's chest, his arm around her waist. *Well*, she thought, *at least the son of a bitch wasn't smiling.*

She hurled the paper to the floor beside her bed, burying herself in a cocoon of bedcovers. Sleep was impossible. She was wide awake when the telephone rang several hours later. In the dark, she reached over the curled form of Cavalier, who lay beside her. In Christopher's absence, the cat had developed a cautious acceptance of her presence in his life.

At the sound of Christopher's voice, she bristled.

"It's late," she snapped.

"I know what time it is," Christopher said. "Only this can't wait."

Something anxious and rushed in his voice made her forego the myriad questions and accusations she had stored within her all day. "What can't wait?" She sat up, switching on the lamp beside the bed.

"Get out of the Wilm deal, Lauren."

The connection was not the best, and his voice came through as if in a tunnel. There was a slight echo after each word, making the transmission eerie, otherworldly.

"Christopher, we've been all through this a dozen times."

"Look," he broke in, "I can't give you specifics because there aren't any."

Meanly, Lauren thought that judging by the photo, he would have been in a marvelous position to have given her plenty of specifics; but she held her tongue and listened while he continued.

"Call it a gut reaction. Only I know I'm not wrong. Holly is going to rip you off."

"Please, spare me that old refrain." Then she asked, "How? Tell me how that would be possible, Christopher, and I'll cancel the whole thing. But first you tell me how."

"I just told you!"

She could feel his frustration even across the miles.

"I just told you, dammit, that I can't pin anything down. I can't provide you with concretes, but so help me, Lauren, I know I'm not wrong about this Holly character."

"I trust you've gotten to know Holly Adler better?" She held her breath, waiting for his response.

There was a hesitation, a beat too long. More

subdued, he said, "I figured you'd find out about that."

"Well, you figured right," Lauren said.

"Yeah, I flew out to Berlin to see her. But it was for your sake, Lauren. I know there were some pictures of us together—I saw them. There were some extenuating circumstances, so don't jump to conclusions. The attraction was one-sided, entirely. You believe that, don't you?"

"Of course, why wouldn't I?" She didn't bother to hide the sarcasm in her voice.

"Look, Lauren, I can't give you specifics because there aren't any, but you've got to believe me about this girl."

"Holly Adler may not be a girl scout, and granted her sexual proclivities, as reported, are a bit on the amoral side, but there's no possible way I can get hurt on this Wilm deal. And I need the Wilm lithos, or I'm going to be out on my fanny in very short order."

"Good. Let the gallery go and come to Italy and be with me."

It had never occurred to Lauren before that Christopher might actually want her to fail, but it did at that moment.

"I'm seeing the Wilm deal through, Chris. I spent eleven years taking calculated risks, so I ought to know what I'm doing."

"I'm impressed," he returned, sounding decidedly unimpressed. "Congratulations. You've won your trophies for being smart, tough kid. But this time, you're dealing with someone who's calculating on you losing."

"It doesn't make sense. If I lose, then she loses."

"Wrong. People like Holly Adler don't lose, Lauren. They never have anything of their own. They only grab and take and destroy what other people have worked for."

They parted with terse good-byes. Lauren did not sleep the rest of the night.

An advertising campaign had been devised by Lauren that evolved in stages, each step in the carefully planned promotion designed to increase in suspense, until by the final week before the Wilm exhibition, critics would be anxious enough to pay for invitations to the event.

Riff had also been busy. His attempts to discredit her before the public had not abated, and now, two weeks before the Wilm opening was scheduled to occur, Riff launched his own counteroffensive aimed at crippling her drive for financial solidarity. On the precise date of Wilm's showing, Riff was to host a lavish fund raiser in the form of a dinner and art auction. Through his family's contacts, he had apparently managed to seduce innumerable Main Line Philadelphia families, a coterie of Southern aristocrats and a sprinkling of Boston and other New England tycoons to part with their centuries' old art caches. The event was to be held in the Grand Ballroom of the Beverly Wilshire Hotel. The list of paintings to be offered for sale were formidable enough to warrant serious consideration by any knowledgeable collector.

Lauren sat at her desk in the gallery. It was after opening hours, and she wore a red velour warm-up suit, having just returned from her evening workout at the gym.

Jacqueline, who had remained late to send a batch of night-rate telexes overseas, entered the office just in time to hear Lauren mutter a string of expletives.

"Did you see this?" Lauren said, slapping the newspaper down on the desk.

Jacqueline picked up the paper. "Ooh la la."

"Ooh la la, my foot," Lauren muttered between

clenched teeth, and glared again at the news feature that Jacqueline returned to the desk.

"You have nothing to worry about," Jacqueline said. "In two weeks all your problems will be gone."

"Either that, or I'll be gone."

Both women looked at each other for a long moment. They were both strong, they were both optimistic, they were both realistic. Neither of them could deny that Lauren was not right.

Chapter 14

THE DAY BEFORE THE WILM EXHIBITION, LAUREN closed down the gallery. The drapes were drawn closed on the front windows and the entire staff was relieved for the day. Only she and Jacqueline were there for the arrival of the lithos, which came by special armored truck with three humorless-looking guards in attendance.

Each litho arrived framed, as Lauren had instructed. There was nothing left to be done but to mount them on the walls.

Weeks of paranoia dissolved as Lauren toured the gallery for a final inspection. Jacqueline marched along by her side.

"Didn't I tell you?" Jacqueline said. "Did I not tell you again and again there was nothing to worry about?"

"You did, you did," Lauren said, feeling well-enough disposed to agree with anyone about anything at that moment.

The lithos clearly represented the finest work Wilm had ever produced. After each work had been completed, Holly Adler had sent Lauren the corresponding trial proof for her approval. Therefore, the quality and content of the series came as no surprise. But somehow, seeing the entire edition there, mounted and displayed as one integral unit, was more than a reflection of the artist's enterprise; the exhibit was testimony to the vastness of her own accomplishment. Her own energy and judgment had prevailed. Christopher had been wrong to doubt her decision to trust Holly Adler. The woman had been faultlessly efficient and accommodating in every way during their dealings. Tomorrow, Lauren planned to make a special toast to Holly Adler congratulating her on her cooperative spirit, and she would make certain that Christopher was beside her when she did.

There was only one cloud left on her horizon, and that was the threat of Riff's gala benefit auction siphoning off potential sales.

"The public will come here," Jacqueline insisted furiously. "They can get those other chaps being shown at the senator's little bash at any time. The man is clever, this Wilm. Rarely does he poke his nose out from that tomb he lives in. When he does, people know they had better be there waiting or they miss out."

"You're right," Lauren said, her spirits risen. "You're one hundred percent right."

"As usual."

Precise to the minute, Kain arrived for his advanced, exclusive viewing of the exhibit. He had dressed in an elegant gray pin-striped suit, a light pink shirt, a tie of luminous silk and a cologne reeking of Madison Avenue's best commercial approximation of power. Kain would, after all, be getting the drop on all the other critics, who would not have access to the Wilm collection until the following day. This would not only allow Kain to beat everyone else to the wire with his review, thus boosting his immediate prestige, but it would also serve to cement his chances of obtaining a syndicated art column. In time, Kain could become the single most authoritative voice in the United States on art.

It was to Lauren's equal advantage that Kain's review would reach the public on the morning of the gallery exhibit, which was also the day of Riff's auction benefit. Those who had committed themselves to attending the McIntyre affair might be compelled to shift allegiance to her showing. They would be fools if they didn't—provided, of course, that Kain's review was favorable.

As Kain scrutinized each litho, Lauren watched him from a discreet distance.

It was maddening but typical of Kain to give no sign of emotion. He merely moved forward and backward, now and then rocking on his heels as he made quick, neat notes to himself on a pad held in an exquisite maroon-leather writing case. When he was done, Kain took a last, rapid, all-inclusive tour of the exhibit. Lauren winced, as with the same terrible vigor reminiscent of his teaching days, he snapped shut his writing pad.

Kain's eyes glowed and his face was a trifle pink as he marched to the door, the pad with his comments—her future—clutched tightly by manicured fingers.

"Maxwell!" Lauren called, stepping after him.

"Yes, Miss Taylor . . . ?" He continued without turning.

"What did you think?"

"You'll read all about it tomorrow, Miss Taylor." Kain was speeding to the front door. Then, surprisingly, he stopped. Turning to her, he paused, then said, "Miss Taylor . . . welcome. Welcome to the world of the established art community."

"Thank you," she said. "I realize we haven't always

been on the best of terms. That it must have been painful to say."

"Yes, actually it is rather. Nevertheless, you deserve the praise."

Although she had every reason to find Kain a thoroughly detestable human being, she found herself grinning across the room at him. For a fleeting moment, she caught the twitch of a muscle at the edge of Kain's primly pursed little mouth. He, of course, did not go as far as to smile; yet in itself, a twitch was a major emotional breakthrough.

On the morning of the Wilm exhibition, Lauren had to stop at the caterers before arriving at the gallery. So it was late, a few minutes past ten, before she finally burst into the main salon with the morning's edition of the *Los Angeles Times*.

"Victory!" she cried and waved the newspaper at Jacqueline, who was just replacing the French telephone on its hook.

"I read," Jacqueline said, her hazel eyes flashing brightly as she matched Lauren's broad smile. "And these are for you to read. Since eight this morning, the phone has been going constantly."

Lauren glanced quickly through the messages, noting with satisfaction the names of the people who had called.

While she filled Lauren with additional details of the morning's activities, Jacqueline straightened the desk. "I've already responded for you. Their names will be added to the guest register at the front."

"Excellent." Lauren nodded. The names she held gave testimony to her triumph over Riff McIntyre's attempted coup at her expense. Names previously associated with the McIntyre camp had defaulted in their allegiance. The messages confirmed their intent to be present at her gallery that night.

In his review, Kain had referred to the Wilm litho exhibition as being the single most important art event to occur in a decade. However, there was scant time available for Lauren to revel in her accomplishment. She was picking Christopher up at the airport in an hour, and in the meantime, she had a list of last-minute details to attend to.

Thirty minutes later, she was hunched over the fine print of a contract when Jacqueline appeared in the doorway of her office.

Creases of anger punctuated the corners of Jacqueline's mouth. There was no necessity for an explanation, however, as the trouble presented itself immediately.

Tanned and patrician-looking, Riff McIntyre pushed his way past Jacqueline.

Lauren rocketed up from her seat.

"I thought it was a delivery we were expecting! He pushed his way in," Jacqueline exploded.

"It's all right, Jacqueline," Lauren said, forcing herself to remain calm. "We'll make allowances for the senator's breach in manners."

Riff closed the door after Jacqueline. "So," he began, remaining where he was, "you've done well for yourself."

"You didn't come here to compliment me," Lauren said. "Get to the point, Riff. And then get out."

"You're right. I didn't come here to applaud you." There was equal frost in his voice. "I came to bring you this." Coming forward, he dropped a brown envelope on her desk top.

"What's in it?" she asked, not in the mood to play his game.

"It's a proposal—from my family. The envelope contains a bank draft for a million dollars in your name. There's also an agreement attached. In essence, the agreement stipulates that upon your signed, notarized concurrence to become my legal wife and to abide by certain other terms and conditions set forth, this amount, plus an additional one million dollars, will be yours in three years—provided we are still married. There are also additional perks, which you'll, of course, immediately recognize once you look everything over. But the main thing is, you announce your intention to be my wife at tonight's Wilm exhibit. I'll have to preside at my own affair tonight. That can't be helped and just as well. The circumstances will lend credence to our mutual regard for each other as individuals."

"How neat. The perfect union."

"Well? What do you say? It means you'll never have to worry about your gallery again. Financially, you'll be virtually impregnable with my family's backing. Naturally no one will have to know you've drawn upon our resources. After tonight, to the public, it will appear that you've made it on your own terms."

"I have made it on my own terms."

"You've won a major skirmish with this Wilm caper."

Lauren laughed. "I've won the war, Riff."

He looked at her coldly. "Lauren," he began, in a tone reserved for the dull-witted, "there's no such thing as ever winning completely. Life is a continuous, ongoing battle. The pendulum swings this way, then the other. Today, this time, it happens to have swung your way. That we concede. We're willing to negotiate with you for very practical reasons."

"Yes, and I know what they are. You're going to look like a laughingstock to a lot of people tonight."

Riff colored.

"I'm not going to negotiate," Lauren continued. "And I want you out of my gallery." She strode across the room, opening the door for him to leave.

Beneath the silence, she sensed the force of his

rising anger. His jaw quivered with tension. He snatched up the agreement still lying unopened on the desk. Stuffing it inside his jacket pocket, he said, "You're only one woman, Lauren. One person, alone. I'm an institution. Of course, you've managed to show that one person can cause a lot of trouble, that's true. You've blasted the hell out of our immediate plans. But you just remember," he said, pointing a finger at her, "it is we who will prevail in the end, if for no other reason than there are more of us."

"I'm glad you at least spared me the rhetoric that your cause is just."

"Being just or unjust has nothing to do with anything. Getting what we want does."

"That's unfortunate, because you can wait until hell freezes over before I'll become available on the market."

Riff's eyes took on a strange light. "The market . . . ah, yes. It was long before our time, of course, but you're familiar with the crash of twenty-nine. All that stock. It became valueless overnight. Nothing but paper." He smiled and left. It was not his words Lauren pondered, but his attitude of assurance.

The McIntyres, the gallery operation and the months of loneliness faded from her mind the moment she caught sight of Christopher, his head high above the passengers arriving out of customs.

He was dressed impeccably, the beige-colored Italian suit cut to perfection, his dark handsomeness in striking contrast to the light material. They greeted one another with a long, silent embrace.

He touched her fingers caressingly, almost wondrously to her face. They stood there together, both silent, both feasting on the other's presence until, aware of their foolishness, they laughed self-consciously.

He pulled her to him again and kissed her. The kiss

began with a quiet reverence and became a hungering need, so that, for propriety's sake, they found it necessary to draw apart.

"Come on," she said, "Cavalier's got a surprise waiting for you."

"A dead mouse perhaps?"

"No, no. Since you've been gone, Cavalier's undergone a major character transformation."

"I'm intrigued."

"Steel yourself to an unimaginable sight," she warned. *And something else . . .* she thought.

While Christopher stowed his suitcases, Lauren brought in the surprise, placing it on the floor by the living room fireplace.

"Well, I'll be." A wide grin blossomed on Christopher's face as he came across the room. Looking down at Cavalier, he shook his head. "Well, you old rascal, you."

Cavalier gave the impression of a proud father as he sat beside the box with the four kittens nursing off their mother, who contentedly eyed her family from beneath half-closed eyes.

"He made her acquaintance in an alley, I suppose, brought her home, and well . . . I don't need to tell you the rest, do I?"

Christopher stooped down for a closer look at the cat family. Cavalier slinked forward, rubbing against Christopher's ankles. "So? Have you made an honest woman out of her, you old tom?"

"Cavy's displayed only the noblest of intentions," Lauren defended. "He's been commendably unselfish, putting off the actual ceremony until your return. We thought a double wedding would be more meaningful."

Christopher turned his head, looking up at her with amused wariness. "Did I hear right?"

"Did you hear a kind of proposal?"

"I took it as one."

"Then you took it right," she said softly, suddenly shy.

Christopher rose, and they came together. She threw her arms about his neck, half-laughing, half-crying from the joy of having at last made the commitment. "I love you so damn much, Christopher Reynolds. What difference does it make . . . us being an ocean away? An ocean's nothing, nothing—compared to what we've got going. I belong to you, regardless of the distance. I'm yours totally, man," she declared seriously, looking up into his black, shining eyes. "Everything's going to work out. Somehow," she breathed defiantly and was silenced by his mouth crushing down upon hers.

During the empty weeks that she had lain awake without him beside her in bed, she had harbored any sane woman's suspicions that the attractive, virile man she loved might find physical solace in the arms of another female. But all fears dissolved as he lifted her into his arms and carried her the full way up the stairs to the bedroom.

It was with tender satisfaction that she clearly read the markings of his sexual abstinence. His eagerness to possess her was barely restrained.

He was lean and hard and totally male. He was also curiously gentle and sensitive. *A woman could never hope for a more perfect lover,* Lauren thought as he slowly undressed her.

He had the same instinctive understanding of a woman's needs as he had of the technique of art. The same way that he brought variations of color to his canvases, he brought forth shadings of desire in her.

He dropped her blouse from her shoulders, letting it fall to the floor. His breathing quickened. His eyes grew even darker, glazed as they were with desire for her. She watched him, delighting in his response. He kissed her deeply, and she parted her lips, exploring his mouth as their need for each other grew.

She arched into his hardness as he traced a finger down her back. Instinctively, he undulated against her. "Oh, my beautiful Lauren . . ." he said, almost as a low, painful moan. "If you only knew . . . I've wanted you . . . wanted you."

She leaned back, looking into his half-closed eyes, knowing that it was taking every bit of self-control he had not to throw her onto the bed and take her for the pure satisfaction of his animal lust. "If you only knew how much I wanted you to want me," she said in return, with both humor and truthfulness.

"Like this?" he said softly and cupped a breast in his palm, tracing his finger lightly over her nipple so that she closed her eyes, taking a sharp breath.

"Yes. Like that."

"And," he said softly, lowering his mouth to take her nipple, "like this?"

"Oh yes . . . like that, yes . . ."

There was more, so much more that she wanted from him, and he satisfied every fantasy she had imagined during her months without him.

Some of the agonizing thrills he drove her to experience had nothing to do with poetry. They were feelings primal and urgent, spreading heat through her loins until her body ruled her mind. The sight of him, the feel of his male strength, caused her to experience an aggressive lust she had never known before.

And Christopher was not shocked by her brazen demands, but encouraged her to take him, to use his body to satiate her desires.

They moved together on the bed in a sensual, natural abandon. He explored the curve of her buttocks, caressing the roundness of her belly, then fleetingly, tantalizingly, bringing sure fingers hard against her until she cried out for him to be with her completely.

But he would not.

Instead, he was relentless, continuing with a new kind of sweet torture. His breath on her body was hot, his hands controlled and expert, his tongue a demon flicking over her skin and making her throb from wanting him. He brought her higher and higher and higher, each time stopping just as the ball of molten fire in the pit of her stomach began to pulse and expand. She would gasp, shudder from the delicious sensations kept always on the brink and then when she was quiet, he would start again.

Gently, he brought her from the bed to stand before him. She closed her eyes to the pleasure as he moved from her mouth to suckle her breasts, sliding luxuriously to her stomach and lower. He explored, he probed. She felt his hot breath becoming quicker against her, his tongue driving and more insistent. And all the while she knew that it was not just animal lust they were experiencing, but love, profound, giving, sharing.

Almost in a frenzy, she ran her hands through his hair and was dimly aware that he was calling her name, telling her he loved her. Then saying, "It's all right. Feel good," he urged her, "feel good for me."

He pressed deeper and harder against and into her, and she was helpless. She felt the walls of her resistance falling, tumbling, and she cried his name out as she was racked with indescribable spasms of glorious release. Waves of rolling, shooting pleasure cascaded through her like sparks against a midnight sky. "Christopher . . . Chris . . ." she cried in short gasps.

She held herself rigid, letting the beautiful agony subside. When the beating of her heart had quieted, a flood of tears rushed to her eyes. They were tears of joy, tears of need, of gratefulness, of wonder and worship for this man whom she loved, who was pressing his face against her belly, as fulfilled in her pleasure as he would be in his own satisfaction.

Loving him, she brought him up, and they kissed. He tasted the tears off her cheeks and drank them from her lips.

Her bare breasts brushed against the light fur of his chest, and she felt him tremble.

"God . . . oh . . . damn . . ." He groaned as she encircled him with her fingers. "You little witch." Then he laughed and lifted her off the floor. He held her up for the briefest of moments, looking into her eyes as if to drink of her beauty.

"I'm going to ravish you, you know—totally," he said, his eyes never leaving her face as he carried her to the bed.

"Am I supposed to complain?" She snuggled into his chest.

"No, cooperate."

She lay on the bed, and he covered her with his body, hot and hard, totally masculine. Shivering, he called out her name in a delirium of passion and need. In response she found herself whispering words of love and giving voice to shameless desires her lips had never uttered in daylight, had never spoken before. . . .

Waves of pent-up male desire rippled through his hard, muscular frame and, at last, he cried out sharply, shuddered violently. She followed him, arching into his heat, feeling their bodies melding into a single explosion of bliss.

Just as the passion had been violent and consuming, the aftermath of their love was sweet. She nestled into the crook of his arm. Her leg was bent, resting upon his stomach, and he cupped a breast in one hand.

"It will always be like this," she murmured. "Every day. Every night. For our whole lives."

He said nothing in response.

She peered up at him, thinking he had dropped off to sleep. But he had not. He was looking up at the ceiling.

"Why don't you say anything?" she asked, suddenly afraid.

"Sorry," he said. "I thought that maybe this was all a dream." He closed his eyes, and she could not tell what he had meant.

Chapter 15

THE OCCASION OF WILM'S EXHIBITION EXCEEDED THE
most elaborate of Lauren's professional fantasies.

To reward herself for triumphing over insurmount-
able odds, she purchased a dress from the designer's
section of Neiman-Marcus's Beverly Hills store. It
was composed of cascading glass beads the color of
pure cerulean, which enhanced her eyes, and reflected
a haze of blue highlights off her midnight-hued hair.

As she moved through the gallery of awed guests,
the dress undulated suggestively, the thousands of
hand-sewn beads moving in counterpoint to the easy
sway of her slim hips.

Several of the art critics were to report in their
reviews that it was hard to determine just who the real
star was that evening of the Wilm exhibition. Surely
the immediate financial focus was upon Wilm's lithos,
with the full run purchased in its entirety before the
evening was half over.

Yet the atmosphere was charged with another type
of excitement. It contained the energy of opening
night at a New York theater, when a new performer
who is destined to make history stands before the

footlights. It contained the anticipatory hush of a crowd of thousands poised as they watched the dark horse hurtle past the favorites to finish first in the derby. It was a feeling of being a part of social history.

Eyes turned and followed Christopher Reynolds moving past in his black tuxedo. He moved with a fluid grace, a magnificent panther in its prime, commanding his territory with assurance. His smile broke easy as people jockeyed to make his acquaintance. The word had spread: Reynolds was hot. He would be Blue Chip. Before long, he would rival even the remote and older Wilm in art circles. Best of all, Christopher Reynolds was young and handsome and still accessible. Everyone there that night wanted a piece of him while he was still within reach. And that night, many people reached . . .

But it was also Lauren's night. She had earned the full respect of the art establishment. She was a winner. People there that night were people who liked winners. There was an old superstition among them that success rubbed off. She had Wilm and she, apparently, had Reynolds. Who would she have next? And would they be in on it? There were many courteous exchanges that night, both financial and social, all of them in Lauren's favor.

She was in the midst of delivering a monologue on Wilm's technique as being distinct from that of Picasso's to a rapt and unctuously polite group of patrons, when Christopher appeared at her side.

Making hasty apologies to Lauren's audience, he swept her away, leading her by the elbow into her office. He closed the door, then made certain it was locked. The seriousness of his expression was chilling. "Christopher . . . tell me. What is it?"

He approached her slowly, the message in his eyes inscrutable. "This," he said, pulling her to him, "and this," kissing the hollow of her collarbone.

She could feel his hand stealthily bunching up the heavy material of her skirt, then through her stockings, the warmth of his fingers against her thigh. She giggled. "Christopher, you're insatiable."

"Yes," he murmured and rubbed himself insinuatingly against her as if to prove it. "It's true, I am."

"That's . . . uh . . . okay." She sighed, suddenly finding the situation less amusing and increasingly compelling. "I think that maybe I am, too."

"That's wonderful." He was nuzzling her earlobe.

She heard the soft whir of her zipper being lowered down her back. With his help, the material slid from her shoulders. She stepped out of her gown. "This is utterly wicked," she said happily, glancing at the locked door to make certain no one would know just how wicked.

"It's shameful," Christopher said, leering suggestively, and with a flourish, undid his pants, throwing them recklessly over his shoulder.

"I'm so, so glad." She held out her arms to him. And while Wilm's lithos made history in the outer gallery, they made love on the sofa in her office.

After her tryst with Christopher, Lauren composed herself and returned to the salon. Shortly thereafter, she lost track of him as they were commandeered by divergent groups of admirers.

The gallery's floor space had become uncomfortably crowded during the evening. Generally at such functions, she would overinvite, and there would be enough last-minute cancellations from the guest list to allow for plenty of extra breathing space.

But tonight's event seemed to have registered as command-performance time. Everyone had shown.

She was delighted when she saw Christopher pressing his way toward her through the milling bodies. As before, he approached with a grim expression.

"There's someone who wants to speak with you in your office," he said, edging her away from two clients.

"Christopher—not again. I'm about to make a sale."

"Now," he insisted.

"I just told you, I'm about to—"

"Lauren," he said, and without so much as an apology to her guests, ushered her aside, "this can't wait."

Nigel Croup was standing with his back to the wall, nervously fidgeting with his formal black bow tie when Lauren found him in her office.

Christopher closed the door. "Tell her," he ordered Nigel.

"Yes, well . . ." Nigel looked from Lauren to Christopher and back again, then prefaced his information with a labored sigh. "I was at the McIntyre affair. A free feed and all, although quite frankly, the stuffed grape leaves were a bit too ethnic for my taste." He stopped short from making further social commentary, obviously menaced by Christopher's glare. "Yes, well, as I was saying, I stayed for the first hour of the auction, mainly to see the Vermeer go. But I did want to be here, where, of course, the real action was."

"That's all right, Nigel," Lauren interjected, feeling Christopher's tension and afraid that if Nigel didn't get on with his story it might be forced out of him. "Just tell me the important part. And," she said, eyeing Christopher, "I trust there is an important part?"

"Right. Yes. Anyway, as I was leaving, the senator was in the outside hall. He was having a beastly row with his father. Of course, it would have been rude to loiter, and besides, I don't think I could have managed it without being seen, but I literally inched my way out. And I heard the most surprising thing. The senator said, quite loudly, for he was in rather a tizzy, that in one week Lauren Taylor would be out of business. For good. He emphasized that—the for good part. It was quite chilling to hear, I'll tell you."

"Thanks," Lauren said. "Thanks. But don't worry. The senator is full of threats. Didn't you know? Wind is a politician's stock in trade." She was rattling. She was worried. Riff wouldn't have said that to Clarence unless he had something to back it up with. But she couldn't imagine what. It was that that bothered her, the fact that she couldn't imagine what he was up to this time.

Christopher had a full week in town before he was to return to Italy. Part of that week was spent in meetings with a concern from London. They were on a search for an artist to execute a triptych for a major new cultural center. It was not only the artist's work they were interested in, but also in his projected future, hoping that in due time the name selected would reflect well upon their institution. Of almost equal importance, they felt, was the artist's emotional stability. It would not do to have someone who might go over the deep end halfway through the work.

The remainder of Christopher's time was spent, Lauren felt, in harassing her.

Two days before the gallery was to offer Wilm's work to the public, Holly Adler had called in her regrets that she would be unable to attend. "Filming," she explained. She would be in contact, she promised Lauren, and wished her well with the exhibit. The only other discussion they had was to reiterate the financial arrangements. Lauren was to forward the money due Wilm immediately, via express mail.

On the day after the exhibit, Lauren attempted to phone Holly at her Berlin hotel.

"Miss Adler has checked out. Over a week ago," the desk clerk added in German-accented English when Lauren pressed him for a date.

Holly called only a few hours later. She sounded elated, having already read a review of the exhibit. "They've all been sold. Fantastic." She immediately asked about the money.

"The check's made out already. I'm sending it out tomorrow."

"Super," Holly said, then offhandedly added, "By the way, the money must be forwarded to a different address." She gave Lauren a post office box. "I've checked out of the hotel—only yesterday," she added. "We finally finished filming . . . at the eleventh hour, or I would have come to the opening. I'm kind of in transit, so the box number is best."

Holly had spoken so rapidly that it took Lauren a moment to realize that she had lied. In spite of all of Christopher's unsubstantiated forebodings about Holly Adler, this was the first time Lauren had actually felt uneasy about her.

"What's wrong?" Christopher asked as she sat pensively staring into her coffee later that night.

"Nothing." But it was a weak nothing, and she squirmed beneath his glance.

"Tell me." He took the cup from her hands and held them in his. "What are future husbands good for, anyway?"

She kissed him then, which was far easier than admitting that he might be right about Holly, after all.

"There's a problem. Holly Adler isn't being upfront with me. It isn't a big thing, of course. I mean, all it was was a small white lie—"

"What lie?" Christopher asked sharply.

"Her address. She's changed her mailing address to a box number, and she's lied about when she checked out of the hotel. She could have any number of reasons, of course, for not wanting me to know when she'd left. And yet . . ."

Christopher rose from the sofa, planting his legs squarely before her, looking every inch the male authoritarian figure to Lauren, who instinctively recoiled from the impression of his dominance. "And yet," Christopher took up, "you refuse to believe me that that girl is going to—"

"Going to what?" Lauren also stood, meeting what she took as his challenge of her judgment. "What could she possibly do now, Chris? The lithos were delivered to me—as promised. And they were all marvelous. The exhibit's over. I've got my money. So what could she possibly do at this stage in the game?"

"Something . . ." The word trailed off, but it still carried Christopher's conviction. Thoughtfully, he walked to look out beyond the glass wall. People across the water had decorated their houses with Christmas lights. They shone merrily against the water.

All that gaiety seemed incongruous, otherworldly to Lauren, as she contemplated the collapse of her own shaky universe. "Something . . . something," Lauren repeated. "There's nothing she can do."

"Did you send the money to her yet?"

"No. I've got the check ready and in the envelope. I was going to put it in the mail tomorrow morning."

"Then don't," Christopher said, turning to her, his expression distant as he worked out something in his mind.

"I can't go against my word," Lauren objected. "That was our agreement."

"Tough," he said. "From what I've heard, Holly Adler's broken her share of agreements with plenty of other people."

"But I'm not one of those people. Holly's been upfront with me all the way in this. Corny as it may sound, I've got this hang-up that when I give my word, that's it. So far, my philosophy has held me in good stead. In fact, I like to think that integrity's had a bit to do with bringing me this far."

Christopher left the window and came to her. "This time your moral code may be your undoing, Lauren. Why can't you understand that being flexible is sometimes as valid a standard as being righteous?"

He sounded frustrated and angry. He also sounded sensible.

She arrived at the gallery earlier than usual the next morning. The envelope addressed to Holly Adler was where she had left it on her desk. Its presence challenged her as if it were a living entity.

But for the time being, she could avoid the show-down between right versus reasonable. The Wilm exhibit had generated a deluge of calls and letters, all of which were screaming to be answered immediately.

The morning had drawn to an end when Christopher appeared.

He leaned in the doorway of her office, his jacket slung over his shoulder, his stance sexy and as natural to him as breathing and making love.

"You are going to be the wife of a famous artist," he said soberly.

"You got it? The London deal?" She was up and rushing to him before he could confirm what was certainly the fact.

He held her, lifting her into the air, kissing her and talking all at the same time. "I return to Italy to finish my project there, and then I go to London. They're even providing me with a flat—a smart flat—as it was put to me."

"Oh, Christopher, that's fabulous. Do you have any idea of what this is going to mean?"

"I do," he said. "It means that you and I are going to get married before Christmas. I was thinking that we'd leave this afternoon for Vegas, but unfortunately, I've got to go over to their attorney's office and sign some preliminary papers, just so they know they've got me and I've got them. I get a bundle upfront, incidentally. Enough to keep my lady in style."

He was speaking so quickly and dishing out so much information that Lauren could barely keep up with him. He looked absolutely radiant. With each new success, he seemed to become taller, more handsome, more in command of himself, and now, as it seemed, in command of her.

"We'll fly to Las Vegas tomorrow afternoon. By tomorrow night, you'll be Mrs. Christopher Reynolds. For ever and ever," he said and kissed her so deeply, so fervently that it brought tears to her eyes.

"All right," she said. "Agreed."

"Jesus." Christopher threw back his head. "I can't believe it. I mean, right up to now, I half expected you to back down."

"No way," Lauren said. "I want champagne and flowers and music and deep, intense looks while we say our 'I do's,' and I want a speech at the end that is filled with romantic mush."

"And I would like to tear off every piece of clothing you're wearing. I would like to run my hot hands all over your beautiful body. I would like to lay you down on that sofa and make such love to you—" He broke off. "But, alas, we famous artists must be off and running. You know how it is." He kissed her quickly and backed out, his black eyes insinuating, making love to her as his body would have liked to.

Yes, she thought, as she walked back to her desk, *I know how it is. It's bloody wonderful being successful.*

She smiled, thinking of the English expression, thinking of Christopher's opportunity in London, thinking most of all of how much she loved him. She loved both of them being famous and fortunate and together. *Life was very good, after all.*

Across from her on the desk, the envelope addressed to Holly Adler seemed to pulse with white life. She closed her eyes, knowing that the time had come to deal with the problem.

Tomorrow night she would be Mrs. Christopher Reynolds. She wanted that; oh yes, she wanted to belong to him. But she did not want to lose Lauren Taylor. She could not lose her identity and have their marriage work. It had been her vision that they would both come into the marriage as one hundred percent whole beings, successful, independent. She firmly believed that this was the only way to make their union work; to make any union last.

She did not believe in the old—and to her—hackneyed fifty-fifty split, where each partner was to fulfill the lack in the other. It sounded terrific, but it didn't work. No, each person had to be complete in and of himself, autonomous. Otherwise, each would be desperate to gather from the other what he, himself, did not possess; and at the same time each would need to cling to that part of himself already owned.

She remembered back to the day when she had met Christopher. He had been the starving artist then, and she had been the fairy godmother. The balance of power was weighted in her direction. Oh, she had been so strong, so decisive, so very independent and sure of herself. She could make miracles happen for him. But since that time, a lot had transpired to undermine that self-confidence. Now Christopher could make his own miracles.

So, she rationalized, eyeing the envelope on the corner of the desk warily, it was important to her and to Christopher as well that the parity be maintained.

She reached across her desk and, curling her fingers around the envelope, stood. Holly Adler would have her money.

Chapter 16

WITHIN THE HOUR, LAUREN HAD SAFELY DEPOSITED THE Adler check in the mail. It would be flown to West Germany by an express service. By tomorrow, Holly would have her money, she would have her sense of integrity and the entire matter would be closed for good.

She felt so marvelous that she even took time out to have a lunch with a friend at Scandia. When she returned to the gallery, she was still under the happy influence of the restaurant's most expensive Brut. She was about to enter when Maxwell Kain—appearing as if from nowhere—lunged at her. The portfolio case he was carrying clattered to the sidewalk, and he stepped on top of it in his haste to latch on to the sleeve of her jacket.

"Maxwell . . . what . . . ?" Her first thought was that he was ill, that he was undergoing some debilitating physical attack.

"I'm going to see you in prison," he hissed.

Lauren tried to pull herself free of his grasp. "Maxwell, let go of me. Are you crazy?" The critic's eyes were diamond-hard, pinpricks of hatred.

"You were never anything but a fly-by-night scam artist." He released the words in jerky, venomous bursts. "You have made a laughingstock of me!" he now screamed. A group of passing pedestrians slowed to stare.

"Maxwell," Lauren said, genuinely afraid of him by this time, wondering if he had not, in fact, flipped out, "why don't we go into my office and discuss privately whatever it is that's bothering you?"

"No," he said, "I want everyone to know about you. Everyone." He shouted this out, turning to the people who stopped to witness the sidewalk drama unfolding.

This gave her the opportunity to break away, and she escaped into the gallery. When she was only a few feet into the room, Kain's voice pealed after her.

"Look! See here?" he yelped. "Look . . . Miss Taylor . . . look and see what I'm going to do!"

Jacqueline and two others of Lauren's staff had been engaged in quiet talks with clients. All conversation stopped and, like Lauren, who turned slowly around, everyone watched as Maxwell Kain opened his portfolio case and removed the Wilm litho he had purchased for himself as an investment.

"This," Kain said, holding up the unframed print, "is the true value of the Wilm lithos purchased by all those other fine fools who trusted this cheat, this fraud."

Lauren had grown sick to her stomach. With his eyes on her, Kain began to slowly tear the top of the litho, ripping it down its center until it was in two pieces.

"Maxwell . . . you are mad," Lauren whispered, not able to find her voice. "You have just destroyed a fortune in art."

"I have destroyed nothing. Nothing yet, that is. But

I will," he said. "I will certainly destroy you." He turned, leaving a mute audience behind to stare at the two pieces of the Wilm print on the floor.

Within the next half hour, the calls began.

Lauren took the first four—one from Brazil, another from Hong Kong, a furious one from Australia and the last one from someone whose anger had rendered him unintelligble in English and who lapsed into rapid and heated Spanish before Lauren dropped the phone into its cradle.

She put her head down on the desk, hiding her face in her arms. She could not cry. But the wail circled mute within. It spiraled crazily. It knotted itself. It flung itself like a ribbon with razor edges, slicing her soul to shreds. Still, she was locked in a paralyzed silence.

The telephone started up again and was ringing off its hook when Jacqueline rushed into her office.

"Mon Dieu," she groaned, seeing Lauren's face as Lauren raised herself and reached to answer the ringing phone. *"Non,* I will take care of this."

Jacqueline's face went white as she listened. At last, she put down the phone. It began its piercing electronic assault almost at once. With quick fingers, Jacqueline disconnected the phone at its module plug.

"What am I going to do?" Lauren's eyes were as blank as her voice.

And for once, Jacqueline, who claimed to have an answer to everything, had to admit, "I don't know."

She was alone in the darkened living room when Christopher came home that night. The door closed behind him with a loud crack. The lights went on behind her. "Lauren?" She remembered she had left her car in the drive.

"Lauren!" He was at the other side of the room. His voice was dim in the empty channels of her mind.

She remained as she was, staring out beyond the wall of glass, seeing nothing, feeling nothing. There was, after all, nothing left.

"Nothing . . . nothing . . ." she whispered the word to herself.

"Hey!" It was Christopher again, his voice bright, upbeat. "What's going on?"

She heard him coming across the carpet, moving toward what was left of her. His hands were on her shoulders. He was turning her to him.

"Lauren? What the hell . . . ?"

He was looking for answers in her expression. But she knew there was none. She could see that to him, her vacant stare must have been more horrible than if she had formed a snarl or appeared before him with a red, swollen face. A face devoid of expression represented a person without hope. *What*, she wondered in her empty way, *could be more terrible than a person without any hope?*

Christopher was shaking her. "Lauren . . . Lauren . . . what's happened?" He brought her to him, holding her against his chest. "Tell me, baby?" He was being so gentle. *Baby*. It was all right, he was saying to her. But he didn't know.

And then she was crying. At first the tears were gentle, coming softly like a purr as she clung to the last vestiges of her dignity. But the tight ball of pain that had been trapped inside her began to unravel.

"I've lost everything," she choked, forcing the words from the well of inner misery.

It was all she said, and it was enough. Christopher held her, riding with her torment, encouraging her to let out her anguish. When the great, racking sobs subsided, she was ready to talk.

She took the glass Christopher gave her. "I don't like Scotch," she said, wrinkling her nose in distaste.

"Drink it anyway. For me."

She did and was glad. It made things not quite so desperate as she recounted the afternoon's events.

"I don't know how, but I know what," Lauren began. She stared dreamily into the distance. "All over the world, the same exclusive prints that I sold my clients were dumped on the public."

"Holly." Christopher smashed his fist on the coffee table. Rising, he poured himself another drink and returned to Lauren. "It could be worse," he said thoughtfully. "You could have sent her the check. Then you'd really be up the creek. But this way, at least you can pay everyone back."

Lauren smiled. She did not think that she was capable of a smile and she certainly didn't feel like smiling, but that's exactly what she was doing. And then the smile turned into a laugh. And the laughter rocked her shoulders, and she clutched her sides, and finally all the laughter stopped. Just the way her life seemed to have come to a stop.

Christopher was staring down at her.

She felt small and weak, and at that moment she hated him, detested him, for appearing large and strong. *And right.*

"You bastard," she said under her breath. "You smart bastard. Didn't you tell me? You told me, you told me."

"Oh . . . no."

She got up and left the room.

It took half a day before the details of Holly Adler's remarkable crime were entirely understood by Lauren.

Holly had been filming a movie; that much was the truth—but little else was.

Holly, as Lauren discovered, had only just begun her shooting schedule when another opportunity presented itself to her. This was Lauren's proposal, and it was something far more lucrative than the grueling, boring work of standing before a camera all day and being barked at by a cranky German director.

Holly had had enough of cranky German men. Sensing that Wilm's enchantment with her had begun to wane, Holly, who was corrupt—but not stupid, decided to make other accommodations for herself. In the event that she would follow the fate of Wilm's previous girl friends, she decided she would not be cast out without a deutsche mark to her name.

Lauren made her pitch. Holly returned to Wilm, managed somehow to reinstate herself into his affections long enough and sufficiently enough to obtain his agreement on the litho project.

Jacqueline listened, sitting crumpled in the corner of Lauren's office sofa. Her sad hazel eyes moved like pendulums back and forth as she watched Lauren pace.

"I do believe, at this point, that Holly would have performed her part of the bargain. Oh, undoubtedly, she would have skimmed a portion for herself off the top. But she never would have had the resources to pull off the whole scheme if it weren't for her coconspirator. That's obvious." Lauren paused, shaking her head.

"Well, to a poor French girl, it is not obvious," Jacqueline interjected. "Please explain."

"Riff," Lauren said. "It had to be Riff. He must have caught those same gossip columns showing Christopher with Holly. It would have been to his benefit to see those two together, which would leave me free and on the rebound, available to fall into his waiting arms and political bed. So, somehow he must have gotten together with the girl. She told him what was what, and Riff conceived of a backup plan to ruin me. When I didn't come around the way he wanted, he decided to implement it."

"He gave Holly the money to pay off the ateliers."

"He would have had to. She couldn't have afforded to pull everything off without a lot of bribery. After quitting her job, Holly contacted selected salons and printers throughout the world. She offered them cash to keep their mouths shut about the Wilm lithos, telling them that she would be bringing them other artists of Wilm's caliber in the future—but only if they could keep it a secret until the day they were to be offered to the public. Then, at precisely the time that I was having my legitimate opening, the doors of these selected galleries were thrown open to the public. She had pledged each owner to secrecy, and each believed that his was the exclusive run. She was brilliant, really. You've got to give the girl credit for expert administration. She accomplished a marketing blitzkreig to rival any I've seen on Madison Avenue."

"But how could she pass off the lithos as being authentic?"

"They were authentic. She took each plate before it had been canceled by Wilm. I don't know what she told him—maybe that I wanted them. Who knows? I'm sure it was convincing, or perhaps he is just so deranged he doesn't care about those kinds of details. Holly struck a deal with a printer, they ran off a slew of them and the rest, as they say, is history."

In essence, what Holly Adler had done was the equivalent of printing paper money without gold to back it. Every print Lauren had sold to her clients, who expected the rarity of the prints to drive the investment prices up, was now worthless. They owned nothing more than paper. She recalled Riff's words to her.

"Holly Adler is very rich now," Jacqueline mused.

"Yes," Lauren said and nodded, "and Lauren Taylor is ruined."

* * *

"No," Lauren said. "No."

"There's no reason why we can't be married. We have nothing to do with what's happened with your gallery."

"We have everything to do with what's happened with my gallery," Lauren said. She was being shrewish, unreasonable, and even she couldn't stand herself. And yet, it made no difference. She felt as if every fiber of her body was electrified, that she was sizzling and crackling and that if she weren't careful she would short-circuit herself out of commission entirely if she didn't get some relief from the pressure. And here he was, aggravating the situation by pounding at her to marry him.

"I only want to love you," he said tiredly.

He had packed both their suitcases before she had returned home from the gallery. The airline tickets for Las Vegas were on the bed along with their coats. She knew he would have a ring on him.

"How can you possibly love me?" she muttered.

"How can you possibly ask that of me?" he returned. "This isn't some sort of game with me. I'm not a barometer, changing with the weather. I'm not the Dow Jones averages, my feelings rising and falling like the stock market. I love you!" This last part was shouted. The raised voice unleashed the fight in her, gave her an opportunity to unload her inturned misery on someone else.

"You are so confoundedly good and right. You haven't even thrown my stupidity in my face. As—I may as well mention—you have every right to do." Her voice leveled. "I have no respect for myself."

"I'd like to be able to say then that's your problem. But I can't, can I? Because it affects me, too."

"I'm sorry, Christopher." *She was sorry.* But she couldn't change her other feelings. She was trapped in a box of her own design. It seemed there was no way out.

"How much money do you owe?" he asked, abruptly changing the subject.

"More than I have."

"What are you going to do?"

"Before or after I'm lynched?" she said bitterly. She continued with a labored sigh. "I'm going to pay back the people who purchased the lithos. I'm going to sell everything I have to do it."

"You won't fight back?"

"With what, Christopher?"

He offered to help her. He said he would beg and borrow in advance on his commissions. She only laughed. Whatever he could give her would be insignificant in light of her monumental debt.

It was that moment, when she turned down his offer for help, that she later felt was the turning point in their relationship.

The first of a series of scathing articles aimed at destroying her appeared in the *Los Angeles Times* the next morning. Kain had never been more brilliantly acerbic.

The gallery was like a tomb. It was as if a sign marked "Plague" had been tacked over her door. No one entered all morning. By noon, Lauren gave her speech to the staff. They were dismissed with apologies. Jacqueline paid them for two weeks.

Lauren locked the door herself. She closed the drapes, and then sequestered herself in her office for the rest of the day going through her accounts. Jacqueline manned the telephone calls, which still came in, even more hate-filled than those on the first day. Kain's insinuations of criminal intent on her part had inflamed the public's ire.

The only person she saw was Phillip Whelen Lloyd. He still believed in her. She declined all favors from him, which included the services of his legal staff to defend herself, funding to continue her enterprise and finally the position of acquisition director for his new museum. It was not just that she was being stubborn and foolishly prideful. She was being realistic. Her professional reputation had taken a beating from which it would not be possible to recover. At least, not for a long, long time. If ever.

Kain had been right; she was destroyed.

Riff had been right; he had been able to beat her.

Christopher had been right; she should have listened to him.

Christopher asked her one more time. "I don't care about your success or your failure. I care about you. Finish things up here, then come to Italy with me. I'll be through with my work in another couple of months. Then we'll move on to London. We don't even have to get married, if that step seems too drastic and confining for you at the moment. Just be with me, Lauren. I need you. I love you."

She was looking at him, but not seeing him. Her mind was playing out visions of the future—Christopher taking awards, Christopher being feted by the art community, Christopher being interviewed by the media, Christopher wealthy. And there, back in the shadows, she saw herself . . . trailing here, trailing there, a nonentity. Finally, in the last frame, she was invisible.

"I can't, Chris . . . I can't go with you," she said.

And that was the last time he asked.

Although they slept in the same bed, they didn't make love that night. She lay awake in the darkness, thinking that she had never been so cold in her life. The next morning she left, as usual, for the gallery.

That evening, she returned home, and everything was the same, as usual, except for one thing: Christopher was gone.

The Christmas season was upon Los Angeles. Lights were strung across streets, looping incongruously over palms that substituted for traditional pines. Lauren barely noticed. With Jacqueline, she arranged for the liquidation of her stock. As the money came in, she would issue checks to those clients who had purchased, and been stung, by the Wilm fiasco. She received no invitations for parties, and the few cards she received were from her old school friends whose concerns ran to new television sets and braces for their children's teeth. If they knew of her disgrace, they would not understand it, and if they understood it, they would find it irrelevant. Her mother's voice had taken on a funereal timber much like a dirge whenever they spoke. Her father was supportive, but seemed embarrassed for her. She could not blame anyone for their feelings.

There was no way she could even launch a counterattack in defense of her position. There was no one to attack.

Holly Adler had not been heard from since she had effected the art scam. For all intents and purposes, she had dropped off the face of the earth. As for Wilm, he either didn't know yet or didn't care about his ill-fated litho run. Those suspicions Lauren held about Riff McIntyre's part in her professional collapse could not be proved. Therefore, all the publicity, and all of it negative, was centered around her.

On Christmas morning, Lauren opened her apartment door to a special courier. She signed for the package, closed the door and, holding the small parcel in her hand, considered not opening it. It was wrapped in brown paper, the stamps on it Italian. She hesitated, then tore away the paper.

There was no accompanying note, only a small velvet box. Swallowing hard, she lifted its lid. A simple gold band shone up from its bed of white silk. Tentatively, her fingers moved to the ring, but stopped short of touching it. Instead, after a long pause, she drew her hand away and snapped the lid shut.

The one thing, the only thing, she had left that Christmas morning was her pride.

Somehow she had managed to survive the holidays emotionally intact.

Survival. The word loomed prominently in Lauren's life. It had become her watchword, her beacon in a dark existence.

Her days consisted of working through her financial problems. Her nights were spent alone. Sometimes she would return to her apartment and, not bothering with dinner, would fall, instead, into bed. Cavalier would drop in beside her, curling into a companionable ball of orange fluff. He, too, had lost his family, the kittens being claimed by neighborhood children, the mother cat wandering off one day to other loves, other adventures. But rather than finding comfort in his soft, mechanical purr, Lauren would be tormented. Her world was cold and bleak. She did not want to be reminded that options like warmth and closeness existed. They were for other people, not her.

Once, at the end of January, when the Los Angeles skies had been haunted with gray for days, she returned home to find that Cavalier had been run over by a passing vehicle. She broke down that night. The next morning, she did not—could not—go to work.

The telephone rang again and again and, knowing it would be Jacqueline, she finally answered. "I have the flu," she said and quickly hung up.

She thought long and hard that day.

At five o'clock, she left her apartment and drove her yellow Porsche to Venice. She walked along the canal. For a long time, she stood on the bridge, staring at the house she and Christopher had shared, had laughed in and made love in and, at last, had parted in.

The rain broke. It came down in cleansing buckets, mixing with her tears as she stood on the bridge.

When she went home, she placed her call to Italy.

She waited, listening to the whir of the phone company's equipment, miraculously transporting her call across vast land masses and bodies of water that had taken years for people to cross not so long ago. In fifteen seconds, she would hear Christopher's voice. She would tell him that it was all right. She would tell him that she would come to him, for she needed him, she loved him. God, yes, she loved him.

The telephone was answered by an Italian man who spoke fractured English, but was able to make himself understood. Christopher was no longer there. He had left over a week ago. He was in London now. There was no telephone number. No, he did not leave a forwarding address.

Lauren had reached the point where she was certain that nothing could surprise her, nor could any turn of events reach her emotionally. She was steel now.

During the first week of February, she had stood across the street watching as her name was removed from over her gallery. Maybe, after all of it, that was the worst—that moment.

So now she was genuinely amazed to find herself

responding with rage to what she was reading in the newspaper.

Riff McIntyre was lauding her. He was championing her. His interview fairly glowed with goodwill directed toward resurrecting her reputation.

"Of course," he said in the article, "I was as shocked as anyone else to discover what had happened with the Wilm thing. But I never doubted that Lauren Taylor was innocent of the charges of fraud levied against her. She's a marvelous human being, a super businesswoman, and I'd stake my entire political career on her innocence.

Lauren hurled the newspaper across her kitchen. "You phony! You yellow-bellied . . . you . . . lying cheat!" she raged. For whatever good it did.

The flowers arrived at four o'clock. Her heart almost stopped as she opened the door to see the delivery boy there. *Christopher had sent them.*

She closed the door, rushed with the box to the kitchen, tore off the top of the box. Red roses. He had sent her a dozen the first time. There were two dozen here. Fingers trembling, she pulled out the white card.

"You bastard!" she screamed. "Lousy bastard . . ."

She dumped the roses Riff McIntyre had sent her into the trash.

Chapter 17

IT WAS PAINFUL BUT NECESSARY THAT SHE TAKE STOCK OF her situation and, most urgently, her financial status. She discovered that she had barely enough money to survive another three months. Of course she would have to do something. But what?

And then there was Riff.

Riff was coming on strong as the white knight. She all but expected him to throw down a gauntlet in defense of her honor. Although they had not seen each other, his interviews gave the appearance that they were heavily involved and that she was dependent on him, poor broken bird that she was.

She would have given her own interview to the press except that whatever she would say would be misconstrued, distorted. In the end she decided it was better to remain the broken bird, rather than becoming a laughingstock.

Lauren recalled the first time she had gone to Phillip Whelen Lloyd's offices in Century City. The elevator she rode then was the same soundless jet. The doors parted, and there she saw the same paintings on the walls. And now she was being led by the same smiling women to Lloyd's office.

But when the double doors parted, she knew that she was not the same person she had been when Lloyd rose from behind his desk to greet her that first time.

"I'm glad you came, Lauren." He held her hand in his. There was friendship and concern in the clasp. She tried not to cry. The one thing she could not face was kindness in large doses. She did not want to feel again. She just wanted to survive.

"You won't have any trouble," Lloyd said. And then, "I'll admit your sterling reputation has become tarnished."

"Tarnished?" Lauren shot him an ironic glance.

"Obliterated," he said. "Nevertheless, I'm fairly certain my name, coupled with my money, will counteract the unpleasantness of dealing with some of your peers."

Lloyd was not boasting. He was a realistic man. Everyone wanted to make a buck. She was buying. It would not do to offend her overtly.

"Nevertheless," he went on, "you're bound to run into a few emotional squalls. Can you handle them?"

"'Can I afford not to?' is the better question."

"I still admire you, you know."

"Then you are a minority of one."

"Incidentally," Lloyd said as he walked her to the door, "I've been keeping tabs on the European front."

She tensed, expecting him to comment on Christopher. But he didn't.

"Wilm's apparently found out about his lithos. He's left his castle. From what I understand, he's gone on quite a rampage. It seems that he's hell-bent on finding his ex-mistress."

"Never," Lauren said. "Holly is fast and smart."

"Don't underestimate a worthy opponent. Wilm is crazy and angry."

"What do you think he'll do if he catches up with her?" Lauren mused aloud, having stored up a few good ideas of her own for exacting personal retribution.

"For starters? Oh, I think he might kill her."

Lauren didn't laugh. It wasn't meant as a joke.

Life resumed again for Lauren.

Her reemergence into the art world was taken as cheeky and spunky and tasteless—by some. And yet, she seemed to provide a curious titillation for others who followed her career in the same way the public followed the fates of the characters whose turbulent lives were played out on television's daytime soap operas.

Lloyd was mostly right, however. Armed with his checkbook, Lauren was accorded civility, albeit slightly chilly at times.

He rang her early one morning. Still dripping from her shower, she blotted herself dry with a towel as they spoke.

"I'd be most grateful if you could check on a splendid acquisition for me," Lloyd said, his excitement evident. "A very nice Utrillo."

"Of course."

"You'll have to travel."

"No problem. Where to?"

"London." Long pause.

"Odd," she said finally. "The Utrillo being in London."

"Yes, isn't it? One never knows where one's next Utrillo may turn up. And we certainly don't want this one to get away."

"The Utrillo."

"Of course." He immediately changed the subject.

*　*　*

There was, as Lloyd had promised, a Utrillo to be had in London.

However, procuring the Utrillo turned out to be a long, drawn-out affair, necessitating countless meetings with the seller. To make her stay more comfortable, Buffy and Phillip Lloyd insisted she leave the Savoy and stay in their fashionable West End townhouse, complete with their staff of servants. It was not difficult for her to accept their hospitality.

London, one of the great cities of the world, seemed suddenly to have shrunk during her stay. The art community was intimate and gossipy, which meant that she heard Christopher's name as often as she heard the local weather report. To make matters worse, he seemed to attract the attention of the press naturally, becoming as publicly visible as Riff, who ironically had to spend hours scheming to get the same coverage. There were pictures of Christopher at various cultural and charity events, even at social sporting functions. Success suited Christopher well; he had never appeared more handsome.

With relief, she made her announcement to Lloyd one afternoon. "I've finished with my work in London. I'm leaving for L.A. the day after tomorrow."

"Wonderful job on the Utrillo, but I was thinking," he said, his voice sounding close, although he was 9,000 miles away, "there's an awful lot of good stuff available over there . . . country estates . . . the nobility suffering lean times."

He insisted she stay. She insisted she return to Los Angeles.

Of course, in the end, Lloyd had his way.

There was nothing she could do to put Christopher out of her mind. His image, the slightest mention of his name, filled her thoughts to the point of obsession.

There was only one way, she decided, to end the fantasies, and that was by meeting reality head on. She had left their relationship undone; now she would settle matters once and for all. The official conclusion of their relationship would be conducted with civility and maturity.

The excuse Lauren had decided upon for dropping in on Christopher was that Lloyd wanted her to see if he might not do something special for his new museum. It sounded plausible to her, but then as desperately confused as she was feeling, anything would have a nice, sensible ring to it. It took her three hours to prepare for her visit. She changed four times. There was image to consider—sexy versus demure, versus efficient, versus just-dropped-by-since-I-was-in-the-neighborhood casual.

But her final choice rested upon the criteria of irony. She had stood before Christopher on that first day they met in Venice so cool, so composed, so fashionable in her St. John knit.

There were rainbows to be realized on that long-ago day. *And in the present, today,* she thought, *there were endings to be had.* So she would pay homage to tradition, celebrate the past in this day's final visit.

She slipped on a soft yellow knit dress. Her hair was full and fluffed, a tumble of luxuriant darkness just above her shoulders, and framing a face that hid from the world another face—one that did not possess the composed, perfect smile that she flashed for the maid's benefit, for the sake of her own bravado, as she left the townhouse.

Christopher's London accommodations were a far cry from his shoddy origins in Venice. It was an impressive brownstone, not as lavish as Phillip's, but one of charm and with a definite air of chic from its few remodeled touches.

She did not think; thinking was too dangerous. She acted, going up the six steps to the stoop, taking hold of the brass fox's head and rapping against the shiny red door. When he did not show immediately, she panicked. Now, plagued by the demons of second thoughts, she turned and started quickly down the stone steps again. She cringed as the door swung open behind her.

His eyes were on her; she knew they were, for she could feel them. Faint, sickened by apprehension, swamped with recriminations for coming, Lauren turned.

His dark eyes melted into her, seeking and destroying every carefully honed artificial resource she commanded within herself. So there she stood, staring up at him, her smile frozen and false, helpless by the honesty of her own heart. It was not possible to end what, seeing his face again, she knew was eternal.

"Chris!" How gay that sounded. "I was hoping you'd be home. Lloyd called me. He wanted me to have a talk with you—about his new museum. We're all so excited about it." The cheerfulness was grating, and he took too long to respond, letting the strident ring of her voice circle in the air between them. Oh, God . . . from that one proud morning in Venice to this shambles of a day in London.

"You're lucky you found me home," he was saying. She was smiling so stiffly that she thought her lips would crack from the effort. "Generally, I've been working at the foundation."

Her hair was blowing across her face, and she brushed it away, holding it back with one hand. A strand had whipped into her eye, and she was tearing. She did not dare to wipe the moisture from her cheek. He would misunderstand. No, Christopher would understand.

"I just took a chance," she said. "I have a few other stops to make."

"Come on in." He was backing into the hallway.

It was not an invitation. It was a suggestion, one that sounded bored and perfunctory. One that made her want to dissolve into the pavement, into the very air. Love. It was so terrible to love.

She went up the steps, following him into the foyer.

"You're sure you can spare the time?" she asked.

"Quite honestly? I can't. But we'll talk while I work."

Déjà vu. She followed him up the stairs just as she had on that first visit to see his work in Venice.

His studio was on the third and top floor. It was a large area, the walls obviously having been destroyed to create one enormous room. The floor was bare of carpeting. Its surface of polished wood was covered in canvas where Chris was painting. There was a large bank of modern windows to one side of the room, another recent renovation to the venerable old building. The view opened on to a back garden. There were trees and green lawn, a proper English garden with beds of carefully tended flowers. No one would realize the scene was taken from the heart of London. One wall of the room was all mirrors. A long tubular wooden bar, positioned at waist level and reinforced intermittently, ran the room's entire length.

"This is really splendid," she commented.

Christopher was at his easel. "A previous tenant was a former ballet star."

He mixed oils. His concentration was directed fully on his work. She might as well not have been there. There were a few canvases, some only half finished, some completed on stands. They were all of superb execution. His style was changing. The man, himself, was changing.

Suddenly, he put down his palette. "Why did you come here, Lauren?"

"Lloyd wanted—"

"No—" His look was cold. "Why did you come here?" he repeated.

"I wanted to see you again." Lauren turned, going toward the bank of glass windows. "We left everything in limbo."

"I didn't think we did. Not after Christmas."

"I'm sorry. I couldn't respond to the ring. There was so much else then, the upheaval in my life—"

"And no answer was answer enough for me, is that it?"

The words ripped through the air.

Behind her, she heard his heels click across the wooden floor, his steps definite, rushed, angry. He was at a small, portable bar helping himself to a drink from a crystal decanter. Her memory flew back to Venice again, seeing the crushed beer cans in the center of his table that first day. There was Cavalier, a hostile fluff of fur, sitting there, king of all the debris surrounding him—Cavalier Cat who had hated her, who had then grown to tolerate her and finally to need her. Perhaps, in the end, he had even developed a cat's brand of affection for her. But Cavalier, like so much else in her life, was now gone.

"Drink?" he offered.

She came back to the present. She nodded. Moving to where he stood, she took the tumbler. Their hands touched. As if stung, she quickly withdrew, concentrating on her cocktail. It went down smoothly, and the liquid instantly warmed her. It coaxed remnants of courage from some cobwebbed corner of her soul. There was a brief flame of hope in the alcohol's glow. She would declare herself. She would tell him she would commit herself.

But even as she formulated the sentences in her mind, he was moving away from her. The flame that had arisen flickered and died.

Christopher had taken his third full glass to the easel with him. He drank as he studied his work. There was no pleasure in his expression.

"Look," she said, "this was very stupid of me coming here." She finished her drink, put it on the bar. "It was stupid and awkward. Misplaced judgment." She shot him a self-deprecating smile, their final link to each other being the unpleasant situation they now found themselves sharing. Starting for the door, she called, "Please . . . keep on with your work—it looks great, incidentally. Great. I can see myself down."

"Lauren," he said sharply. "All this was, was pointless. That's all. Just very sad and pointless."

She glanced his way, expecting to read either bitterness or self-satisfied triumph in his expression. But there was no meanness there. Instead, there was the intelligent sensitivity that he brought to his work, that he had previously brought to their relationship. It was that nobility of spirit that burned into her, crippling her ego, which would have preferred the chance to exchange poisoned barbs of dialogue in parting. Instead, he had made things so very difficult. He had covered her in gentle rejection.

She made it to the bottom landing. Her hand was on the lock, twisting it back when his hand clamped over her wrist.

"Don't," he whispered. "Don't go."

They came together slowly, their eyes equally questioning. His mouth softly brushed her lips, grazed like butterfly wings over her forehead, caressed her earlobes, fell lightly upon her closed lids. The passion rose instinctively, of its own accord. An unmistakable and familiar current passed between them, and word-lessly, she went with him, up the stairs.

His bedroom was on the second floor. It was sparsely furnished with excellent antiques, as if the room was either being added to gradually or was being disassembled piece by piece. A fireplace faced the four-poster bed. On the mantel, a French clock imprisoned in a glass-domed casing ticked loudly, marking their movements as they removed their clothes.

Supine, they touched each other's bare flesh for the first time since Los Angeles. The beginning was tentative, both of them unsure. But the sweetness soon became lost to the urgency of mutual need. His mouth was fire on her breasts, on her stomach, against her thighs. Any threads of self-conscious restraint binding her, he was severing one by one, just as he had always done.

He was above her; she ran her hands along his back, tensing to the feel of his taut muscles, to the firm sweep of his hard buttocks. His skin glistened like silk shot through with light, the sweat of his excite-ment sweet to her senses.

She wanted to tell him how much she loved him still, but fearful that she would be speaking too honestly, too soon, the words remained frozen within her. Instead, she attempted to show him through touch, through response how she felt.

With a fierce hunger, he covered her mouth with his. His tongue moved between her parted lips, his fingers twining desperately through her flowing mass of dark hair spread against the pale pillowcase. His eyes were closed, the features of his handsome face contorted by desire.

Gradually, words of love came from him, gentle and personal. Her name on his lips sounded like music to her ears as his hands slipped over her breasts. He was no longer merely an assured male animal but her Christopher again.

"I've missed you so," she said at last, arching into him as his mouth found her nipple.

When he said nothing in response, she felt a wild desperation well within her. To love him so much, to realize how wrong she had been all along rejecting paradise for the promise of empty wealth and the illusion of fame, seemed horrible beyond imagining.

His face turned, and she caught the look in his eyes. It was sad and dark, and this frightened her even more. Fevered and demanding, his body was clearly desirous of her, but then why would he not want her? She was an available woman, a woman who clearly wanted him.

"What's wrong?" he said suddenly. His voice was so gruff, the question so unexpected that she stiffened. He was looking into her eyes, obviously seeing the turmoil of her mind.

"Nothing . . . nothing . . ." she answered. "Just hold me," she said and brought her lips against his with fierce possession.

She could not be certain what he said in response, but she thought he whispered low to himself, "But for how long?"

She was swept in a tide of passion, of remembrance of other times they had loved, and there were moments as they explored each other's bodies, pleasured each other in ways only they knew how to, that she imagined it was long ago. . . .

They had fallen into a twilight sleep, and when the telephone rang, Christopher sat up with a start.

Lauren caught his face, interpreted the dread. "Jesus . . ." He grabbed the phone. "Sorry," he said to his caller. "I, uh, got caught up in something." He was looking down at her as if trying to remember how she came to be in his bed. "I'll be there in"—he looked at his watch—"twenty minutes."

When he hung up, he began to dress. She sat up, watching him, feeling discarded. A coldness that had nothing to do with the room's temperature swept over her. *Fool,* she thought, getting out of bed herself and beginning to find her clothes. *For a minute, she had been stupid enough to think enough love could turn back the clock. Fool.*

He was looking at her now, his face arranged into a polite mask of apology.

"It's all right," she said, putting her shoes on. "I know. You've missed an appointment because of me."

"It was idiotic of me," he said.

From the look in his eyes, she knew he was arranging words to soften his abrupt and untimely departure. She thought of the experiences of some of her friends, victims of the one-night-stand syndrome. After a perfect evening of wine and roses, deep looks and impassioned kisses, the morning would dawn, filled with lost eye contact and just-remembered appointments. She almost smiled as she saw Christopher's eyes flit to the wallpaper, avoiding honest confrontation.

"Good-bye, Christopher."

He looked forlorn and beaten to her.

"Lauren . . ." The single word contained a world of pleading within it.

"No, really," she said, "things are different now. I can see that. Situations change, people change. But the world goes on. As they say." She started to the door.

"Lauren . . . it was stupid of me to . . . bad timing. I had this thing this afternoon. I know how it must seem to you. But I've got to go. Please stay. Wait for me."

"No, really, Christopher . . . our initial conversation this afternoon seems to have been appropriate to our situation." Turning, she slipped quickly through the bedroom door. She was downstairs, her hand on the doorknob, before he caught up with her.

"Stop it," he said. "You're right. Things have changed. I've changed. I'm successful now. But that should help us, not keep us apart."

"I don't want to wait in a corner for you to fit me into your life," Lauren said, her voice a low, desperate whisper as she tried to control herself.

"I never thought I'd see you again, Lauren . . . much less have the occasion to find you in my bed. I made a life for myself the best I could, and now I have to live it."

She could not contain the rage and fear and insecurity she was experiencing. She had nothing to offer him anymore. Nothing but herself, and that would never be enough for him now. Now he had meetings to attend. He was destined to be the guest of honor at parties where she, pariah that she was, would never be invited. His life was entwined with others; there was no room for her.

"Well," Lauren said, her fingers twisting the door's handle, "you've places to go . . . people to see . . . as they say."

"Lauren, wait."

The door closed behind her, cutting off the rest of his speech. She hurried down the steps. This time he did not come after her.

She had left instructions that no one was to disturb her when she returned to Lloyd's townhouse. She was on her bed, staring up at the ceiling, when one of the maids tapped lightly on the door.

"A special messenger," the voice said, "from Mr. Lloyd."

Lauren slipped on a robe and opened the door. The maid handed her the large brown envelope and, sensitive to Lauren's black mood, disappeared quickly and silently.

The envelope contained the morning's issue of the *New York Times*. Lloyd must have had it flown directly to her. But for what purpose? She returned to her bed and studied the front page. There was the usual batch of world disasters, but nothing that would particularly interest her.

Impatient with Lloyd for making her play guessing games, she snapped the paper open to the second page. At first she just stared, then let out an audible gasp.

There was a photo of Holly Adler and a separate one of Fredrich Wilm. And there beside them was the smiling countenance of Senator Riff McIntyre.

Lauren's eyes raced over the black ink, her heart beating double time. Fredrich Wilm had caught up with Holly. He had managed to break two of her ribs, and she was reputedly suffering from a dislocated jaw and a broken nose, and had lost two front teeth.

She had formed the conclusion that the man was a fiend when she read further and changed her opinion.

Holly, it appeared, had led the attack on Wilm, clubbing him with iron bars and smashing him on the head with vases. He had repeatedly tried to leave, deciding to deal with his grievances through a third party, his attorney, when the girl turned mean and went on a psychotic rampage. Wilm was only protecting himself from total annihilation.

According to the report, Holly had not only admitted to her crime, thus exonerating Lauren, but she had also named Riff McIntyre as being in collusion with her. The senator had made no comment on Holly's accusations and was reputedly sequestered in his family's compound outside of Cleveland. There would be an investigation.

The article concluded with a blurb on Lauren, making her out to be a victim and one of the world's basic heroic, sterling individuals.

"Well . . . hot damn," she drawled, breaking into a wide grin before yelping at the top of her lungs, "well, hot, hot damn!"

During the next few days, she was almost regretful that she had been reinstated into the art world. She was called constantly by former colleagues who sought her forgiveness, who offered compensating boons for their previous defection to her cause. One of the bonus gifts turned out to be trade gossip. Christopher's name was often repeated. It was, of course, assumed that their relationship was long over; after all, they hadn't been linked together publicly for months. Assuming that it would be all the same to Lauren, his name was mentioned in the same passing tidbits as the cultural center's opening.

"The opening's two days off, and I want to be out of here by then," Lauren said to Lloyd, adamantly refusing to stay no matter what his current objection was. "Every paper, every news show, every mouth in town, is going to go on about the cultural center and along with it, the fabulous wonder-artist, Christopher Reynolds. I don't need that aggravation, thank you. I don't need that heartache. All I want is to return home and lose myself in doing good works for your nice, quiet museum enterprise."

And so she would have, except that the following

afternoon, Buffy called her personally, asking the first favor she had ever asked of Lauren. It was to be Lloyd's birthday, and she wanted Lauren to pick up a special painting for him—a Max Ernst he had admired for years. Of course, there was no way she could refuse Buffy.

So Lauren canceled her plane reservation and began the steps to acquire the Ernst. It turned out to be a frustrating task. Not until the day of the cultural center's opening was she able to make the final arrangements to acquire the painting.

As soon as the deal was concluded, she called the airline to find out if there were any night flights from London. There were not. Paranoia crept into her world.

An hour later, Phillip intruded upon her depression with a call. "I'm so relieved you're still there in London," he began.

"Well, don't be. I'm trying my damnedest to get out."

"Look, Lauren, I know how you feel about attending the cultural center opening, but it's imperative that you go. I couldn't make it myself and I really do need a representative. It's rather shabby, according to Buffy, that our new endeavor is not represented on a social level. I happen to agree."

"Phillip, you've been very good to me, and you know I'd never do anything to let you down. But I can't go there tonight. I don't want to see Christopher."

"Of course, it's your life, Lauren, and I won't press you into doing something you feel that strongly about."

"I appreciate that. I'll see you when I get back."

After Phillip's call she paced through the big house. A drizzly rain had begun, adding more gloom to her already downtrodden spirit. She indulged in fleeting visions of herself suddenly appearing at the cultural center opening, dressed exquisitely—a seething, sensual creature inviting praise from all quarters. But to harbor such fantasies was foolish. They only fueled her misery as each scenario included recapturing her past bliss with Christopher.

By ten-thirty, her mind had become a torturous weapon out of her control. Deciding that she could not bear to launch into another obsessive musing, she found her raincoat and went for a walk. The drizzle suited her just fine.

She returned forty-five minutes later and found the phone ringing. She let it ring. It stopped. A couple of minutes later, it began again and, because the caller was so insistent and the hour late, she grabbed the receiver.

"Yes?" she answered, the aggravation in her voice clearly evident.

"Lauren?"

"Phillip? It's so late here."

"Yes, my apologies, dear. I wouldn't bother you, of course, except that something quite extraordinary has come up. One of my snitches has put me on to something too hot to pass up. This can only happen once in a lifetime, and I'm not about to let the Getty people snatch it away. Thank God," Phillip said, sighing mightily with relief. "Everyone else is at that cultural thing tonight. So you see, it was our good luck after all that you stayed home."

He gave her the information, and yes, it was startling. A Botticelli had been found in an old lady's attic after she passed on. The heirs—rather simple people, not involved with art—had not known what to do with their inherited painting and had contacted one of Phillip's art informers, who had in turn contacted him.

"But tonight, Phillip? Can't it wait until tomorrow morning? I'll dash out of bed and be there by six."

"No," he said. This was an emphatic "no." "It must be done now. *Now.*" The "now" also registered as nonnegotiable. "I can't allow that painting to slip out of the museum's grasp."

"It's nasty out, it's late, and I'm definitely, but definitely not in the mood, Phillip. But I suppose I owe you one. In fact, maybe like two or three or a thousand favors."

"Good girl. This means a great deal to me," he finished.

She kept her word. But first she had to wait fifteen minutes for a cab to arrive. It took another twenty minutes to cross town.

She felt like a spy in a late-night movie. There was mist and drizzle, darkness, lonely, crooked streets, a foreign city; she was in a raincoat palming a hastily scribbled address on a small piece of white paper.

"Wait for me," she said to the cabbie when they had reached the destination. She had the urge to add, "And if I'm not back here in an hour, call the Falcon." She managed to suppress herself.

The place was an artist's garret. The painting was supposed to be in the possession of Phillip's snoop, an artist with less talent than avarice. According to Phillip, who rarely misjudged character, the man would put the Getty group on to the Botticelli if Phillip didn't make his claim immediately.

She was not in the mood to be tough, relishing, instead, the concept of a good, satisfying midnight cry into her pillow. Nevertheless, for Phillip's sake, she did some internal squaring-of-the-shoulders and marched forward through the mist and up to the darkened building.

There was only the faintest glow in an upper window, the sole sign that anyone would be waiting.

The outside door was unlocked, and she took narrow wooden steps up to the second floor. She arrived at a large and shadowy room, its ambience that of a warehouse.

There was nothing much to be seen other than the three framed canvases positioned on easels in the room's center, their blank sides to her. They were flooded in white light from directional cannisters above.

She stood just inside the door. "Hello?"

Her voice carried through the empty space like a shot in the wilderness. There was no answer, and she moved into the loft's center, her heels providing a companionable clattering sound in the quiet.

Entering into the pool of light surrounding the paintings, she made her way to their front, ready to cast a discriminating eye on the reputed Botticelli for offer.

Only there was no Botticelli.

There were three canvases belonging together in a series. The artist's style was naturalistic, the flow of unity within the three paintings masterfully executed. The mix and patterning of colors were luminous and original. A woman's likeness had been captured in oils. Her expression was enigmatic in the first, defiant and noble in the second and vulnerable and open in the third.

"What do you think of the artist?"

The voice came from the shadows behind her.

"He's got talent."

She did not—could not—move her eyes from the canvases. She had never been so moved by an artist's work since the day she had first seen Christopher's abstracts in Lloyd's office.

"He had a very good subject to paint," the man said, his voice closer.

"He could be a star." Lauren's voice caught.

"I am a star." He was standing so close that she could feel his breath on her neck. "You made me one." Lauren turned. His face was a blur through her tears. He was wearing a black tux and a white formal dress shirt. He had also just arrived. He was damp from the rain, and a strand of dark hair fell forward on his forehead.

"You were quite a sensation tonight," he said. He glanced at the paintings. "But they weren't for sale."

"They'd bring a fortune."

"I'd like to paint you again," he said softly.

"Christopher . . ."

"I want to go on painting you the rest of my life."

"Oh, Christopher . . ."

But he would not let her speak. Moving closer to his work, he said, "This is what kept me from going mad, from becoming as demented as poor Van Gogh. I couldn't have you with me in the flesh, but at least I had your memory. I tried to bring you into my life. I had never thought I'd hold you, touch you again. But, at least," he said softly, so that she had to strain to make out his words, "at least, I could always love you."

Moving away out of the light, she looked into the dark shadows. It was cold where she stood, and she clutched her arms over her chest, hugging herself. A single step into the dark, where it was frigid and lonely; a step into the light, and it was warm. It was so easy now. It was all up to her.

She spoke from where she stood, the dark a good covering for what she had to say, or not be true to herself.

"I found out that there are things that count in this world. It's impossible to dismiss their reality—no matter how crass it may seem. There's the reality of money. And power." She saw the towering buildings in Century City. She saw Maxwell Kain. She saw Riff and the sign with her name over her doorway on Rodeo gleaming in the sunlight. "There's who you know and what you know, and where you're going and where you've been. There are balance sheets with black ink and red ink, and there's first class and third class in this world. There's crystal and then there are beer cans with their sides crushed in." She took a small step back toward the light. "And all that reality is a damn crock."

She took the final step into the pool of light where Christopher stood waiting.

"The biggest . . . no . . . the only reality is love. And I love you. I do," she cried, rushing into his arms.

He lifted her high, neither of them having to speak. Holding each other was everything.

Silhouette Intimate Moments

Available Now

Serpent In Paradise by Stephanie James

At first Jase Lassiter had promised Amy paradise, offering her nights of love and days of sheer delight. But then she thought he'd betrayed her and she wondered if paradise would ever be found.

A Season Of Rainbows by Jennifer West

Christopher Reynolds was a genius on the brink of realization—realization that beneath Lauren's cool exterior beat the heart of a woman waiting to be awakened by passion!

Until The End Of Time by June Trevor

The private wilderness of Rafiki was Reed Kincaid's haven, until Elise brought the outside world to his door. He hadn't wanted to love again, but she was woman enough to change his mind.

Tonight And Always by Nora Roberts

Kasey was an anthropologist, but her knowledge of men in general hadn't prepared her for one man in particular: Jordan. Together they did research for his novel, and found something even more precious than knowledge.

Silhouette
Intimate 💐 *Moments*

more romance, more excitement

Special Introductory Offer $1⁷⁵ each

#1 ☐ DREAMS OF EVENING
Kristin James

#3 ☐ EMERALDS IN THE DARK
Beverly Bird

#2 ☐ ONCE MORE WITH
FEELING Nora Roberts

#4 ☐ SWEETHEART CONTRACT
Pat Wallace

$2.25 each

#5 ☐ WIND SONG
Parris Afton Bonds

9 ☐ SERPENT IN PARADISE
Stephanie James

#6 ☐ ISLAND HERITAGE
Monica Barrie

#10 ☐ A SEASON OF RAINBOWS
Jennifer West

#7 ☐ A DISTANT CASTLE
Sue Ellen Cole

#11 ☐ UNTIL THE END OF TIME
June Trevor

#8 ☐ LOVE EVERLASTING
Moëth Allison

#12 ☐ TONIGHT AND ALWAYS
Nora Roberts

LOOK FOR *THE PROMISE OF SUMMER*
BY BARBARA FAITH AVAILABLE IN AUGUST
AND *THE AMBER SKY*
BY KRISTIN JAMES IN SEPTEMBER.

SILHOUETTE INTIMATE MOMENTS, Department IM/5
1230 Avenue of the Americas
New York, NY 10020

Please send me the books I have checked above. I am enclosing
$_____ (please add 50¢ to cover postage and handling. NYS
and NYC residents please add appropriate sales tax.) Send check or
money order—no cash or C.O.D.'s please. Allow six weeks for delivery.

NAME _____

ADDRESS _____

CITY _____ STATE/ZIP _____

Silhouette Intimate Moments

Coming Next Month

Edge Of Love by Anna James

Jennifer had expected to find new artists on her buying trip to Europe. She hadn't expected to lose her heart to the most difficult of them all: Jake Marshall. Together they would create a lasting memory of beauty all their own.

Reckless Surrender by Jeanne Stephens

Each was keeping something from the other. Over their double deception hung the ugly specter of suspicion. Its resolution would either destroy their newborn love or give to it the strength and luster of a diamond, the stone that means "forever."

Shadow Dance by Lorraine Sellers

Solo St. Clair had built her life around dance to escape the painful memory of Ben Savin. But neither time nor distance could ease the pain. Only one last dance shared together, could perform the healing magic that would unite them through all the years to come.

The Promise Of Summer by Barbara Faith

Alejandro Cervantes was a matador who danced away unscathed from the horns of charging bulls. One day watching him, and April's life was changed forever. They would work to break the tradition that a bullfighter's wife was a woman with tears in her eyes—or break their hearts in trying.